FORGED IN BATTLE

THE TOWN OF Helmstrumburg has stood for many generations, founded after a crushing defeat of the beastmen hordes.

Things have changed since those times of heroism. The legions of Chaos are amassing in the north and town has grown complacent, lorded over by a corrupt burgomeister and his crooked militia bodyguard. Now, the beastmen are gathering their forces once more, carrying out devastating raids on remote farmsteads nearby. Sigmund, leader of the Ragged Company, must organise his ragtag soldiers to defend both his home town and the farmstead. With time running out and a monstrous legion of beastmen at the gates, Sigmund must organise the defence of his town and get to the bottom of a mysterious prophecy.

War-torn fantasy from the grim world of Warhammer, *Forged in Battle* sees the Black Library debut of Justin Hunter.

More Warhammer from the Black Library

· GOTREK & FELIX BY WILLIAM KING ·

TROLLSLAYER
SKAVENSLAYER
DAEMONSLAYER
DRAGONSLAYER
BEASTSLAYER
VAMPIRESLAYER
GIANTSLAYER

· THE AMBASSADOR NOVELS *

THE AMBASSADOR by Graham McNeill
URSUN'S TEETH by Graham McNeill

· OTHER WARHAMMER ·

RIDERS OF THE DEAD by Dan Abnett
MAGESTORM by Jonathan Green
HONOUR OF THE GRAVE by Robin D Laws
SACRED FLESH by Robin D Laws
THE BURNING SHORE by Robert Earl
WILD KINGDOMS by Robert Earl
VALNIR'S BANE by Nathan Long

A WARHAMMER NOVEL

FORGED IN BATTLE

JUSTIN HUNTER

*For Cris and Giles, who shared the adventures with me
to the Keep on the Borderlands and Griffin Mountain*

A BLACK LIBRARY PUBLICATION

First published in Great Britain in 2005 by
BL Publishing,
Games Workshop Ltd.,
Willow Road, Nottingham,
NG7 2WS, UK

10 9 8 7 6 5 4 3 2 1

Map by Nuala Kennedy.

A CIP record for this book is available from the British Library

ISBN 1 84416 153 6

Distributed in the US by Simon & Schuster
1230 Avenue of the Americas, New York, NY 10020.

Printed and bound in Great Britain by
Bookmarque, Surrey, UK.

See the Black Library on the Internet at
www.blacklibrary.com

Find out more about Games Workshop
and the world of Warhammer at
www.games-workshop.com

THIS IS A DARK age, a bloody age, an age of daemons
and of sorcery. It is an age of battle and death, and of the
world's ending. Amidst all of the fire, flame and fury
it is a time, too, of mighty heroes, of bold deeds
and great courage.

AT THE HEART of the Old World sprawls the Empire, the
largest and most powerful of the human realms. Known
for its engineers, sorcerers, traders and soldiers, it is
a land of great mountains, mighty rivers, dark forests
and vast cities. And from his throne in Altdorf reigns
the Emperor Karl-Franz, sacred descendent of the
founder of these lands, Sigmar, and wielder
of his magical warhammer.

BUT THESE ARE far from civilised times. Across the
length and breadth of the Old World, from the knightly
palaces of Bretonnia to ice-bound Kislev in the far north,
come rumblings of war. In the towering World's Edge
Mountains, the orc tribes are gathering for another assault.
Bandits and renegades harry the wild southern lands of
the Border Princes. There are rumours of rat-things, the
skaven, emerging from the sewers and swamps across the
land. And from the northern wildernesses there is the
ever-present threat of Chaos, of daemons and beastmen
corrupted by the foul powers of the Dark Gods.
As the time of battle draws ever near,
the Empire needs heroes
like never before.

PROLOGUE

Two and a half thousand years before the present day

WHITE BANNERS OF mist hung around the clearing. The thick frost gave each blade of grass a cruel edge, the tree-line was as dark and impenetrable as a shield wall. In the centre of the clearing a gruesome splinter of black rock stood at a crooked angle. From niches carved into it, the eyeless sockets of skulls stared out and crude totems hung limp in the freezing air. With their backs to the stone, the last of the beastmen herds stood close together, their breath misting the chill air, their furred fingers clamped on the shafts of their spears.

They were surrounded.

From the still banners, all the tribes of Sigmar's new Empire were represented: mail-clad chieftains with their jostling warbands behind them. Despite the cold many warriors were naked, their pale skin inscribed with swirling blue tattoos. A few gnashed their teeth, the frenzy of battle overcoming them.

From the Imperial ranks one man stepped forward. His white beard hung nearly to his waist, but there was nothing frail about the way Johann Helmstrum, first Grand Theogonist, raised his mailed fist and pointed towards the hated foe.

Sigmar had been gone for ten years, but the furnace of his passions still glowed in men like Johann. From Sigmar's own tribe of the Unberogens, he had followed Sigmar until his disappearance – and like others of the man-god's warband, he now led armies of his own to destroy beasts like these.

For too long had people lived under the threat of death. Fo too long had nightmare beasts haunted the night. For too long had the people along the Stir River been prey to the occult rituals of these creatures, foul amalgams of man and beast.

Hefting his dented warhammer, Foe-crusher, Johann picked out the largest beastman and fixed him with a merciless stare: warlord to warlord. 'In the name of Sigmar,' his voice carried across the clearing, gathering power as he spoke, echoing over the ranks of warriors. 'I claim these lands for man. Your kind has no right to laws or life. I hereby pronounce your execution.'

The Unberogens beat their spears and sword-hilts against their shields. The beastmen shuffled uncomfortably; even their leader, eight foot of rippling muscle, bowed his horned head.

Johann Helstrum lifted his warhammer again and turned back to his men. 'For Sigmar!' he roared and led the charge.

THE CLASH OF armies was like two waves breaking upon each other. Through months of battle and slaughter, the beastmen had been harried and hunted to the very edge of their tribal lands, and now with their backs to the mighty River Stir, they had nowhere left to flee. It was around the last of their herdstones that they fought, and the arcane monolith, of a stone known to no man, gave them renewed strength and resolve.

They fought with all the ferocity of trapped animals. Three times the men of the Empire were thrown back, but each time the white-bearded figure of Johann Helmstrum led them back into the charge, and as close around him as a mailed fist went the men of his bodyguard, led by Ortulf Jorge and his brother, Vranulf.

It was mid-morning when the men fell back in confusion for a fourth time. There were heaps of dead on both sides, but a knot of a hundred monstrous beastmen survived: berserk with blood-lust, their snouts stained red, their weapons dripping blood.

Men collapsed from exhaustion and the sight of the enraged beasts was enough to make the bravest man falter, but Johann's encouragement sent the fire of Sigmar from man to man, and gave them the energy for one last fight. One last charge would surely break them.

The old man's warhammer cut a swathe through the beastmen. He wielded the warhammer as if it weighed no more than a hatchet, and with his bodyguard round him he cut a path right to the base of the herdstone, where goat-horned shamans still desperately prayed to their capricious gods.

The closer they came to the monolith, the more the men could feel its evil. It pulsed at the priest's approach, made the arms of his bodyguard heavy and leaden. Ortulf found that simply raising his weapon to parry was a terrible effort; Vranulf was almost run through as he struggled in mortal combat.

Only Johann seemed immune to the arcane power of the stone. He killed both shamans and splattered the herd-stone with the remains of their horned skulls. With their death, the beastmen's spirit seemed to waver – but the war-gor let out a huge bellow, like an enraged bull, and charged through the battle. Ortulf and two other body-guards stood firm, but the aura from the monolith made their legs and arms shake with the effort. The beastman shrugged off their sword and spear thrusts, battering them aside as if they were sticks. He cut Vranulf down and reared up over the venerable warrior, knocking Foe-smiter from his hands.

Ortulf shouted out as he saw his brother cut down, struggled to get back to his feet. As the wargor raised his axe Ortulf tried to pick up his sword, but it slipped from his fingers.

'Sigmar!' the Grand Theogonist shouted and drew his sword, but his voice was weak and the beastman batted the blade away as if it were a child's toy.

The wargor had dragged the old man to the herdstone. He took a handful of beard and pulled his head back, exposing his throat. The monolith hummed with pleasure as the knife was raised.

'Sigmar...' Ortulf prayed, and just the name gave him strength enough to stand. He dropped his shield, picked up his brother's spear from the bloody grass, and staggered towards the wargor. The pain in his head was like hammer blows. Ortulf saw the raised dagger and thrust with all his remaining strength. The spear head went in next to the creature's spine and up under its ribcage. The wargor let out a bellow of pain, but instead of falling it turned and Ortulf realised he was defenceless. His fingers grasped for a weapon or shield – but his hands were slippery with blood and sweat and could find no purchase. The wargor picked him up and threw him aside. Ortulf's body hit the monolith with a sickening crunch. But in that brief moment of respite, Johann Helmstrum's fingers found the haft of his warhammer. He had fought a hundred campaigns against the enemies of humankind. It was not his fate to die here. The face of Sigmar came to him, whispering quiet words of encouragement, and gave him the strength he needed to raise his warhammer one final time.

Johann Helmstrum swung Foe-smiter down, and buried the blunt head deep into the wounded beastman's skull, between its curled horns.

The monster staggered and raised its axe once more, but sank slowly to its knees, and fell face down at the Grand Theogonist's feet.

* * *

WITH THEIR SHAMANS and leaders slain, the last of the herds were quickly routed and hunted down. Johann Helstrum had men loop ropes around the vile stone and tear it from the ground, roots and all. They built a great pile of wood over the thing and set fire to it, and when the fire at its hottest and the stone was glowing a dull red, they carried freezing water from the Stir River and drenched it. Steam filled the clearing for a whole day, and when it cleared they saw the stone had shattered into a thousand pieces.

Johann led them all in prayers to Sigmar, and then he declared the land to be free of the enemies of man.

WHEN THE DEAD had been buried and the wounded tended, the Grand Theogonist's army struck camp. The people watched them leave, astonished to find that the woods and hills were clear of enemies. In the crowd that watched them leave was Griselda Jorge, young widow of Ortulf. She let her tears flow, reliving the moment she and the other women had hurried through the piles of dead and dying to find her lover: crushed at the foot of the herdstone. But where that accursed monolith had once stood was now a high burial mound, where her husband's and her brother's broken bodies had been laid: their weapons at their sides and the heads of their enemies piled about them. Griselda sat there until evening, watching the shadows grow, her cloak tight around her, pressing their son to her chest.

'Your husband was a brave and honourable man,' the Grand Theogonist had told her, and she repeated his words to her son, over and over. 'Your father killed many of the enemy. He was a brave and proud and honourable warrior.' But inside she cursed his bravery and his pride and the honour that had left her widowed and her son fatherless.

At last one of the local women came out to her. The woman patted her hand. 'Your husband is with Sigmar now,' she said and Griselda nodded and wiped away her tears. He would be happy here, she thought and let the old woman lead her back to the new village they had founded, named in honour, not of her dead husband, but of the Grand Theogonist: Helmstrumburg.

CHAPTER ONE
The present day, spring 2521
Helmstrumburg

VASIR CROUCHED LOW and blended into the patch of ferns. A twig snapped underfoot. The trapper cursed silently, but the mistake was momentary. He kept breathing slowly, stayed perfectly still – and his quarry relaxed and renewed chewing.

Taal's bones! This one would get him a good price.

Vasir fitted the arrow to his bow. Another sip of water, that's it, Vasir smiled. And have something to eat, why don't you? He pulled the bow taut, let his breath out and then loosed the arrow which flashed briefly in the sun-dappled green.

The beast dashed off into the undergrowth, and Vasir leaped up after it, crashing through the undergrowth and the snapping branches. He found the stag, twenty yards off, lying on the ground, flanks heaving, the arrow embedded deep into its side. The fletching had broken off in the chase, there was no way to pull it out. Vasir drew his knife. The stag tried to struggle to its feet again – but its legs flailed weakly on thin air. The creature coughed and red foam began to bubble from its open snout.

Vasir said a prayer to Taal, then put the blade against its throat and opened up the artery with a deft nick.

AFTER SKINNING AND gutting the deer Vasir hiked up to the crag called the Watching Post and washed a skin in the cold melt-water stream, then laid it out on a rock to dry. From this rocky outcrop, on the shoulder of The Old Bald Man, he could look down the town of Helmstrumburg.

Though he'd been trapping in these hills all his life, Vasir never tired of the view: The Old Bald Man, Galten Hill and the snow-clad slopes of Frantzplinth – the three mountains sat high above town, their ridges descending to the valley, where the ancient stone-walled town of Helmstrumburg stood beside the river.

Helmstrumburg had grown rapidly in the past few years, now spilling over the western wall, rambling along the banks of the River Stir.

Vasir watched fat barges push their way downriver a thousand feet below, their sails tiny squares of white in the distance. He had heard it from boat hands in the inns in Helmstrumburg that it was nine days' sail to Altdorf. Maybe when he had enough money saved he would go and see the capital city of the Empire, Kemperbad and the miraculous bridge at Nuln. He would travel all through the lands that Sigmar had cleared for humans, a thousand years ago or more.

THAT NIGHT, ALONE in his cabin, Vasir threw a few pieces of split wood onto the fire. The wood smoke eddied round the simple room as it searched for the hole in the thatch that served as a chimney. He ate a few slices of stale pumpernickel and dried sausage then lay down to sleep. Outside, the trees whispered to each other in the evening breeze.

Vasir slept as the trees whispered back and forth. Even if he could have heard them he would not have understood.

But there were many that could. On the rocky crags, from the mouths of mountain caves, in the bleak pine forests, high on Frantzplinth – many ears heard the whispers and looked to the west, where they had long waited the sign.

A twin-tailed star. Burning red on the horizon.

Announcing the End of Times.

ELIAS SHOULDERED HIS pack and struggled to keep up with the other forty men of the Helmstrumburg Halberdiers as they struggled along the forest track. When he joined up he had expected glory and excitement and a fine uniform. He'd had no idea how much marching there would be, and how little fighting. And the uniforms were old and faded and ill-fitting – and to make it worse there were not enough to go round: some of the men wore the uniform trews; others the jackets: once quartered with red and gold – but now so patched with leather that they were more patch than original.

A ragged company other men had dubbed them, but for the Helmstrumburg Halberdiers it was a symbol of pride. They were *The Ragged Company*.

WHEN ELIAS HAD heard that the Helmstrumburg Halberdiers were returning to town to refill their ranks, he had joined up. That first day he had sworn service to the count and felt tall and strong: now as he hunted through the dark forests for the third day, all that courage and confidence had gone.

His sword slapped awkwardly against his thigh. He put his hand down to touch the hilt and reminded himself that he was a soldier now, in the pay of the Elector Count of Talabecland.

'Keep in rank!' Osric called as they passed through the scattered forests, and Elias hitched up his pack. His halberd caught on a branch above his head and nearly pulled him over. Osric gave him a shove to move him along. 'Get on you useless bastard!'

Elias felt his face redden. His shame increased when Sergeant Gunter stopped and waited for Osric. 'If you have a problem with one of my men then come to me.'

Osric nodded without a word. Gunter pushed Elias forward, next to Gaston and took his place.

'Now get going!' Gunter hissed. 'And don't mess up again.'

THAT NIGHT THE halberdiers bivouacked in a wooded hollow, lit a fire and mixed their hard-tack with water and fried it for flavour.

'I'll be glad to get back to town and get some real food,' Osric said as he chewed. 'And some beer.'

'I'll be happy when the captain feels like leaving these cursed hills,' Baltzer, one of Osric's men and the company drummer, said. 'I joined up to see Talabecland, not the woods round Helstrumburg!'

A few men smiled, but Elias kept his mouth shut.

Their banter was interrupted by a sudden shout from the trees. 'Sigmar save us!'

Gaston was on his feet immediately, sword drawn. Sigmund looked in the direction of the shout. It was one of the men they had posted at the edge of the camp to keep watch. 'Freidel?' he called.

'Oh – Sigmar save us!' the shout came again. Osric shook his head: Freidel was one of his men, but he was tired, and had only just got comfortable by the fire. It was probably just a false alarm.

Sigmund, their leader, drew his sword and started running up the hill. Dark branches whipped his face as he pushed through the trees to the rocky outcropping that Freidel had been posted on. From here, there was a fine view down to the Stir River below, and the twinkling lights in Helmstrumburg.

'What's the matter, Freidel?' Sigmund demanded, and the halberdier pointed to the western horizon.

'Look!'

Sigmund kept his sword unsheathed as he turned to look. The Stir River was a ribbon through the darkness, rippling with moonlight. Low in the sky on the left hung a star with two tails. It glowed with a dull red light, menacing and sinister.

Sigmund shook his head. It was the star of Sigmar.

'WHAT IS IT?' Osric called when Sigmund returned.

'The sign of Sigmar, the double-headed star!' Sigmund said, and rammed his sword back into its sheath. He looked shaken.

'I don't believe it!' Osric retorted but Baltzer, who had followed Sigmund, confirmed what the other men had seen: it was definitely a twin-tailed star.

The firelight caught Gaston's face, casting half in shadow. 'What does it mean?' he asked.

No one answered.

'Will Sigmar come again?' Schwartz asked, finally.

Osric laughed at them all. 'If he has, there'll be some to-do in some far flung place and the news will take six months to reach Helmstrumburg,' he said, his thin face half lit by the dying firelight. The men nodded. That was how it always happened.

Baltzer tossed a stone into the fire. 'I tell you what it means – it means that bastard–' he nodded towards the fire where Sigmund sat '–will be taking us on a lot more of these damned patrols!'

Osric laughed and threw a stone at Baltzer. He was always bitching about something.

THE NEXT MORNING the men of the Ragged Company were up early: hitching their heavy packs onto their shoulders, halberds resting on their left shoulders. It was damp in the early morning mist, and the woods were strangely quiet.

Gunter's men assembled on the left of the clearing; Osric's on the right.

'All present?' Sigmund called and Gunter replied, then Osric. 'All present and correct!'

'Gunter!' Sigmund commanded. 'Lead your men out!'

* * *

FOR THE REST of the day, the Ragged Company pushed on
along forest paths and high mountain roads, where it was
said that beastmen had been seen – but they saw nothing
except a crazy old trapper, who was carrying a freshly
caught badger.

Baltzer moaned about the endless walking. When the men
paused by a stream for a lunch of cold hard-tack and water
he pulled off one of his boots and socks to examine his foot.

'Sigmar's balls!' he cursed, and took out his dagger to
pop an enormous blister that covered half his heel. 'How
much more walking do we have to do?'

'Shut up for once!' Freidel snapped. He spoke for a lot of
them.

'Since when did you become the model trooper?'

'I'm just sick of your bitching!'

'I'm sick of wearing my feet out!'

'Well,' Freidel said, 'I'm sure the captain has good reason.'

'Bollocks!' Baltzer said. 'He's just tired of the burgomeister telling him what to do.'

'Who isn't?' Edmunt said and the men all laughed. The
burgomeister had done much for Helmstrumburg: bringing
in trade and expanding the town outside its historic confines – even barges from the port of Marienburg called into
Helmstrumburg now – but he hadn't made many friends in
the process. His manner excited even less admiration. He
had turned the town watch into his private army, raised
taxes, and was rumoured to be involved in all manner of
dubious business deals, possibly even smuggling. 'Except of
course,' Edmunt smiled, 'those who take his coin!'

Baltzer and Osric and many of the halberdiers had been
part of the town watch before they joined up. 'Used to!'
Baltzer snapped.

'Oh – I didn't realise you'd stopped,' Edmunt said and
pushed the drummer off the log, sending him sprawling
into the ferns.

'Dumb log-splitter!' Baltzer spat.

* * *

LATE ON THE following day of their patrol the halberdiers found the Old Post Road, an ancient track that led towards more civilised parts. The road was overgrown with weeds but it allowed the men to move quickly under the leaf-cover.

Sigmund wanted to reach the cabin of Osman Speinz before nightfall. Osman kept a boarding house of sorts, selling ale and food, and he had stables which he rented out as lodging. If there were any rumours going around the trappers about beastmen gathering, Osman would know them.

'How much further?' Elias asked Gaston.

Gaston shook his head. 'A mile or so.'

'And what's Osman like?'

Gaston shrugged. 'He keeps a good cask of ale. Not cheap, but better than stream-water.'

Elias nodded. He'd been orphaned earlier than he could really remember, and had been taken in by Guthrie Black, proprietor of the Crooked Dwarf inn, and raised as a son. He'd spent his life carrying barrels of beer up and down to the cellars or mopping the stale beer from the flagstones in the morning. He'd never thought he'd miss beer as much as he did when on these patrols. A stein would take away the aches in his feet and his shoulders. He could almost taste it as the Old Post Road twisted off the ridge down towards the cabin of Osman Speinz.

As they walked Elias could not stop thinking about the luxuries that Osman's cabin offered. After eleven nights sleeping rough, a night in stables seemed like luxury. The promise of ale made the weight of his pack disappear.

'Do you think he's still renting his daughters out?' Freidel asked.

No one answered: they were all thinking the same thing.

THE SUN WAS casting long shadows when they reached Osman's sign, pointing towards his lodge. There was no writing, few men here could read. The worn sign was composed of hammered planks, daubed crudely with a barrel of beer and an arrow.

'Not far now!' Osric told them and the men lengthened their stride, and even Gunter started to laugh and joke. The trees pressed in on either side, then opened out to a couple of small fields, with spring-green shoots of winter wheat starting to show. The road curved across a stream and then they were in the clearing where Osman lived.

As they broke the tree-line they could see that something was terribly wrong. The cabin was surrounded by a simple palisade, but the crude timber gates of the farmstead had been torn from their hinges, the cabin door had been broken through, and the front yard was littered with shredded clothes.

The company was silent as they followed Sigmund up to the ruined gateway. There was a strong scent of animal musk.

'Beastmen!' Edmunt spat. It was a scent a man would never forget.

Elias followed the men into the yard. The stink was overpowering. There were clothes everywhere, as if the half-goats, half-humans had gone into a frenzy of looting.

So much for the beer, or even Osman's daughters.

'Gunter – clear up this lot!' Sigmund snapped, pointing to the mess. 'Osric check around the back. Elias, Petr and Gaston – stand guard!'

Petr had joined up with Elias. He was a tall, quiet man with his hair pulled back into a ponytail. He had missed out on a uniform altogether, and wore a strip of cloth tied around his right arm.

Elias leant on his halberd and stood close to Gaston. No one spoke as they worked. Each rag hit the pile with a wet slap. Elias looked back up the road that they had come down. The leaves rustled, but it was just a bird, flapping through the undergrowth. He looked back at the men clearing up the mess, then at Gaston, who was leaning on his halberd shaft.

'Beastmen?' Elias asked.

Gaston nodded.

'Do you think they escaped?' Elias asked.

Gaston pointed with his chin towards the scraps of clothes. 'I don't think so.'

Edmunt overheard the comment. He stood up to his full height and held out a dripping rag at arm's length: it was not a rag at all, but a tatter of human skin.

Elias stared back at the front yard in horror. They were not rags at all, but body parts. Out of one torn sleeve he saw part of a hand. Another had some nameless body part – little more than shreds of muscle and a snapped bone sticking out of it. That was a part of a child's head, there was a foot. He looked down and almost yelped in shock: wedged next to the palisade was the head of a young boy, not much younger than himself. The dead youth's teeth were clenched, his eyes were open and staring. No, not staring, Elias realised, and this made his stomach lurch uncontrollably. The man's head had been skinned – and from the terror in the eyes, and the set of the jaw, Elias could tell they had been skinned alive.

Sigmund picked his way across the yard, pushed the broken doorway open and stepped inside.

OSRIC CAME BACK round the house to find Elias bent over retching.

The pile of body parts was almost waist high. Osman and his family had been torn to shreds. There were strange symbols daubed in blood on the cabin walls. He tried not to look because they made his head hurt, but they kept drawing his attention.

Osric looked from the pile to Elias and back again. Gaston waited for him to say something, but not even Osric could make a joke out of this.

'Sigmar's balls,' Osric said at last, and shook his head. 'They made a mess here.'

The door of the cabin swung open and Sigmund came back out of the doorway. His face was deathly white, his jaw clamped against some greater horror inside the cottage. 'Gunter!' he said. 'I don't want anyone else going in here. Get a fire started, we'll burn this place down.'

Gunter nodded and his men started piling brushwood against the cabin walls. 'We'll find these creatures!' Sigmund called as his men worked. 'And we will pay them back!'

A few of the men nodded, but Baltzer caught Elias's eye. 'Let's hope we don't!' he muttered under his breath.

Elias looked away, but Osric pulled him over to the corner of the yard. 'Look at this!'

The beastmen had sprayed and defecated round the edges of the enclosure: the dung looked as if it had been kicked about to spread out their pungent stink.

'It's like they're marking their territory,' Freidel said and his nose wrinkled at the thought of the filthy beasts. 'Abominations!' he spat.

Osric kicked a pile of dung that was the size of a cow pat.

'Look at the size of that one!' he said. 'I personally don't want to see anything that made that.'

Elias swallowed hard. He also hoped that the beastmen had gone back into the high hills and stayed there. He didn't want to see the creature that made that either.

THE HALBERDIERS SET off following the path of the beastmen, but after an hour's march Sigmund called a brief halt by a stream. While the men filled their flasks and drank long gulping mouthfuls of water, Sigmund went forward with Edmunt. The giant woodsman was crouched on the ground staring at the forest floor as if it were a book he was unable to read. 'I am no tracker,' he said at last.

Sigmund nodded. None of them were: from their clothes they were soldiers, but in their hearts they were still tailors' assistants, woodsmen, farriers, farmers' boys. And miller's sons, Sigmund told himself.

'If you had to guess, which way do you think?'

Edmunt looked to the left and right: briars and ferns clogged the space between the tree trunks and the ground was thick with moss and well-rotten leaves. Dusk was closing in around them. On all sides the forest appeared impenetrable. Edmunt shook his head. He couldn't tell. It seemed impossible that the beastmen had come this way and not left any sign.

'I don't know,' Edmunt said after a long pause, 'but if I had to guess I would say that they went that way, to the left. There are a couple of farmsteads over the ridge, about half way to Gruff Spennsweich's land.'

He pointed to where the stream splashed down a stair-case of slippery black stones. A fern waved as if caught in a breeze and Sigmund's skin prickled. Since they had left the hut he felt as if they were being watched. He cursed him-self. It was impossible hunting beastmen like this: they could disappear as easily as wild animals; to the untrained eye they left less trace than a passing ghost. And night was already setting in.

'We'd better get to the nearest farmstead and raise the alarm,' Sigmund said. Edmunt nodded.

'Does Farmer Spennsweich rent out his daughters?' Petr asked and Edmunt laughed out loud.

'Touch one of his daughters and he will use your guts for sausages!'

Behind them the men were filling their water skins. Sigmund felt his skin prickle again. 'Keep your arms to hand!' he hissed, the tension showing in his voice as they started forward again.

SIGMUND LED THE way down along the stream bank. The stones were rough but slippery; they turned under foot and made the going difficult.

Osric shouldered his pack. This was stupid. The only way they knew which way the beastmen had gone was the trail of burnt cottages and farmsteads, the dead bodies of women, children and men. He waited for Elias to go before him. No point having the new guy take up the rear, but tak-ing the last spot made Osric too aware of how exposed they were, strung out like pack-horses in the thick forest at dusk.

'We'll be the ones caught next,' Osric muttered.

As they filed through the forest, Osric kept muttering. Elias didn't know if he should respond or not. 'These are not deer we're hunting,' Osric said, and Baltzer overheard and turned to join in the fun.

'These animals hunt you back,' he whispered. 'We could be walking into a trap. In the forest, at night...'

Elias started to look around him.

Gaston stopped on a stone in the middle of the stream. 'Leave off him.'

Osric gave him a half-smile, half-sneer. Gaston let him go in front, took the position of end man himself, but not even the presence of Gaston could soothe the new boy.

As the first stars began to glimmer through the leaves above, Elias could sense the forest watching and waiting, a hundred eyes behind each tree.

As Morrslieb rose behind the stark crags of Frantzplinth, the Ragged Company broke through the trees onto a walled field. They had come down to more civilised parts. Sigmund paused and conferred with Edmunt. He had grown up near this place, in a cabin deep in the woods.

'If we go that way,' Edmunt said to Sigmund and pointed down towards a patch of tall cedars. 'We will cut out a couple of miles.'

Sigmund nodded and the men scrambled down the hillside, over a dry stone wall, and through the cedar copse. He did not tell anyone what he had seen inside the house. He tried to scrub the memory from his mind: but the unbidden sight kept appearing of the fresh hides of Osman Speinz and his three daughters, hair and face and legs, nailed across the inside of the wall.

When the dogs started barking, Gruff Spennsweich went out to quiet them down. The animals were tugging at their chains, teeth bared. He could see shadows moving in the trees. The horses started to toss and neigh in the stables and the farmer's skin prickled.

'Who's there?' he demanded. The shadows moved and he shouted again, louder this time in an attempt to bolster his nerves: but he felt more frightened than ever. A horn blew and Gruff ran back to the house. A strange scent hung in the evening air, vile and musky.

'Dietrik! Olan!' he called the farmhands from the barn then hurried back inside, took the old crossbow from above the fireplace and began to wind it.

Valina, his eldest, stared at him as if he had gone mad.

'Father, what are you doing?'

He had kept the mechanism oiled, but it was still stiff from lack of use, and he began to sweat as it jammed.

'Sigmar's balls!' he hissed and Gertrude, his youngest, and Shona and Werna, the blonde twins, blushed.

Olan and Dietrik stood at the door, uncertain whether to come into the house or not.

'Here! Dietrik,' Gruff said and the farm boy stepped inside and took the crossbow hesitantly. 'Olan, get a pitch-fork. Watch the trees. Shout if you see anything.'

Dietrik held the crossbow reverently while Olan hurried across to the barn, a worried look on his face.

'Don't point that at me!' Valina cursed him. The farm-boy blushed and pointed the crossbow out of the doorway.

Gruff took no notice. He was digging through his chest for his blunderbuss. He unwrapped the oil cloth, and the smell of polished iron rekindled memories of hunting when he was a young man, up in the hills. He didn't like to use too much blackpowder – it was expensive – but this time he poured a good measure in and then rammed home a good few handfuls of pellets and smithy scraps.

'THIS IS POINTLESS!' Osric dared to raise his voice. Silently the rest of the men agreed, even Edmunt. They had somehow missed the road and were caught in a defile that seemed to be winding its way back into the mountain. They could barely see anything in the darkness, but if they could hit the road then at least they could make their way to a farm and get some shelter and protection. None of them fancied sleeping rough with a band of beastmen raiders nearby.

Sigmund came and stood next to Edmunt. 'Any idea which way?' he asked. Edmunt shook his head.

Sigmund looked left and right. None of the ways seemed good. 'We'll double back,' he said, 'and follow the stream down.'

It was as good a plan as any. Osric imagined what tales he'd be able to tell Richel and the other handgunners all about the latest chase that Sigmund had led them on. He would have a platter of roast beef and the largest flagon of ale at the Blessed Rest inn. Then he might visit the House of Madam Jolie and see if she had any new girls in.

'Quiet!' Gaston hissed. Osric snarled, but crouched down like the rest.

The men huddled down low and listened. Even though the trees deadened noises, there were men shouting, the distant clang of metal. Then the unmistakable sound of a gunshot. Sigmund sprang forward and his men followed – slipping on the ground and tripping on the under-growth.

Elias tripped over a tree root and fell face forward into a tangled knot of briars. He felt a hand dragging him out and he yelped with terror, expecting a beastman to tear him apart. A rough hand grasped his shirt and hauled him to his feet, then Edmunt's broad silhouette jogged ahead of him.

Elias followed Edmunt's silhouette through the trees. They ran as quietly as they could until they broke through the foliage and the open sky above seemed almost as bright as daylight. They had found the road. They saw two carriages, their horses lying in pools of blood, and around them were dead human bodies and cavorting goat-headed figures carrying spears and crude shields. Sigmund was at the front. He led the halberdiers in a ragged charge: all of them roaring furiously. Elias opened his mouth but had no idea if he made any noise at all, he just concentrated on following Edmunt's hulking shape. Suddenly a beastman loomed in front of him. He jabbed and felt the blade smack through fur and flesh and then the beastman went down and Elias kept running and screaming.

Elias caught another beastman in the gut, but this time the creature did not go down so easily. Elias was so terrified of being killed that he thrust the point of his halberd at it again and again, until it hung, impaled upon the side of the carriage. Elias tried to pull his halberd free, but it was stuck. He had a terrible fear that he would be caught and drew his sword, but when he looked around there were only halberdiers.

The fight seemed to have lasted no more than a few seconds, but suddenly a gun flashed again, and the retort was so loud Elias dropped his sword in fright.

THE CARRIAGE STOOD amidst the ruin of its former occupants and attackers. From the spread of bodies it appeared that the carriage driver had attempted to crash through the beastmen, but the beastmen had torn out the throats of the horses, and with such superior numbers against them the defenders had been doomed. The driver's blunderbuss had crudely beheaded one beastman and turned the creature's shoulders into a mangled mess of lead shot, gore and bone. But he and his two guards lay gutted and dead, their eyes staring blindly up into the starry sky.

The two survivors had run down the road, and it was there that the last beastman was cut down. Sigmund pulled his blade free, turned the body of the creature over with his foot, and cleaned his halberd on the shaggy fur. In their frenzied attack on the carriages, the beastmen had smashed all but one of the lanterns. The remaining lamp swung back and forth, casting eerie shadows. The largest beastman lay on its front about ten feet from the second carriage. Its horns were broad and straight, curling forwards at the ends like the horns of a bull. It had a bull's neck, pale and creamy and thick with muscles. There were many stab wounds on its front, Sigmund knew. He had made half of them himself. It was the one that had killed one of the new boys, Petr – it had cut the lad almost in half.

Osric had already covered Petr with his cloak, but from beneath the cloth a red pool was spreading. Sigmund shook his head. The boy had forgotten all his training and had been an easy kill.

'Is anyone else hurt?' he called out.

No one answered. They gathered together, hushed by the sudden relief of surviving battle.

GUNTER LED THE two men who had survived the attack back down the road.

They were dressed like merchants, with silk cloaks and velvet hats. The taller man was the one with the pistols, one of them in his belt and one hanging – spent – from his hand. Even in the glimmer of lamplight, they could see the quality of their manufacture. The hilts and barrels were worked with silver filigree, but there was nothing delicate about the shots they fired. The barrels were as wide as Sigmund's thumb. A short range, but deadly.

Not far off was proof of its power: a beastman lay on its front, the gaping exit wound raw and bloody. The shot had driven flesh, bone and cartilage before it, and then ripped out of the monster's back, leaving a hole a hand's breath wide.

'Who are you?' Sigmund asked to the merchants.

'Are you free company?' the shorter man said. He had a Reikland accent, refined and arrogant. The man had a finely cut beard and his bone structure was delicate. His hands were gloved with the finest kidskin, his deerskin boots trod silent as he strolled up to the halberdiers' captain.

Sigmund pulled himself up to his full height to compensate for his patched jacket. 'Captain Sigmund Jorge, Helmstrumburg Halberdiers,' he said. 'And I want to know your business.'

'Well. How lucky that you came along,' the man said, but there was something about his tone that made Sigmund bristle. If these fools had not been out at night then he would not have lost one of his men. He watched the Reiklander tilt his head towards the dead beastman at their

feet. 'Otherwise we would have been in a more than a little trouble.'

'You would be dead,' Sigmund said. 'Now, what were you
doing on the road at night?'

The smaller man gave the halberdier a look that suggested he had no right to question him. 'What business is
it of yours?'

'I am Marshal of Helmstrumburg,' Sigmund said.

The smaller man gave an affected titter.

'Marshal? Can't you afford a proper uniform?'

Sigmund ignored the jibe. 'What business do you have in
Helmstrumburg?'

It was the other man, with the pistols, who spoke next. 'I
apologise, marshal. We have a message of some import to
deliver.'

'Who to?'

'That, I believe,' the smaller man said, 'is none of your
business.'

Sigmund refused to rise to the insult, but Edmunt took a
step forward. Gunter put his hand out to stop him. The
Reiklander looked up at the towering woodsman with a
mixture of amusement and fascination.

'Are you going to attack the cousin of Baron von
Kohl?'

Sigmund stared at him for a moment then turned his
back on the merchants deliberately. 'Gunter!' Sigmund
called his sergeant forward. The grizzled veteran's beard
looked even more silvered in the lamplight. 'Take five men
and bury these bodies. Edmunt organise the rest. We'll
escort these,' he paused and indicated towards the two merchants, 'two to town.'

Elias was still standing with his sword drawn, his hands
shaking uncontrollably.

'You can put that away now,' Sigmund said. Elias nodded
but did not move. 'The sword,' Sigmund said, 'you can put
it away now.'

Elias reddened and slid the blade into his scabbard.

'Where's your halberd?'

Elias looked back towards the carriages, where the beast-man he had killed was still pinned to the painted woodwork.

'Let's go get it,' Edmunt said and led the boy back to the farthest carriage, where the beastman had been impaled through the shoulder. The body hung off-centre, Edmunt pulled the blade free and clapped Elias on the shoulder.

'Looks like you got one!' Sigmund said and gave him back his halberd.

Elias nodded. I got two, he thought. I got two, he told himself and grinned.

WHEN THE BEASTMEN corpses were dumped to the side of the road, Elias could not resist going to have a look. They were not much larger than children, with the beginnings of horns through the matt of fur, like young kids. Apart from the vertical pupils and the needle-sharp teeth, they had a strange beauty about them.

'Just wait till you see the big ones!' Freidel told him as he threw the last corpse onto the pile. 'There's nothing pretty about them!'

Edmunt took a cloth and dipped it into the blood of a beastman.

The men chuckled as the new boy was pushed forward. Edmunt smeared blood on both Elias's cheeks.

'Now!' he said. 'You're a real halberdier!'

GUNTER'S MEN WERE assigned the job of burying the dead. They set to with crude picks, scraping away half a foot of dead leaves and then moving away as much earth as they could before they hit a tangle of roots.

'That's enough!' Gunter said. The halberdiers took each dead man by the feet, dragged them over to the pit and dropped them in. The dead coachman's neck had been cut through almost to the bone. His head flopped unnaturally as they put him down.

Gaston leaned down to straighten the head.

'Why did you do that?' Schwartz said as they walked to get the next. 'It won't make any difference where he's gone.'

'I'll remember not to do it for you.'

'Now I didn't say that,' Schwartz said as they lifted the guard from the back of the coach. The dead man's hands still gripped the blunderbuss. He looked to have been in the process of reloading when a spear thrust had run him through.

He was fatter than the coachman. Gaston and Schwartz lifted him like the others, but there was a grunt, and they dropped the body in surprise.

'He's still alive,' Gaston said.

'Never!'

The man's guts were spilling out from under his shirt. Belly wounds were the slowest and most painful sort. Better cut your throat than wait to die of a gut wound.

Gaston drew his knife and held the blade over the man's mouth for a few moments. When he took it away there was a film of condensation.

'He's breathing,' Gaston said.

'Poor bastard,' Schwartz said.

Gaston sighed. There was no point taking the man with them. He'd die if they tried to move him. If they left him where he was then he'd die anyway.

'We can't bury him alive,' Gaston said, and bent over the man's head.

When Gaston stood up the man's neck had been slashed. The deep cut oozed fresh blood. Gaston wiped his knife on the guard's coat. He and Schwartz mumbled a quick prayer to Morr, then lifted the dead man and laid him on top of his erstwhile companions.

THE LAST to go into the pit was Petr. Baltzer went through his pockets and took out a silver hammer from the thong on his neck.

'For his family,' Baltzer said but no one took much notice. None of them knew who his family were. As long as Baltzer didn't go near their pockets they were fine.

By the time they had finished disposing of the bodies, Morrslieb was rising up through the dark trees trunks.

'Hurry now!' Gunter shouted as they shovelled the dirt back over them all, then they piled up stones and branches to stop wild animals from digging the bodies up again.

THE MERCHANTS' BELONGINGS consisted of some wooden crates and heavy packs.

'Get these men's bags!' Osric shouted but no one volunteered. 'Come on! Freidel! Elias! You two!' he shouted, meaning Schwartz, a stable lad before he joined up, and Kann – a quiet man who had been friends with the man they had just buried. 'Pick this stuff up!'

Baltzer started to chuckle as Freidel lifted one of the satchels onto his shoulders. Elias lifted a case, but as he did so he felt a stabbing pain in his arm and dropped the crate.

'Careful!' Gunter cursed, but when Elias tried to lift it again his arm refused to take the weight.

'He's wounded!' Freidel called out and the men gathered round and saw the slash on the underside of Elias's jacket: the spreading stain of blood.

Gunter hurried over to inspect his new lad. The cut was not too deep, but it was bleeding freely. 'Freidel – bind this up!'

Freidel took a dirty strip of cloth and bound it around Elias's arm. Elias could barely feel the pain. He could still feel his heart racing.

Freidel tied a knot in the cloth and Elias dropped his arm to his side. 'Is it bad?'

Freidel told him, 'Don't worry, you'll live.'

ONCE THEY HAD walked a little way along the road Edmunt began to get a sense of their bearings. They were higher up the valley than he had thought. It was only a few miles down the road to Gruff Spennsweich's farm.

They paused to pass the merchants' belongings around, and as soon as the loads were redistributed Sigmund was off again, with Edmunt at the front.

Elias felt the blood on his cheeks drying to a scab. He put his hand to his face and looked at the blood on his finger-tips. It was red, just like human blood.

He swallowed. He was disappointed with his first battle. He'd been terrified. The thought of being in combat again made him start to sweat.

'Come on, wounded soldier,' Gaston encouraged and Elias forced a smile and went in front of him.

SIGMUND LED THEM down the road towards Farmer Spennsweich's farm. Osric's company led, Gunter's fol-lowed. Even though it was dark, the men's legs swung freely now, and they made good going.

The trees pressed in on either side, dark and silent. The men strained their eyes in case one of the shadows should leap out in ambush – but nothing moved and this time no alarms were given.

The road dipped down and forded a stream. They splashed through the water and climbed up a gentle rise. The closer to the top they came the stronger was the faint smell of wood smoke and cooking. Many of the men expected to find the place devastated, like the farm they had seen earlier that day – so when they saw the lights inside the shutters and the thread of pale grey smoke hang-ing over the cabin, there was a noticeable wave of relief. The soldiers laughed and joked and Baltzer suggested Freidel ask how much Gruff's daughters were for the night.

GRUFF SPENNSWEICH SAT by the door, a piece of straw in his mouth and the loaded blunderbuss across his knees. He had chewed the end down to a sodden mess of fibres ans spat it onto the floor.

Valina didn't like him spitting in the house, but he was too preoccupied to notice her frown.

When they heard the tramp of many footsteps Beatrine gasped. 'What's that?'

Gruff Spennsweich had worked all these years to raise his family and now savage animals – animals with just enough intelligence to understand hatred and vengeance and cruelty – were coming to kill all his pretty daughters. He stood holding the blunderbuss, both hands shaking as he checked the bolts on the doorway, then opened the shutters on the window and thrust the gun out.

'Get off my land!' he bellowed. 'Or I'll blow you back to your damned pits!'

Osric saw the gun first and ducked and then all the halberdiers started to run for cover.

'Farmer Spennsweich!' Sigmund shouted and the blunderbuss waved in his direction for a moment. 'Farmer Spennsweich it is Captain Jorg of the Helmstrumburg Halberdiers!'

There was a curse from inside the farm and the blunderbuss was withdrawn. Osric started laughing and all of a sudden the tension of the day's march disappeared and they all started laughing.

AFTER INTRODUCTIONS, GRUFF sent Dietrik out to show the halberdiers where they could sleep for the night.

The barn was split level, with crude wooden enclosures for the livestock. On the top floor straw and sacks were piled up. The press of animal bodies meant the air was warmer, but also was strongly scented with manure, straw and tightly pressed livestock. Dietrik herded the five cows into one of the enclosures and they jostled against each other, nervously attempting to turn to watch the men come in. The halberdiers piled their packs against the wall.

The men climbed the ladder up to the second level and threw armfuls of straw over the floor, then spread their cloaks over it to make crude beds.

Dietrik came back and Gruff told him to tap a firkin of ale for the men to drink. Valina selected a pair of hams that were drying in the upstairs room and Dietrik carried them out one at a time to the barn. The men started to carve the meat up, chewing the salty meat slowly as the beer was left to settle. Dietrik brought all of Farmer

Spennsweich's best pewter tankards which were then filled and passed around.

As THE HALBERDIERS relaxed and toasted the generosity of their host, the cows slowly settled down and began to chew their cud.

Outside, the moons cast enough light to illuminate the farmstead. There was a vegetable patch behind the house. The barns were on the other side of the yard. They created a 'U' shaped compound that was typical of the more isolated farmsteads, the three buildings creating a wall that made the settlement far more defensible.

Osric's men were on sentry duty. Due to the danger of a beastman attack the sentries were doubled.

Elias, Schwartz and Kann stuck together as they patrolled round the back. Baltzer and a pair of brothers, Friedrik and Frantz, stood at the gateway, staring down the road that they had come on. The woods were silent, but an occasional bat swooped down around their heads.

Baltzer's nerves were on edge. There was a loud rustle of branches.

'What was that?' he asked.

The rustling continued. It sounded like something large, crashing through the undergrowth. Baltzer's fear was contagious. Soon all three of them were standing alert, their halberd blades pointing into the darkness, but the crashing stopped and a long silence followed.

'Do you think it was anything?' Frantz asked.

'Could have been a bird,' Friedrik suggested hopefully.

Baltzer didn't want to talk about it. His eyes were straining to catch the slightest movement. Frantz yawned and then Friedrik yawned too.

'Will you shut up!' Baltzer hissed.

'Anything?' Kann asked when they had completed a circuit.

'We heard something,' Friedrik said. 'Seen anything?'

The other men shook their heads. Baltzer stood a little way off. This would be the best moment to attack, when the sentries were distracted – but however hard he stared at the moonlit tree-line, he could see nothing.

WHEN THE SOLDIERS had been fed and watered, Gruff locked and bolted the doors and windows and made all the girls bring their mattresses into the living room where he could watch them. Beatrine huffed as she helped the twins lug the mattress the three of them shared from their bedroom. Gertrude was too young to know what was happening. She held her sister's hand.

Valina looked at her father, embarrassed by him. 'They're not criminals,' she said but Gruff didn't pay any notice. He had no intention of saving his daughters from beastmen, just to see them plundered by halberdiers.

AFTER THEY HAD drunk the beer was down to the yeasty dregs, the halberdiers lay on their cloaks and slept. Gunter's men were upstairs in the straw, while Osric's men were down next to the cows.

Sigmund and Edmunt stayed up, their faces bottom lit by the fire.

'It's not like beastmen to come so far down the hills. They've always kept themselves to the high lands. I never heard of them coming down in herds like this,' Edmunt said.

'Why do you think they came so far down?' Sigmund asked.

Edmunt shrugged

'The ones we killed. Do you think they were the ones from Osman's farm?'

Edmunt tossed another stick onto the fire. 'No,' he said at last. 'I do not. Nor did Gunter. There were prints of large beastmen at Osman's, but the ones we killed were all small.'

They sat in silence for a while longer. Behind them one of the men coughed and turned over. 'That means there's more than one band.'

Edmunt nodded.

There was a long pause.

'I don't know about you,' Sigmund said, 'but I cannot believe that this has nothing to do with the fiery star.'

As SIGMUND AND Edmunt talked, the two Reiklanders made their beds upstairs, away from the halberdiers.

They had insisted that their packs were brought upstairs, and the crates and bags piled together.

Gunter's men left them to themselves. They had no interest in the men's airs and attitudes, nor in their heavy merchandise.

Half an hour after Sigmund and Edmunt had put out the fire with the last dregs of beer and turned the lanterns down to low and hooded them, Theodor checked his pistols were under the crude pillow of his rolled cloak.

He listened until he could hear the halberdiers snoring. When he was sure that they were all asleep he turned to peer at his companion.

Eugen's eyes were wide open. They caught a stray beam of moonlight and glittered strangely in the darkness.

Theodor whispered, so quietly it was almost inaudible. 'Why were we attacked?'

The pale eyes turned down to him slowly, as if Eugen was in a meditative state. There was something disconcerting in his companion's manner.

'I thought everything was agreed!' Theodor said.

Eugen moved silently, and Theodor felt a hand rest on his cheek.

His companion's eyes were dark as he turned towards him, but his teeth glittered with malice. 'Do not question me again.'

The voice was sad, but as his companion spoke he ran a fingernail across Theodor's throat, then the Reiklander lay back, and did not speak again.

CHAPTER TWO

A JAGGED SKYLINE of three and four storey buildings lined the broad cobblestoned marketplace of Helmstrumburg.

One of the many watering holes was Crooked Dwarf inn: a crooked timber-framed building with ferns growing in the gutters. Its owner, Guthrie Black, a portly bachelor, was standing in the doorway. He wiped his hands on his apron and smelled the fine morning air. There was a strange hush. Not even the town crier sounded as pompous as usual. It was all this talk of the fiery star. Guthrie's gut swelled as he took in a deep breath, and let it out in one long sigh.

'Josh?' he called. Where was that boy when there were jobs to be done? 'Josh!'

Josh didn't reappear for an hour. By this time Guthrie had swept the bar himself, carried three barrels of ale up from the cellar, and now rested in one of the chairs, mopping sweat from his brow.

'Where have you been?' he demanded as Josh slunk into the room.

'Nowhere,' the lad said. If Guthrie hadn't been so tired he would have stood up and boxed the boy's ears. 'If you were a little closer!' he said and shook his fist as he always did, but he never did hit any of his boys. He said 'his boys', but they were no one's boys really.

The lad scuffed his foot against the oak bar. 'I wanted to join the town watch,' he said at last.

'And?'

'And they said I was too young.'

Guthrie tousled the lad's hair. Since his oldest, Elias, had left, all the others wanted to join up. 'Whatever this fiery star means,' Guthrie reassured the boy, 'it'll have nothing to do with us here. Even if you could join the halberdiers, all the excitement would be over before you even got there!'

Josh pouted. 'Promise?'

Guthrie smiled and pinched the boy's cheek. 'Promise!' he said

THE HALBERDIERS WERE up before dawn. The eastern sky was already paling, but in the west, late stars still glimmered above the tree-line. The two-tailed star was nowhere to be seen.

The air was still, and their breath misted in front of them. The halberdiers lined up in the courtyard of Farmer Spennsweich's house, dark shapes in the half-light. Osric yawned as he pulled his backpack higher on his back and leaned on the halberd shaft for support. There was no sound from the cabin. Not even the dogs were awake.

Sigmund stood to the side, silently watching his men rank up. They distributed the merchants' crates and packs amongst themselves, and then stood, halberds on their shoulders, ready to march.

'All ready?' Sigmund called and the men hurried to their ranks. They waited for a moment as the parade roll call was called. Each man answered to his name.

'All present!' Osric called first, then Gunter.

Sigmund nodded. 'Halberdiers – forward!' Sigmund called and Osric's men began to tramp out of the courtyard.

THEY WERE A third of the way down the hill when the sun rose on their left. There was no warmth, just brilliant light that made the shadows deeper and more impenetrable. Elias was sweating and tried to adjust his pack. High above him the crags of Frantzplinth began to catch the first rays of sun, the snow shone brilliantly and clouds began to run aground upon the sheer peak.

Below them the River Stir was a gold ribbon, sparkling with reflected sunlight. None of them paused, but they all looked down to see the magnificent curve of the river: the orchards that lined the banks and the dark brown patch of Helmstrumburg, its tiled roofs gleaming in the morning light.

THE HALBERDIERS KEPT a fast pace all morning, making Eugen and Theodor hurry to keep up with them.

'Captain, would you slow your men down?' Eugen called but Sigmund took no notice.

'Captain, sir!' Eugen called again and his aristocratic tone made Sigmund's teeth grind. Gunter cast a sideways glance at Sigmund, but Sigmund did not make any sign. It seemed to Gunter that he might have even lengthened his pace a little. 'I must protest!' Eugen called, but then he realised how far behind he'd fallen and broke into a trot to catch up.

THE LAST STRETCH of the road led through orchards. Under the apple trees, chickens were picking though the grass. Edmunt called forward to Osric.

'Do you think the burgomeister would miss one of those birds?'

Osric didn't even bother to respond, but Baltzer did. As the unit drummer Baltzer always stood in the front rank. He and Osric had both been in the burgomeister's town watch before enlisting. The burgomeister would give them all the chickens they wanted if they did what he said. 'I didn't think you were one to accept payment from the bur-gomeister!' Baltzer called and Edmunt laughed the comment off.

'It'd take more than chickens!' he laughed, but although a few of them smiled, they all knew that it paid to do what the burgomeister asked.

As THE WALLS of Helmstrumburg came into view the packs on the halberdiers' backs seemed lighter, their footfall was longer. Helmstrumburg had been walled with stone hun-dreds of years ago, but since then the settlement had overgrown the walls along the western bank. Around the new town there was an earthen rampart, topped with a nine foot timber palisade.

'Look smart!' Sigmund called and the usual traffic of farmers and idlers stepped aside to watch the Ragged Com-pany march through the gates.

Holmgar and Richel – a couple of Vostig's handgunners – stood sentry at the gate. They stood to attention as the halberdiers marched up, but as Osric passed, Richel mut-tered: 'You scruffy bunch of bastards!'

Osric's jaw tensed. He would box that idiot's ears when he came back to the barracks.

DESPITE HIS PATCHED uniform, Osric puffed out his chest. He winked at a pretty blonde girl who turned and giggled with her friend. But they were pointing at Gaston. With long blond moustaches, pale blue eyes and high cheek-bones, he looked good in the worst of uniforms.

Osric's cheeks paled when he realised. Baltzer sniggered and Osric gave him a sharp glare.

The two files of halberdiers marched through the new town, and passed through the old stone wall, which sprouted ferns and grass from the ancient stonework. Sig-mund stopped at the marketplace. 'You two! Come with me!' he ordered, gesturing to the two merchants. The two men obviously weren't used to being spoken to like this and their faces darkened with anger, but Sigmund paid them no attention. 'The rest of you, back to barracks! Get some rest. No drills till the afternoon. Parade at two!'

The men started to march off.

'Elias!' Sigmund called. 'Get that cut seen to!'

'Sergeant Gunter!' Sigmund said and Gunter turned back for a moment. 'Make sure he does.'

'HOW MUCH FURTHER?' Eugen asked after they'd been going for five minutes. The shorter man had been limping since they'd entered town.

Not used to walking, Sigmund thought. 'Not far,' he said.

Eugen tried to hurry the captain along, but Sigmund kept a constant marching pace, and turned onto the docks.

The cobbles here were strewn with rotting scraps of food and rubbish. Men shouted and bargained as sacks and barrels of grain, ale, meat, furs and wood were loaded onto the barges in exchange for metal pots, fine clothes, cheap knives and arrow heads, and a few precious barrels of blackpowder.

The harbour was a hundred feet long, with a thirty-foot stone pier thrusting out into river, protecting the boats from flood or floating debris. The long jetties were lined with barges and sail boats that plied up and down the Stir and the Reik. One boat had red-striped sails and a high prow and poop-deck, such as the men of Marienburg used to sail along the coats of Bretonnia.

'You trade with the men of Marienburg,' Theodor noted.

'The burgomeister will trade with anyone,' Sigmund said.

The three men started to push through the bustle. In the middle of the pushing crowds the stink of stale sweat was overpowering.

'Ho, Sigmund!'

One of the labourers, a man with a sweat-stained shirt and a pot belly, pushed through the crowd.

'Frantz!' Sigmund laughed.

Frantz nodded towards the two Reiklanders. 'Who are these two?'

Eugen tried to overhear the men's conversation, but Sigmund's Talabheim accent thickened and it was hard to make the words out. 'Beastmen,' he heard, 'patrols' and then he heard the word 'burgomeister' and at that the labourer's face darkened and he turned to appraise the two outlanders, then spat into the ground at his feet.

Eugen put his perfumed handkerchief to his nose and cleared his throat loudly. The stink of sweat and rotting fruit was unbearable.

'Please!' Eugen said, but Sigmund refused to be either intimidated or hurried. When he had finished talking to the labourer he turned to the two merchants.

'Please, follow me.'

THE GUILD HALL stood at the east end of the docks. It acted as both centre of power and fortification: designed to be able to withstand the mob and act as courthouse and seat of government. It was built of hard red brick and was four storeys high. In the centre of the building was a paved courtyard, around which the outside walls rose up without windows until the second floor. The windows held glass, but they were narrow and high and were barred with black rods of iron.

On the river side of the guild hall were loop-holes for handguns. A pair of cannon had once sat atop the building, until the burgomeister had sold them. Or so the rumours went.

The doorway of the guild was guarded by a couple of town watchmen. They wore white ribbons tied about their arms and carried long wooden batons at their belts.

Seeing Sigmund approach, one of them slouched over to the entrance and called inside.

Roderick, the watch commander, appeared at the doorway. He had taken over command of the town watch when Osric had enlisted. He was a tall handsome man, but there was a cruel glint in his blue eyes. Sigmund had no reason to disbelieve the rumours about Roderick: that he'd stabbed a rival merchant to death when he tried to replace the burgomeister. Of course, no one was arrested for the murder and no one talked about it any more. Not in public anyway.

'Captain Jorg,' Roderick smiled without warmth. 'How can we help you?'

'I have important matters to discuss with the burgomeister.'

'Who are these two?'

'Messenger boys.'

Eugen bristled at the contempt with which Sigmund referred to them.

Roderick smiled and bowed a little. 'Greetings, gentlemen. Please follow me.'

Sigmund pushed past the watch man. 'I'll see them in.'

THE OUTER DOOR opened into a central courtyard. On the other side, a heavy oak door opened into the guild hall.

Sigmund strode across the courtyard into the guild hall, where the burgomeister was sitting, at the end of a long oak table, talking with a scribe.

'Captain Jorg,' the burgomeister said without any hint of emotion. He was a tall thin man, his bony hands folded on the table in front of him. His fingers were covered with gold rings set with all kinds of coloured stones. Around his neck hung a gold chain of his office. 'What news from the hills?'

'Not good, lord burgomeister. The rumours are true. Beastmen are banding together and they are coming lower than we have ever seen before. Osman Heinz's house was destroyed, and–'

'Osman Heinz? There are a hundred men who would have burnt his house with pleasure.'

'It was beastmen,' Sigmund said. The memory of what he'd seen there made him shudder.

'So you tell me,' the burgomeister said. 'But that is just your opinion. I have other matters to take into account. Anyway, who are these people?'

'Your captain was kind enough to help us when we were attacked,' Eugen intervened.

'We killed all the beastmen, and I lost one man,' Sigmund said.

'So you dealt with the offending creatures. What is the alarm? I am sure they will have learnt their lesson. They will not dare to stray back down near human settlement.'

Sigmund was thrown for a moment. 'But I do not think the beastmen we killed were the same as those who–'

Again the burgomeister cut him off but Sigmund refused to be silenced. 'Sir!' Sigmund said, his voice rising as he rested his hands on either side of the ledger and glared at the burgomeister. 'I am sure that this was not the party who slaughtered the Osman and his family. I believe we must call for reinforcements and until then the outlying farmers must be brought into town for their protection.'

The burgomeister looked up at the halberdier for a moment and then laughed. 'Captain Jorg – I think you have been listening to these stories about Sigmar's star. Meanwhile I have a town to govern. I cannot waste time with superstitions!'

Sigmund slammed his hand onto the table. 'Beastmen killed Osman. More will be killed unless we get reinforcements and bring those living in the forest down to Helmstrumburg!'

The burgomeister put up his hands and closed his eyes. 'Please, captain. I have heard your request and will consider it. If it is half as bad as you think then I suggest you go and find those last few beastmen!'

'If you will not request more men then I insist that we put in place a policy to bring the outlying villagers into town for their own protection!'

'No,' the burgomeister said emphatically. 'Now I have other things to consider.'

Sigmund bit back his anger. 'Sir–' he managed.

The burgomeister smiled politely. 'My dear Captain Jorg,' he spoke as if to a child. 'I do not think we need more troops around Helmstrumburg. You and your men are protection enough!'

Sigmund was furious, but he bit his retort back, and strode from the hall.

* * *

IN THE BURGOMEISTER'S hall Eugen, Theodor and the burgomeister listened to Sigmund's footsteps depart.

The burgomeister rose in one fluid motion, swung the door shut, and bolted it. He glared at the two merchants. 'You were supposed to come in secret!' he hissed. 'In secret!' he repeated, his face purple. 'I cannot think of a less ostentatious arrival than to get yourselves attacked and be rescued by that dolt and his team of drill-ground thugs.'

'Isn't there a better way to greet your guests?' Eugen smiled as he pulled himself a seat.

The burgomeister's mouth clamped shut. He flopped into his seat, his arms hanging at his side. Eugen drew a hand from under his jacket and extended it over the table. He opened his fist and there was a loud thud as the leather purse he'd been holding landed on the table top. The burgomeister stared at the purse for a long while, but did not reach out to take it.

'Now,' Eugen said as he leaned in and spoke slowly and softly. 'I trust the second part of the agreement is in place?'

The burgomeister's eyes did not leave the purse of gold. Theodor cleared his throat but the burgomeister's eyes did not flicker.

'Lord burgomeister,' Eugen said. 'I trust you have fulfilled your half of the bargain.' He spoke a little more hurriedly this time, stress raising the pitch of his voice. 'Lord burgomeister–' he began one last time but the burgomeister put up his hand.

He drew in a deep breath and pulled himself erect in his seat, took the purse. 'It is,' he said.

SIGMUND WAS STILL fuming as he marched across the courtyard and took the stone staircase down to the vaults, where Maximillian, the treasurer worked.

Not bothering to knock, Sigmund pushed open the heavy oak door. Beyond, in a low-ceiling room, a man sat hunched over a large table covered with ledgers. Maximillian was the long-suffering treasurer of Helmstrumburg. A true-blooded bureaucrat, he ignored Sigmund for as long as possible, then put his quill back into its ink pot and let out a long sigh.

'How can I help you?'

'I have come to take three crowns from your chests.'

'You lost a man?'

Sigmund nodded, but immediately felt uncomfortable with his flippant manner. How many times had he done this now?

Ten – eleven? He couldn't remember. The first man he'd lost was Arneld, a childhood friend. That had been the hardest. It had been his own fault. Not only had he persuaded Arneld to join but he'd failed to save him. He still remembered turning and seeing Arneld's horrified face – frozen forever in that brief moment before death – when the greenskin chieftain disembowelled him.

'Name?' Maximillian said and Sigmund snapped back to the present.

'Petr von Blankow.'

The certificate was signed and stamped with red wax. Petr's death would earn his relatives three crowns. That was the price for each dead man's life. Sigmund realised how hardened he'd become to loss. It was a soldier's bedfellow. Edmunt was the only one he would truly miss now, he thought.

THE TWO MERCHANTS were coming out of the guild hall when Sigmund came back up the stairs into the central courtyard.

'Delivered your message?'

The two men started. 'Captain Jorg. Still here, I see?'

'Indeed. I suppose you're here for the fur?' Sigmund said.

Eugen didn't seem to understand.

'The furs,' Sigmund said. 'Helmstrumburg is famous for the quality of the furs.'

Eugen nodded. 'Of course. How forgetful of me. We are interested, but I have to say that there are other things that interest me more.'

'Will you be partaking of our Helmstrumburg hospitality for long?'

'I doubt it,' Eugen replied, and Theodor laughed.

SIGMUND WAS RELIVING the argument with the burgomeister when he stepped inside the Crooked Dwarf inn. There were a couple of regulars, sitting at the bar, tall steins of beer in front of them. Sigmund acknowledged them as he walked up to the bar.

'Now then, Guthrie,' he said and leaned his arms on the smooth wood of the bar. 'What's new?'

'Nothing new.' Guthrie continued drying his tankard. 'I hear you brought my lad back alive.'

'I did,' Sigmund said.

'Coming home with living men is a good habit for a captain to have,' Guthrie said. 'Keep it up.'

'I intend to,' Sigmund snapped, surprised by the animosity of the jolly ostler. Turning round, he saw Edmunt sitting in the corner with a steaming platter of beef, bowls of pickled cabbage and good thick trenchers of rye bread. Sigmund walked over to him, pulled out a stool, and sat down.

Edmunt nodded to Sigmund to help himself. The two men had been friends long before they'd enlisted. That feeling still blurred the distinctions between captain and halberdier.

'I saw Frantz,' Sigmund said.

'How was he?'

'Good.'

They ate in silence for a few moments.

'The burgomeister refused to ask for more men.'

'Did you expect anything else?'

Sigmund shook his head and kept eating.

'Did you deliver our friends to him?'

'I did,' Sigmund said and smiled. 'Strange pair.'

'They are.'

'What do you think?'

Edmunt took another bite of bread. 'Who can tell,' he said at last, cut a piece of meat and began to chew.

Sigmund put his beer down. 'I don't trust them.'

Edmunt nodded. They ate in silence for a while. After they'd finished wiping their bowls clean, Edmunt let out a belch of satisfaction.

'How's Elias's cut?'

'We cleaned it. He's resting.'

Sigmund nodded. 'I'll go see him,' he said and stood up. On his way out of the door he paused and looked back at his friend. Edmunt had grown up in the high country. He'd known Osman, and even more than that he'd known the trader's daughters. He watched his friend take a long swig of his tankard. After what they'd seen in the hills they were all a little shaken. Getting drunk was one way to forget.

THE HELMSTRUMBURG BARRACKS backed onto the river. Ringed by a stone wall, meant as much to keep the soldiers in as angry fathers out, there was a wide drill ground and then a 'U' of buildings with their back to the river, the long draughty barrack formed the right wing. The left housed kitchens, the armoury and a stable, which was used to store grain and blackpowder, and the two nags that the soldiers used to collect their provisions from the docks.

Across the top were the officers' rooms, sick room and shrine, with its small statue of Sigmar. While Sigmar may have cleared the forests of greenskins, it was Taal who created them, and Taal who had named this land, and Taal who owned the hearts of the men of Talabecland. He shared his shrine with his brother, Ulric, at the base of a tree near the river. It was a crude thing, which passing soldiers had built up over the years. The coloured strips of cloth upon which they'd written their prayers were completely faded.

The barracks had been strange at first to Sigmund, but now the smell of oiled metal, sweat and waxed cuirboili breastplates seemed like home.

Sigmund hailed Vostig, sergeant of the handgunners, who was sitting with his men, cleaning their guns. They'd been shooting that morning and their clothes and faces were dark with soot.

'You should try washing your clothes some day,' Sigmund told them and Vostig grinned.

'When you get proper uniforms,' he bantered, 'then we'll wash!'

SIGMUND WAS STILL chuckling as he stooped to pass through the sick room doorway. There were five beds, crammed together, and on one of them sat Elias, looking bored.

'How's the arm?'

'It's alright,' Elias said but he didn't look good.

Sigmund felt the young man's forehead. The lad was feverish. The wound must have gotten infected. 'Let me have a look at that,' Sigmund said and began to unwrap the bandage.

As the last wet wrapper came away he saw that the wound was oozing green pus. Sigmund frowned. 'Who cleaned this wound?'

'Freidel.'

Sigmund shook his head, stood up and moved to the doorway. He could see Schwartz coming back from the latrine. 'Get Freidel!' Sigmund shouted. 'I want him to fetch the apothecary. And run!'

VASIR DID NOT dare sleep, but at some point he must have dropped off and jerked awake as dawn began to bleach the sky. Beneath him he could see shapes moving: horned shapes.

Vasir was so frightened he stopped breathing. They have come for you, he told himself as the enormous figures passed not more than a hand's reach beneath his perch. They've tracked you here, he told himself, but that was impossible. He'd crossed streams, ducked through stinking patches of wild garlic, taken circuitous routes through rock fields. It was impossible to follow a scent through all that.

Impossible, he told himself. If they'd tracked you then one of them would be looking up this tree straight at you.

Ill fate has brought them here. Nothing more. Don't move, don't breathe, and don't let them smell me!

It was several minutes before all the beastmen had passed. Vasir thanked Taal for his benevolence.

THE BEASTMEN KNEW a different world to that of men: found their way by sacred rocks or twisted and macabre trees that were imbued with a dull sense of hatred for living things. They'd lived in the hills since time immemorial: had ranged right down to the river – until the Great Slayer came and killed their chieftain, and destroyed their most sacred herdstone.

Since then they'd brooded, nurturing their hatred as carefully as a flame: feeding it, letting it grow. Deep in the hills they'd been gathering their strength, and now the two-horned star had been seen, the prophecies were true.

It was time for the gathering.

THIS SACRED SHRINE had once been in the heart of beastman country, but now humans had come up even into these hills: cut down trees and planted seeds in the ground. The beastmen could smell their fires, smell cooking meat, and knew that the time had come.

Azgrak knew that this was his time. As soon as he'd seen the two-horned star, animal impulse had compelled him to follow the summons. He stood, stark albino white, glowing in the half light of dawn. his fingers flexing over and over in some mad impulse. Behind him his bodyguard stood, bearing the banners they'd found on their way to the gathering: the skinned bodies of men. Around the circle he saw the other tribal leaders. Fat Potgut – the Red Killer, whose belt was made of linked human heads, their hair plaited to form a gruesome belt.

Brazak – the bloated beast, whose skin bubbled with suppurating sores that boiled and popped and oozed a sticky white pus.

And of course, Uzrak the Black who had ruled the plateau since Azgrak was weaned from his mother's udders. But

Uzrak's fur was starting to grey. If the star had come a few winters earlier then Uzrak might be the undisputed leader but now...

Azgrak let out a low growl. It was involuntary: the blood-lust was coming onto him again as the shaman strode into the middle of the square. All the tribe leaders knew what they were here for: to choose a leader. Any who contested leadership had to fight for it, or die.

The shaman shook his man-skull rattle. It was time.

Uzrak stepped into the crude ring of stones – daring any to challenge his leadership.

Azgrak growled again, unable to keep the fury inside. He snorted and flexed his hands, his muscles so tense that ten-drils of veins stood out from his arms and neck and forehead, right up to his horns.

Uzrak the Black glared at the display of dissention. He'd fathered this whelp ten years before on the brood-goat of some dead chieftain. He put back his horns, snout to the sky, and let out a roar that made the trees above his head shake – but when he looked back down he saw that one challenger had stepped into the ring. The contester glowed white in the dawn.

Neither of the beastmen moved for a moment, but all around the circle the other beastmen began to snort and stamp their hooves, tense and excited.

Blood would be shed tonight.

In the clearing the two combatants – black and white – were locked together. The white shape thrust his horns in one more time, and the black body slid slowly to the ground, to lie at his feet like a pool of darkness.

There was silence. In the memory of all there, there had never been such a fast and brutal fight. And none imagined that Uzrak the Black's thirty-year reign had ended on the horns of one of his son – this cursed albino – that should have been smothered at birth.

Azgrak glared round the ring, sensing the disquiet, but no others dared challenge him. They looked towards the shaman to ban this abomination but the shaman shook the man-skull rattle and began the rites of lordship; after what they'd seen, there was no doubt that the albino had been blessed by the gods.

CHAPTER THREE

THAT AFTERNOON VOSTIG'S men were drilling. Sigmund stood to watch, making sure they were lined up close together.

'Prime the pan!' Vostig shouted. The men moved as one, filling the pans with powder.

'Close the pan!' The men flipped the pans closed and blew away any loose powder.

'Charge with powder.' The men poured a measure of blackpowder down the barrels.

'Prime with shot!' A lead ball the size of a walnut was dropped down the barrels. The bullet and charge were rammed home. Each gun had a slow-burning fuse attached to the trigger. They blew on the fuse to make the end glow and then when the order came to 'Present handguns' the handgunners lifted the butt to their shoulders.

'Prepare to fire!' Vostig shouted. The men flipped the pans open.

'Give fire!' Vostig called. The men pulled on the triggers and the fuse struck the powder in the pan, which belched and ignited the charge within the barrel. The guns flared flame and smoke in a ragged fusillade.

As the smoke cleared Sigmund turned to look at the length of cloth, a foot high and ten foot long, that had been pinned up along the back of the barrack wall, at chest height. Twelve ragged holes showed where the lead shots had ripped through. Three men had missed. There were new chips on the brickwork, well over head height.

Vostig cursed. 'Again!' he shouted, and the men scrambled to remove the fuse from their guns and use the ram rod to clear any embers from the barrels. 'Damn your hides!' Vostig cursed. 'I want fifteen holes each time! Now – prime the pan!'

SIGMUND LEFT THE handgunners to their practice and walked through the barracks to the sick room.

Elias did not look any better. His face was pale and sweaty. As he inspected the young man, Sigmund smiled to hide his concern. Where was that damned apothecary?

'How do you feel?'

'A little sore.' Elias seemed exhausted by the effort of speaking. His ragged breaths filled the room. He looked suddenly frightened. 'If I die will you tell Guthrie that–'

'You're not going to die,' Sigmund told him, quickly.

'Promise?'

'I promise,' Sigmund said, trying to hide his concern. Surely no normal infection could have taken hold so quickly and so violently? And there were no medicines for the supernatural.

As SIGMUND SAT with Elias, keeping him company, the sick room door creaked open. The woodsman, Edmunt, stood uncertainly by the door, his lips moving silently in a prayer to Taal.

Sigmund bowed his head. He knew why Edmunt had come. The woodsman's face was white. He stared at Elias and nodded.

'The same,' he said, and then turned to go.

* * *

OSRIC'S MEN LOOKED up as Edmunt came out of the sick room and walked past where they were polishing their halberds. Edmunt didn't meet their gazes but walked straight past, across the drill ground to the barrack gates.

Baltzer spat. 'What's up with him?'

'Give it a break,' Freidel said. To anyone who knew the woodsman's history, it was obvious.

THE APOTHECARY ARRIVED at the barracks just before dinner. There was a fine smell of lentil broth coming from the kitchens and the men were standing around expectantly.

The apothecary nodded to them as he walked up to the door of the sick room. He paused at the door before knocking and stepping inside. Sigmund left the side of Elias's bed to make way for him. The apothecary walked over to the bed, where the young man was dozing listlessly. He leant over, adjusted his spectacles, and pulled back the blanket to inspect Elias's arm.

'He has been wounded by a poisoned blade,' Sigmund said and the apothecary nodded. Slowly and carefully, he unwrapped the bandages which were sticky with fluids. The wound was swollen and putrid, and a green pus oozed out.

The stench made both men's eyes water. The apothecary took a pomander from his robes and held it close to his nose.

'Can you fetch me a bucket?' the apothecary asked. Sigmund hurried out to the kitchens and came out with one of their buckets, which the apothecary signalled he should put by Elias's bed.

The apothecary lifted his case onto the bed next to Elias's and took out a copper mixing bowl. In it he mixed red Tilean wine vinegar, mixed with salt, and used the mixture to clean out the wound. The procedure must have been painful, but Elias hardly seemed to notice what was happening. When the pus had been cleaned out the apothecary took a short knife from his case and bent over the wounded man. Sigmund watched with a morbid curiosity as he pared away the infected flesh and dropped it into the bucket. When true red blood began to flow freely the apothecary knew he'd hit living tissue and he washed the wound again with a fresh mix of salt and vinegar.

Sigmund watched the apothecary mix medicinal herbs and more vinegar. He made a thick paste to spread over the wound – binding it tight with fresh bandages, then he let out a long sigh.

'There,' he said, but his voice did not sound hopeful. 'That is the best I can do.'

THE APOTHECARY HAD been in the sick room for nearly an hour when Osric and Baltzer came out of the kitchen, their bowls full of steaming stew.

Richel was just coming back from sentry duty and his stomach was screaming for food.

'Richel!' Osric said. 'Good to see you.'

Richel smiled nervously. 'I don't want any trouble,' he said.

Osric marched straight up to the handgunner. 'I'll give you trouble!' he said, pushing Richel roughly against the wall, then putting his hand on the handgunner's chest. 'Now,' Osric said, 'who's a scruffy bloody bastard?'

Richel could barely breath with the weight on his chest. 'Who?'

'Me!' Richel said.

'Who?'

'Me!'

'I can't hear you.'

'Me!'

'Me what?'

'I'm a scruffy bastard!'

Osric took his foot off and gave Richel a kick. 'Remember that – damned gun-boy!'

EDMUNT TOOK HIS bowl of stew round the back of the barrack building, to the short jetty. He'd grown up with his parents high up in the hills, on the edge of the high moors. To think he needed real quiet and solitude: and here, staring out over the grey water was about as quiet as it got.

He shovelled a spoonful of broth into his mouth, and took a bite of bread. It tasted stale, as always. He chewed it anyway, and took another spoonful of broth to wash away the taste.

When he was a boy his mother had been attacked by beastmen. Somehow she survived, but the wound had eaten her alive, in much the same way that it was eating Elias. The smell was the same: fetid and bitter, like the stench of the red stinkball in the forests. In the end the sickness had driven her mad. Her skin bubbled with boils and her tongue swelled up to fill her mouth.

It had taken Edmunt and his father a whole morning to dig her grave at the back of their cabin. They wrapped her body in her favourite shawl: a red-dyed woollen one, with fancy embroidery around the hem.

Years ago, when he'd first enlisted in the halberdiers, Edmunt had been wandering through the market one morning when he found a trader selling embroidered shawls.

'Two for ten pennies,' the trader had told him, but Edmunt had just wanted one. 'Seven for one,' the trader had argued.

There was nothing Edmunt disliked more than a Reiklander with attitude – but it was the shawl he was concerned with. He paid the seven pennies and took it. The trader had assumed it was a gift for some trollop at Madam Jolie's, but when he joked Edmunt's glare had silenced him.

Only seven pennies, he thought. After his mother had died his father never spoke much. His wife's death had taken the purpose from his life. He hadn't spoken much when she was alive. After she was gone he had barely spoken at all. Four years after they'd buried his mother, Edmunt had had to dig a pit for his father as well. Woodcutting was a hard life. He'd buried his father next to his mother, raised a cairn over him and said the prayer of

Taal over his grave. And that afternoon he'd carried on cutting.

HIS MEAL EATEN, Edmunt tossed a stone into the broad, fast waters. There was a brief splash and ripples, before the current of the river swept them downstream. From here the Stir became the Upper Reik and then the Reik, and then it flowed into the sea at Marienburg. All his father had wanted him to be was a woodsman, but his mother had been more ambitious for her son, proudly imagining him in a smart uniform: feathered hat, puffed sleeves of silk and felt, an outrageous codpiece of striped cloth. He imagined her eyes filling with joyful tears as she put her hand over her mouth to laugh at her son dressed so well – then he threw another stone and stood up and turned to go back towards the barracks.

THE BARRACKS WERE quiet as the men sat on their beds and ate.

Freidel took a bite of his bread and cursed. 'Can't we get something that's not full of pissing weevils?'

'When you stop being an ugly bastard we'll give you weevil-free bread!' Gunter told him and the men laughed and dipped the bread in the stew.

AFTER DINNER SIGMUND and Vostig sat at the gate of the barracks, which was set on the crossroads that led towards Altdorf Street. It was always busy at this time of day as people hurried home before dark. There were women with baskets of shopping; a ploughman, leading two shire horses in for shoeing; two old men, deep in conversation.

'Does it ever make you sad?' Vostig asked. 'Watching all these people in their ordinary lives?'

'No. It makes me glad to be a soldier!' he laughed.

Vostig let out a sigh. 'I left the army six years ago. Didn't know that, did you? I couldn't face it: normal, life that is. I've been a soldier so long I don't know what to do unless someone tells me to eat, shit, sleep and shoot.'

Over the sounds of the town, they could hear a marching tune. Sigmund turned to see if Baltzer was anywhere near, but the drill yard was empty.

'Do you hear that?'

Vostig nodded.

The sound got louder and louder, and the two men stood up to see better. Down Altdorf Street marched a column of men. Their striped uniforms were clean and neat; they carried large round shields with red and blue quarters; on their shoulders rested seven-foot spears, the leaf-blades alone a foot in length.

Sigmund stood up as the men marched up towards him. Their sergeant was a tall thin man with a pencil moustache. He raised his spear and then gave the order, 'Company! Halt!' He stepped forward. 'Hanz Spurig of the Vorrsheim Spears. We are to join the command of Captain Jorge,' the man said in a thick mid-Talabecland accent.

Sigmund grinned. 'Captain Sigmund Jorg of the Helmstrumburg Halberdiers! Welcome!'

The man glanced at Sigmund, trying to hide his surprise at the captain's shabby appearance. 'My apologies!' he said. 'I did not recognise the uniform.'

'It's a long story…' Sigmund said.

Hanz smiled, but he seemed bewildered.

'Head straight in,' Sigmund clapped him on the back. 'And welcome to Helmstrumburg!'

THAT EVENING, THE halberdiers sat outside the barracks, their equipment piled up in front of them. Gaston was polishing his steel cap, while Edmunt was diligently buffing the brass fittings to a shine. Osric had his whetstone out and was grinding an even blade onto his sword – but the cheap blade was bent slightly out of shape and he gave up. 'Why don't they give us something decent to fight with!' he cursed, tossing it on the ground.

At least the halberd blades were good Reikland steel. Freidel smiled as he saw his own dim reflection in the black polished surface of the cuirboili breastplate. Layers of

stitched leather, stiffened with wax, the cuirboili breastplates wouldn't stop a handgun shot, but they would stop
all but the heaviest blows, and more than that they were a
quarter of the weight of a steel breastplate. When he could
see his own reflection Freidel put the breastpiece aside and
picked up his braces and began to work, but then he heard
the sound of marching feet and looked up and saw a company start to march across the drill ground.

'Ho! Look at this lot!' he laughed.

The halberdiers of both units put down their whetstones
and oil clothes and gathered to gawp at the newcomers.
The spearmen looked as if they'd just walked out of a tai-
lor's shop. Their uniforms matched, and instead of plain
jackets and trews, their clothes were slashed and lined with
fine striped cloth.

Osric shook his head and laughed to see such finely
dressed soldiers. 'Do you think they can fight?' he asked.

'I want to see them after Captain Jorg has taken them out
into the hills,' Osric said and stood up to his full height.
'They'll not look so fine after that!'

HANZ DID NOT appreciate the fact that his commanding officer looked little better than a tramp. The halberdiers
snickered as his men marched up to the barracks. More
galling still was to be told that there was no room for his
men in the barracks.

'My men are tired! There is no food and no place for
them to bed down! What kind of outfit is this?' he
demanded angrily.

'Helmstrumburg,' Osric said.

'And who are you?' Hanz snapped.

'Sergeant Osric von Blankov. Second Company, Helmstrumburg Halberdiers!' He jutted out his chin and dared
the new sergeant to say anything.

'Where are my men supposed to sleep?'

'In the stables.'

'My men sleep in the stables when your rabble are in the
barracks?'

'Yes!'

Hanz put his hand to his sword, but just at that moment Gunter stood up to intervene. 'I'll take over!'

Hanz's cheeks were red with anger, his men were tired and hungry. There was a tense silence as Gunter strode up to them and inquired which unit they were.

'Vorrsheim Spears!' Hanz snapped.

'Cold Beck, Fritzburg and Dravin's Wall. A fine history your unit has!' Gunter said and they were so astonished that they forgot to be angry. 'Now – we could clean the stables out for you, but they're cramped and there are rats. You' probably be more comfortable bivouacking.'

Hanz was completely disarmed by the gruff old sergeant.

'You lot!' he gestured. 'Get up and help these fine warriors put up their tents!'

Osric cursed as his men stood up. He refused to lend a hand and glared at the fancy cockerel that was their sergeant.

THE SUN HAD barely set when Roderick arrived at the guild hall to bring news to the burgomeister about the reinforcements. He could tell from the silence that followed his news that the burgomeister was not happy. As Roderick started to move towards the door, the burgomeister slammed his palm onto the table.

'The town is paying for enough troops as it is. Why should we pay for more?' he said, his tone rising as his anger flared. 'All these rumours of attacks! Scaremongering!' he insisted and banged his fist on the table again. The guild hall echoed with the sound. Seeing the man's anger, Roderick now he wished he'd sent someone else to bring the news.

'Can't you send them back to wherever they came from?' he suggested.

The burgomeister seemed to consider this for a moment.

'It would take too long,' he said, finally. Would it change things or not?

* * *

IT WAS THE turn of Osric's men to be on sentry duty that night. Six men manned each of the town gates, working in shifts. Two manned the gatehouse while two walked the walls and the other two rested. When dawn came the shift would change and the town watch would take over the day to day running of tithes and tariffs that the burgomeister charged.

The night hours were long and slow; the walls were quiet, dark and empty. In the guardhouse of the west gate Osric sat up with Kann and Schwartz playing dice.

Kann was on a winning streak and Osric was not in a good mood.

Schwartz sided with Osric. He was the sergeant after all.

'I don't know about you,' Osric said, 'but I don't want to meet those beastmen!'

Kann took his winnings again. He shared the sergeant's sentiment. He remembered the size of the beastman dung they'd found near the ruined farmstead. No one wanted to meet beastmen that size.

Schwartz was indignant. 'There's no way we should go out with warbands around. We could be ambushed at any moment!'

Kann was impatient to roll again. He got a double 6 and grinned so wide Osric could see his missing back teeth. Osric let out a sigh and pushed another three pennies across the table.

'If anyone's going out it should be those Vorrsheimers!' Osric snapped as the door of the guard-room opened. It was Sigmund. The men jumped to attention. Osric froze, in case his comment had been overheard.

'All's well?' their leader said.

Osric nodded. 'All's well.'

Sigmund nodded and shut the door behind him. Osric let out a long whistle and Kann elbowed him in the ribs. 'You lucky bastard!'

IT WAS THE officer on watch's duty to make sure all the inns were free of soldiers. After he'd checked the north gate, Sigmund walked down to Altdorf Street to check on the usual haunts of the men. The streets were dark and quiet, rats scurried from piles of rubbish, watched and then returned after he'd passed by. The only light was that cast by the moon and that which spilt out from the tavern windows.

The Blessed Rest was busy with a party of miners from Burholsen, a little way up country. In the Talabec Arms there were a few old men, smoking their pipes and talking in low voices.

He walked down towards the marketplace and stopped off in the Saddler's Rest. Two Ostlanders, Sigmund guessed from the accents, were drunk and singing songs of their homeland. At the Crooked Dwarf inn there were maybe twenty men inside; dim candlelight and pipe smoke made it difficult to see too clearly. Sigmund stooped under the door, and the drinkers saw his uniform and a hush fell over the place. Sigmund could not see Guthrie anywhere. He nodded towards Josh.

'Can I have a word?'

Josh nodded.

'It's Elias,' Sigmund said. 'His wound is infected. It doesn't look good.'

Josh nodded nervously. 'I'll tell Guthrie,' he said.

Sigmund nodded to the other drinkers and as he turned to leave he noticed the two Reikland merchants sitting by the fire, gave them a strange look and then stepped back out into the cold.

WHEN SIGMUND GOT back to the barracks there were three neat lines of five white tents arranged in the courtyard. He strode to his room and imagined leading them out on patrol, but then he saw Gunter coming from the sick room. From inside he could hear moaning, and the noise dampened his excitement at getting reinforcements.

'Nothing more we can do?'

Gunter shook his head. He'd been a soldier for fifteen years, and in that time he seen death so often that its footsteps were like the approach of an old friend. 'All we can do now is call the priest and have him say his prayers then we can let this boy die in peace.'

WHEN GUTHRIE HEARD the news about Elias he left Josh in charge of the bar and hurried to get his coat. The two Reikland merchants watched the innkeeper hurry out. Eugen finished the beer with one long draught, and grimaced. There were gobs of yeast floating in the bottom of his tankard. The beer here was the same as the people: more than a little rough.

'I better go.'

Theodor waited until Eugen had left before he went upstairs. With his accomplice gone he could get some real work done. Ten minutes later Theodor slipped outside, paused for a moment to let his eyes get accustomed to the dark and then followed Guthrie down the road to the barracks.

GUTHRIE CAUGHT SIGMUND up in the streets and grabbed him by the shoulder and turned him round.

'What do you mean it doesn't look good? That boy is my son!'

Sigmund said nothing. There was nothing he could say.

Guthrie glared and then ran on ahead. Sigmund let out a long sigh and followed in his footsteps.

GUTHRIE CRIED OUT when he saw Elias: the boy's skin was beginning to fester and his forehead streaked with sweat.

The man's sobs echoed around the barracks, making the men uneasy, but after and hour, the man left.

BALTZER STOOD AT the barrack jetty and listened to the footsteps depart. The lanterns around the barrack square cast long shadows out across the water. There was a mist rising over the river. Baltzer shivered. He missed the times when Osric was captain of the watch. Those were good days with lots of easy money to be made.

'I need a piss,' Baltzer said and Freidel nodded.

Baltzer felt his way into the darkness, down to the jetty.

'What time do you reckon it is?' Freidel called from the other side of the trees.

Baltzer shook himself and buttoned his trews up again. 'Late.'

As Baltzer reached for his halberd, he saw something at far end of the jetty. There was someone there. He was sure.

He kept as low as possible so he could keep the intruder silhouetted against the reflections of the river. It was a man, a large man. Definitely not one of the halberdiers. Baltzer had sharpened his knife that afternoon. Its blade was sharp enough to cut right through this intruder's neck. He slid it from the sheath, and took another step forward.

The man was tying his boat to the jetty. His back was turned and Baltzer slid the last few steps. 'A fine evening!' he hissed and the other man flinched at the feel of cold steel on his neck. Baltzer pressed a little harder. 'Please tell me this is not a love-tryst?'

The man cleared his throat to speak.

Baltzer recognised the voice. It was one of the merchants they'd saved in the hills.

'I'm visiting a friend,' the man said. Baltzer saw the flash of gold but he did not take his sword away. Another gold coin landed next to the first. And another.

'The burgomeister sent me,' the man said. 'And – if you are still making your mind up – understand that I have no more gold.'

Baltzer took his sword away. He didn't want to interfere in the business of the burgomeister.

'Be quick!' he hissed. By the time he'd snatched up the coins the man had gone. There was just the empty boat, bobbing on the water.

Baltzer hid the coins in his boot. He could guess why the Reiklander was here. The burgomeister liked to get his way in everything. It was a shame, but after Sigmund was dead, then Osric would buy the captaincy.

* * *

FROM THE EDGE of the barracks gate, Theodor could see three rows of five tents at the far end of the central courtyard. The barracks were quiet, and there appeared to be no one guarding the gate. Theodor crept inside, keeping close to the shadows of the walls, being careful not to catch his foot on one of the guy ropes.

From the sounds of snoring men inside, the room he'd just gone past must be the sleeping quarters. Theodor slipped silently along it, paused to check the door was not ajar, then hurried on.

Imperial barracks were usually built to a common design. If this was the sleeping quarters then the other side must be the kitchen and the armoury. At the top should be the room he was looking for.

There were three doors. It was customary for officers to have one or two rooms to themselves; he guessed one must lead to the sick room.

Theodor stopped at each and listened carefully. When he was sure he'd found the right room, he took out a flask and dropped two drops of oil onto the heavy iron hinges then waited a few moments. The last thing he wanted was for a squeaky hinge to betray his presence. There was too much at stake.

When the oil had had time to work, Theodor lifted the latch as slowly as possible, and opened the door just enough for him to squeeze inside. It took a few seconds for his eyes to grow accustomed to the dark.

He made out a sleeping figure lying on one of the beds. That must be the man. Theodor drew something from under his cloak and crept forward. The floor of the room was packed dirt and his feet only made the slightest scrape as he crossed the room and bent over the prostrate form.

Theodor opened the pouch a little. Just a little, he thought, was all that was needed. He thought of their reaction in the morning made him smile.

EUGEN TOOK OUT the paper that he had been given that afternoon, unhooded his lantern and read the instructions.

The horse was where it had been agreed it would be. It was nervous and a little skittish as he approached. He wondered where it had come from – stolen, he guessed – and how it had survived thus far.

He soothed the animal as he took its reins from the branch of the tree around which they'd been wound. There was some crude knot that Eugen did not recognise holding them. He tried to tug at either end – but it looked like a child had tangled the whole lot over and over and around and through. It would take him half an hour to unpick it all.

He took out his knife and cut through the leather. He could not afford to be late.

Eugen mounted quickly and kicked the horse into a trot. White stones marked the trail, as the instructions had said, but in the darkness it was difficult to make them out at times, especially from horseback.

He had to double back a couple of times and at one point he thought he'd missed the trail completely – but Mannslieb rose above the trees and cast enough light to make the stones glow ghostly white.

After an hour, Eugen saw the split oak that had been described to him, silhouetted on the top of a hill. He couldn't see anything there, but kicked his horse. Surely he wasn't too late, he thought.

Eugen reached the split oak and paused. No one. He turned the horse around and cursed.

He would have to retrace his steps, he thought and turned the horse when a horned figure stepped suddenly out of the shadows. The horse reared up in terror.

Eugen struggled not to be thrown, and wrenched on the reins to force the horse back down.

The figure had a white hood pulled down over its face, and a rattle in its hand – a skull-headed rattle – that it shook in Eugen's face.

It spoke in broken Dark Tongue, the syllables distorted by the inhuman lips. 'Late!' it hissed. 'We wait!'

'I'm here now,' Eugen said.

'We wait!' the thing said, but its tone was almost celebratory, as if waiting was a pleasant experience in itself.

'We're agreed?' Eugen tried to say to the thing, but it was involved in a strange dance, stamping its hooves and shaking its curled rams horns to either side and jiggling the rattle. The dance lasted for a few minutes, and Eugen felt his skin prickle and realised that he'd been surrounded by a ring of horned figures. His horse sensed this too and snorted nervously, then the shaman's dance ended suddenly and it shook his gruesome rattle in Eugen's face.

'Agreed!' the shaman told him, its face so close to Eugen's that he could see the goat lips curl back from the teeth in a gruesome smile.

'I will do what we agreed,' Eugen said slowly and deliberately.

The shaman shook its horns and started to stamp backwards. 'Waiting for you!' it called out and Eugen saw the circle of warriors disappear as well.

Eugen let out a long sigh of relief. He hated dealing with creatures like these. They had different understandings of a pact. They were just as likely to eat you as wait to eat a hundred people tomorrow.

When Eugen turned his horse it reared up in terror.

Eugen had to fight to bring it back under control and then he saw what had terrified the animals so. Standing not two feet behind him was a huge beast, almost tall enough to look Eugen in the eye. The creature had bull's horns which swept forward in a deadly curve and a shaggy mane of knotted fur hung down over monstrous knotted shoulders. What made it most terrifying of all was that the whole creature was an albino: head to foot it was stark white.

The snout opened in a snarl, and Eugen swallowed. As if in answer to his prayers, the beast took a step backwards, still facing him as it paced away until its ghostly white form disappeared from sight into the shadows.

CHAPTER FOUR

FOR A THOUSAND years, under the dripping stalactites and the crude cave paintings, legends had been told about that which had been stolen. From the high peaks of Frantz-plinth, beastmen warriors had stood on the rocky crags, their manes ruffling in the mountain winds, their horns stark against the thin, blue heavens: staring down at the curve of the river, and the brown irregular shape of fields and farmsteads, and the semi-circle of the thousand-year man-camp.

Now, as the sun's rays caught the peak of Frantzplinth, those warriors took their shields from the crude racks. Ancient banners of stretched manskin were taken from the cave walls. The poles of heads, some dried and crinkled with age, stared with sightless eyes as the migration gathered pace.

The beast herds moved down ancient mountain paths and began to flow together, ancient animosities laid aside for the common cause. They flowed together like streams running into a river, growing in strength and momentum, until a mighty flood flowed silently through the high mountain forests.

IN THE JORG family mill, a few miles east of Helmstrumburg on the Kemperbad Road, Andres Jorg woke with a start and found that he'd fallen asleep across the kitchen table. Bright sunlight streamed in through the open shutters.

His neck was stiff, his back ached, his mouth tasted of stale spirits and his head felt as if a dwarf had been hammering it all night. To top it all his leg was aching. Not his actual leg, but the leg he'd lost more than twenty years ago on a surgeon's table while stray cannon and gunshot whizzed all around. From his knee downwards, there was no shin: just a finely polished piece of oak, shod with a steel cap.

Andres pushed himself up, stumped over to the water barrel and took the dipper and drank it dry. He drank another one, and felt a little better, cursed the spirits he'd been drinking.

Never again, he told himself, as he'd sworn so many mornings before.

ANDRES STUMPED THROUGH the kitchen, past where a kettle hung above the cold fire, to the open doorway, where the sunlight streamed in. He blinked in the sudden light and shut his eyes for a moment. It made his head feel worse.

The mill stood at the edge of the Stir. There was a sluice a quarter of a mile up the river that channelled water out of the river and took it to a holding pool. From the pool the water ran over a weir and down a steep stone-sided shoot. The force of the water turned the enormous water wheel, which ground the stacked sacks of wheat to a fine white flour.

He had to stop drinking like this, Andres told himself, but each night he'd have a small measure and begin to think about the days of his youth, then he'd get lost in drink and memories of his time as a greatsword.

The greatswords were the largest men in the army, with greatest physical strength. They were paid twice the salary of the other soldiers: they lived hard and died young. Always leading charges; always the last to leave the battlefield: dead if need be, their motto ran.

There was no scabbard long enough for the sixty-inch blades so they carried them wherever they went, resting on the shoulder. But, when wielded in battle, there was nothing cumbersome about them. Perfectly balanced, the ten-pound blade could out-reach any other swordsman and could smash through shields and armour with ease. They were used as shock troops to smash the enemy lines. Often they charged halberdiers, the blades easily cutting through the shafts of the weapons and leaving the halberdiers defenceless. And then there was a long leather ricasso, allowing the zweihander to be used up close.

Andres's zweihander hung over the fireplace. It was the best polished thing in the house. Made of the finest Reikland steel, decorative swirls were etched into the steel. The cross-piece curved towards the hilt, each guard ending with a closed fist. The heavy round pommel balanced the blade perfectly, allowing the blade to be spun round with ease. The undulating flamberge blade glimmered with a dull light. The edges had long since lost their sharp edge, but zweihanders didn't rely on the edge of the blade, the strength of the wielder was multiplied ten times by the weight and length of the blade.

Andres smiled as he remembered the first time he had cut a man in half. The power of the greatsword was formidable. It had saved his life a hundred times. He revered it like a lover: hard and cruel and deadly to his enemies.

He patted the weapon and then stumped across to the open doorway, and watched the water wheel creaking round and round. And now he was a fat, drunk miller.

THE CLAMOUR OF excited voices woke Sigmund. He threw off the woollen blankets, slung his jacket over his undershirt, and strode to the door.

The sun was rising over the barrack walls. He saw Edmunt come out of the sick room with a wide grin on his face.

Sigmund dared not feel hope. 'How is he?' he asked.

'Taal be praised!' the woodsman laughed. 'You should come and see this!'

Sigmund strode down to the sick room to see for himself. He pushed into the room where Elias was lying and – by Sigmar – there he was! Sitting up as if he were a lord waiting for his breakfast in bed.

'Sigmar be praised!' Sigmund said. 'I never thought to see you looking so well!'

Elias grinned sheepishly. He could hardly remember anything after the fight with the beastmen; he couldn't even remember getting wounded.

'I remember falling over into some brambles,' he said, looking at the scratches that still covered his hands and arms. 'But other than that...'

Sigmund shook his head. 'Well, you've saved the count three gold coins!' he said. 'We should all be glad of that!'

Later that morning, when the apothecary arrived, he was so astonished to see the young man's recovery that his spectacles fell off the end of his nose. 'I never expected to see you so alive and well!' he said, recovering his spectacles. He removed the bandages from Elias's arm and inspected the wound. Where there had been rotten flesh there was now a dull red scab and the reddening around the edge of a healing wound. He peered more deeply and stabbed the end of a knife through the scab.

Elias winced as the apothecary pressed but no pus came, just thick red blood.

Again the apothecary shook his head.

'I have never seen anything quite like this,' he said. 'To be sure.'

Sigmund nodded. 'So he's not going to die quite yet?'

The apothecary didn't like to state anything he could not be absolutely sure about. He thought of the twin-tailed star and shook his head. 'Not from this wound, anyway.'

ONE DAY A week the men were given an afternoon off. At the end of the morning the men lined up for a parade and kit inspection. Afterwards Sigmund dismissed all the men except for Vostig's handgunners, who were on sentry duty.

The other men had been in the hills for days. They needed a break. As for the spearmen – well – it seemed good to let the two companies out to get to know each other.

THE MEN WERE all laughing and joking as they strode through the barrack gates. As they jostled into the street, the townsfolk stepped out of their way. Osric saw this as respect, but Sigmund knew their behaviour was more down to fear. Soldiers were fine as long as there was an enemy to fight or they were safe in barracks. Loose in the town they were something to avoid.

Behind Osric's men came the scattered groups of Gunter's company heading for the Blessed Rest.

Elias, miraculously recovered, so it seemed, went to the Crooked Dwarf where Guthrie started crying with joy.

'I never saw you looking so ill!' he said. 'And I never thought I'd be so happy to see you walking around with bandages on!'

They were still hugging each other when Osric and a group of halberdiers wandered in and sat down. Guthrie brought the soldiers a tray full of beers.

'On the house!' he grinned and the men cheered. Elias felt embarrassed to think that the man who had rescued him from the streets and raised him was now serving him.

'Here!' Guthrie said and put a stein down in front of Elias. 'This will help you get better!'

WHEN A BAND of tall Vorrsheimers in their smart uniforms came in and began to make their way across the bar, a few of the local women looked at them with interest.

'I hope you're not going to steal our women!' Osric shouted across the room, and the Vorrsheim men laughed nervously.

'I don't think they realise he's not joking,' Freidel said. Kann and Schwartz laughed. They'd soon find out about Osric's sense of humour.

By the time Eugen came back from his visit to the burgomeister, the soldiers were quite drunk. He noticed the
halberdiers sitting in the bar and walked towards the stairs,
but looked back. When the halberdiers noticed him staring
he half smiled then turned away and hurried up stairs.

He and Theodor shared a room overlooking the street. It
was noisy, but served their purposes, and it wouldn't be for
long.

Eugen knocked three times and the door was opened.

Eugen slipped inside and then shut the door behind him.
Their room was small and cramped, with two simple beds
on either wall and a window overlooking the street.

Their crates were stacked under the window. On the left-
hand bed Theodor was cleaning his pistols. The ram rod and
oiled cloth were set out on a cloth on the blankets. The bores
had been unscrewed and polished. The broad barrels were
fearsome. The balls they shot could stop a charging bull.

'I saw something downstairs,' Eugen began.

Theodor looked up from the barrel he was cleaning.
'What?'

'*That* boy. He is downstairs.'

Theodor didn't bother to pretend he didn't know what
Eugen was talking about. 'I saw him too.'

Eugen sat on his bed and put his hands together as if he
was praying, then put them to his lips. 'I do not understand
how he has survived,' he said, 'unless you were somehow
involved.'

Theodor did not look away. 'I was,' he said.

Eugen pursed his lips and shook his head. 'Why?'

Theodor peered down the barrel to make sure that it was
clean, and then began to screw it back onto the firing
mechanism. 'He helped save us.'

Eugen frowned. He didn't understand this peculiar sense
of honour.

'I cannot think that you chose to endanger our mission
by bringing such attention to us.'

Theodor aimed the pistol out of the window and pulled
the trigger and the wheel-lock snapped down on the pan.

Satisfied that all was working properly, he put that one down and began to screw the other back together.

Eugen hated to be ignored. 'This is endangering us,' he said, his voice rising in pitch. 'Endangering me!'

Theodor nodded. 'It will be fine,' he said. 'I bribed the man. He was one of the burgomeister's men. It will be fine.'

Eugen paused for a long time as if considering whether to say more on the matter.

'I suppose it was because of us that he was wounded.'

'Just what I thought,' Theodor said. 'If anyone intervened that would have been my line.'

Eugen nodded, opened his mouth to say more, but relented. There were more important matters at hand. And once those were completed it would not matter about the burgomeister or any of his men. And then he could also deal properly with this insubordination.

'So now we go onto the next phase,' Eugen said. Theodor dry-fired the second pistol out of the window as he'd done with the first. 'You understand what you have to do?'

'I do. Four barrels.'

'Good. And tomorrow I will light the fires around the Sacred Heart so we are sure that they get the right man.'

'Which one?' Theodor asked and slipped both his pistols into their holsters and hung the belt from a peg on the wall.

'The one with the water mill,' Eugen said.

Theodor nodded. The water mill it was.

DOWNSTAIRS IN THE bar Osric pushed his way unsteadily across the bar to where four of the spearmen were sitting with the women. The stein in his hand sloshed beer over his hand. He licked it clean then pointed his tankard at the men's striped uniforms.

'So, how did you get this fancy rig?'

'Vice-Marshal Trappe paid for it,' one of the men said, 'for our bravery.'

'Bravery, huh?' Osric sloshed more beer down his front. He tried to rub it away with his sleeve, but the wet stain only made his uniform look more dishevelled. One of the girls, Fat Nadya, laughed. She'd squeezed her ample bosom into a garish pink dress. She had too much face powder and rouge on her cheeks.

Osric had had a brief thing with Nadya when Osric was still a lowly town watchman. As soon as he'd been promoted to officer of the watch he'd dumped her straight away – and she'd held a grudge ever since.

'When you lads have earned it maybe you'll get a proper uniform!' Fat Nadya cackled and looped her arm through that of the nearest spearman.

Osric couldn't hit her so he hit the spearman instead. The man barely had time to turn to face the blow before the fist crashed into his chin with the force of a hammer. He crashed against the wall and Fat Nadya screamed. Two of the other spearmen jumped in but instead of punching Osric they held his arms and stopped him hitting anyone else.

Baltzer, Freidel and a few other men were sitting on the other side of the room. They leapt up, but Guthrie stepped forward and held up his arms

'For the love of Sigmar, stop!' he shouted and the halberdiers paused.

The spearmen held up their hands.

'Cowards!' Baltzer cursed, but Osric dusted down his uniform.

'That man insulted me and I have paid him back! No need for any further fighting!' he said and his men returned to their seats and the spearmen carried their friend out.

THE MEN CAME home, loud and drunk. Lying on his bed, Sigmund listened to each group return: the unsteady footsteps and the loud banter of drunk men.

A long time passed. He didn't hear anything, and dozed off. He was woken by the sound of footsteps coming across the yard, the sound of a door squeaking, then more footsteps coming up to his door. There was a loud knock.

'Yes?'

The door opened. Sigmund blinked. The lantern was so bright he could not see who was holding it.

'Sir!' a man said. 'There's a man just in from the hills. He says he's seen beastmen.'

The voice sounded familiar. 'Is that you Holmgar?' Sigmund asked.

'Yes, sir!'

'Then take that damned lantern from out of my face!'

'Sorry sir!'

SIGMUND FOLLOWED HOLMGAR out into the yard. There was a light on in the kitchens. The kitchen door was open. Sigmund took the lantern from Holmgar, and went in. The kitchen had the lingering smell of pickled cabbage. In the gloom Sigmund could make out the huge cast iron cauldrons that were used to cook the daily rations, hanging from the beams. The walls were hung with brass dippers and knives. There was a platter of bread and cheese on the table, next to the lantern. A man stood there. He was short and dirty. He certainly looked and smelt like a trapper.

'Who are you?'

'Vasir,' the man said. 'I am a trapper. Up in the hills. Under Frantzplinth.'

'What have you seen?'

'I went to Goethe's place, and–'

'Jonn Goethe's place? On the western spur?'

Vasir nodded and carried on with his story. 'They were all dead. Skinned – like hunted animals! I ran. When I came to Burhens, the village was silent. Human skins hung from the trees. There were strange symbols.' The man clutched himself. 'I never thought I would make it here alive!'

Sigmund shook his head and seemed to make up his mind. 'Alright, rest here tonight. Holmgar – look after this man. He can sleep in the stables.'

Holmgar nodded. Sigmund walked back to his room and lay down. Burhens was on the slopes of The Old Bald Man. It was twenty miles from there to Osman's shack on Galten

Hill. He must bring the people down, he told himself and lay down to sleep with that single thought in mind.

THE NEXT DAY at morning parade the four sergeants came to get their orders for the day. Vostig's men were to clean the stables and count the supplies of food and blackpowder. Hanz was to supply the sentries for the day. The rest of his men were to cut up the loads of firewood that were stacked by the docks. Gunter's men were to practise their sword-play. Osric was to take the cart to buy wheat for the stores.

When he was finished, Sigmund set out to the guild hall. The streets were busy with morning traffic as farmers brought their goods into the marketplace.

When Sigmund got to the guild hall there were four watchmen on guard. They eyed Sigmund warily, but made no move to approach him. He strode past them and knocked on the oak door.

'Yes?'

The burgomeister seemed surprised to see Sigmund.

'Good day,' he said, and shuffled the papers in front of him as if he were anxious to hide the papers he was read-ing.

Sigmund had no interest in the burgomeister's petty business dealings. 'A trapper came to the barracks last night. He said that Burhens has been destroyed. I insist that we raise the alert!'

The burgomeister frowned. 'You want to raise the alert on the basis of one man's report?'

'I believe the man. It fits in exactly with what my men found.'

The burgomeister sighed. 'I think we have every right to expect you to defend us, rather than huddle in the city. Don't you think, Captain Jorg?' Sigmund started to speak but the burgomeister cut him off. 'Stop this talk of running and hiding and evacuating! Take your spearmen and do what you are paid for – Captain Jorg. Defend the town!'

* * *

VOSTIG STOOD IN the doorway and watched his men sweep horse dung and used straw out of the stables. Holmgar and Richel carried sacks of pulses and oats from one side of the stables to the other to count them.

'Twenty-three of oats. Fifteen of pulses.'

Vostig nodded. He chewed a piece of straw and waited for Osric's men to come over. The two horses snorted as they were led out and hitched to the cart by Baltzer and Kann.

Osric climbed onto the driver's seat. Vostig told him how much they needed and Osric nodded and lashed the reins and drove the cart out of the barracks.

'Now, get those sacks back over there!'

The men carried the sacks back across the stables.

Richel tripped and swore loudly.

'Language!' Vostig said.

'There's a boulder in here,' Richel said and began to pull the heaped straw aside, but when he uncovered it he laughed. 'You should have a look at this!'

The men came over to see what Richel had found. Buried in the old sacks and straw was a primitive kind of firearm. It was three feet long, and made of bands of copper around a steel barrel, with a primitive open powder pan for firing.

'What is that?' Holmgar said with awe.

'It's a swivel gun,' Richel said. 'You dumb oaf!'

Vostig came over to look. 'I've seen this kind of thing mounted on boats,' he said. 'But I can't imagine what it's doing here.'

The men shook their heads, and then Vostig told them to cover it over again. 'No use to us,' he said.

ALONG TANNER LANE, smugglers managed a good trade, sneaking goods across from Stirland under cover of darkness. It was into one of these dens that Theodor went. The stench of ammonia hung over the street. Theodor ducked into one of the tanneries. Inside the gloomy building the tanning vats bubbled poisonously. Cattle and calf skins dried over racks.

A man in a stained apron swirled one of the vats. Theodor slipped a gold crown into his palm. 'I'm looking for the Otter,' he said.

The man bit the coin and slipped it into the folds of his shirt. He nodded over his shoulder. Theodor walked over to the back of the room, to where skins hung in rows, drying.

'How can I help you?' a man's voice said.

Theodor pushed through the dripping skins, but he couldn't see anyone.

'Are you the Otter?'

'None of your business. What do you want?'

Theodor explained what he needed. There was a pause.

'Ten gold coins,' the man said. 'You are staying in the Crooked Dwarf, are you not? I will have it delivered there.'

'No, there is an old stable at the back of the water tower. Have it put there.'

'I will leave this here,' Theodor said and dropped the purse onto the floor.

'The goods will be there tomorrow,' the unseen man said.

Sigmund spent the rest of the afternoon watching the Vorrsheim spearmen drill. They seemed to be a solid group of men. When the drilling was over, Sigmund let Gunter know he was going out. He'd a little time before he'd to be back at barracks to check that the sentries were assigned their duties. If he was quick he could get to his father's mill and back before then.

The Kemperbad Road ran parallel with the banks of the river. To either side there were rich meadows and scattered trees. Sigmund's stride ate up the distance. The watermill appeared around the edge of the hillside and for a moment he flashed back to his youth, when he remembered how proud he used to be of his father. He wasn't sure when the disgust began to replace it. Maybe it was when he was old enough to understand that his father was a drunk; that the man he'd idolised for so many years was a fraud.

The road dipped down to cross a stream, then up again to his father's fields. The mill was a low building about twenty feet from the river bank. Just below it the water sluice rejoined the river. About fifty feet up the bank was their farmhouse. There were stables to the side and in front of it were a couple of ploughed fields.

Sigmund could hear the creak of the wheel as the water drove it slowly round, the shouts of the men who worked there. As he approached the door, Sigmund called out. His mother's face appeared in the doorway and she lifted her skirts and hurried outside.

'Mother!' he said and held out his arms to embrace her.

He was so used to soldiers that it felt strange to feel her large soft body. She looked a little older and more tired. There was more grey in her hair than there had been a year ago, when he'd first enlisted. She worried about him, he knew.

'You look well!' he said.

'So do you!' she told him, even though he looked thinner and tired. No doubt there were all kinds of things he'd to sort out. What with Sigmar's star appearing again.

'Come in! Come in!' she said. 'I have a stew on the boil!'

THE HOUSE SEEMED smaller and more rustic than Sigmund remembered. Although his father was thought of as a rich man, it was a hovel compared to the richest houses in the town, which were filled with luxuries from Kemperbad.

Sigmund shook his father's hand, embraced his brother, and started to tell them about the news from town, and further afield.

'I should get back to barracks,' he said after about an hour, when he heard the bells of the Temple of Sigmar ringing, but his mother looked crestfallen.

'Surely they'll be able to manage without you for one evening?'

Sigmund nodded. He didn't really want to go, but he knew he shouldn't leave his men. He was their commanding officer, but it was important he explained the danger to his family.

'Maybe I will stay,' he said at last, but felt torn between family and duty.

Over the meal he brought up the matter of their moving to town. 'I do not think it is safe for you to stay here.'

His mother paled but Andres waved his hand in dismissal.

'Why should we do that when we have you to protect us? The beastmen have never come so far down the valley. All they dare do is steal and run away,' he scoffed, refilling his glass. 'They'd never dare attack somewhere like this. There are seven strong men here. We'd easily beat them off!'

Sigmund could see the zweihander, hanging as always over the fireplace. He shook his head in exasperation. 'It's not safe here. If you are too stupid to understand that then at least let me at least take mother and Hengel into town.'

Andres slammed his wine cup onto the table and the room went silent. 'I will not be spoken to like that in my house,' he spat. 'I thought you became a soldier to protect us all – not to tell me that I should flee. What are you a coward?'

SIGMUND SLAMMED THE door behind him in rage, and stood for a moment, trying to control his anger. There was nothing he could do to make his father change his mind. As he strode off down the hill, his mother rushed after him to catch him up.

'Your father's drunk. He doesn't mean what he says!'

Sigmund nodded, but he was too angry to be understanding. His father had called him a coward!

'When he's sober, try to make him see sense.'

His mother nodded. Both of them knew how seldom Andres was sober.

'I will try,' she promised.

Sigmund nodded. 'If you can, bring yourself and Hengel into town tomorrow, and I'll find you lodgings. Now I have to go!' he said and kissed her on the cheek, then began to jog down to the bridge, heading along the water meadows, towards the east gate of Helmstrumburg. As he ran he thought of the beastman bands and hoped that his father lived long enough to regret his stupid pride.

CHAPTER FIVE

IT HAD BEEN a thousand years since they had smelled the scents of life. For too long they had been buried. Hammers had shattered them. Fires had burnt their surfaces, water had cracked them deep. But not quite stone, they had lain long in the earth, slowly repairing themselves, moving slower than worms to reunite the fissures, and now it was time. They could feel it in the deep burrows of the world.

One by one, tentative at first, they began to push for the surface. The turfs broke and split open, and the black stones began to rise, the jagged tips rising like mushrooms from the ground. There was strange writing on their sides such as would make any man who could understand the words go mad. Such was their power that the beastmen tribes had waited this long for their return. They were the slaves of the stones.

And as the stone circles and monoliths retook their rightful place, between earth and sky, the beastmen knew, in the manner of migrating beasts, that it was time to move towards the river.

ON THE SLOPES of The Old Bald Man, Fritz Shorr's dogs began to bark. He came out of the cabin door and shouted. 'Shut up, damn you!'

The dogs strained on their chains. Fritz shook his head. Dumb curs. As he went back inside he noticed an odd smell.

'A dead fox or something,' Fritz told his wife, who was breast-feeding their youngest by the fire. The other two children were already in bed, their blond hair visible in the bed that the whole family shared.

'Worst-smelling fox I ever heard of,' Fritz's wife said after a few minutes. She was right, the smell was getting worse. Fritz stood up, but as he turned to the door it flew open and a hooded figure stood in the doorway. Obscenely fat, the thing filled the doorway.

Fritz gagged on the overpowering stench. One of the children woke up and started to cry. The stranger stepped over the threshold and Fritz saw horns curling around its head. The figure had the legs of a goat; they ended in brown hooves. Fritz's wife screamed, clutching the baby closer to her for protection. The creature took a sharp skinning knife from its belt and took another step forward.

THEY MOVED SILENTLY through the forests, pausing every few minutes to smell the air, nostrils flaring as they closed in. They had pushed on ahead of the other bands, but it was not far now.

Red Killer moved at the head of band. His belt was plaited with fresh heads. Man-gore dripped down his thighs, and he gave a low snort of warning as he stopped at the end of the clearing.

The stones had risen from the ground. There were four of them: black and jagged and throbbing with power. Red Killer would be the first to draw on their power. With the strength that the stones gave him, he would be able to challenge the Albino Abomination that had usurped the leadership.

Red Killer snorted. His men began to herd the prisoners forward. They had gathered them as they marched down from Frantzplinth. There were fifty of them, their tongues torn out. Ready for sacrifice.

ON THE UPPER slopes of Galten Hill, Gruff went out into the cold night air and paced across to the latrine. Just as he was about to bang the wooden door shut, he noticed the flicker of flames a little way down the hill.

That was the Larsen farm. He was about to call his farm hands to come with him and see if they could help out when he heard a horn blowing: strange and eerie high in the forest. More beastmen, Gruff thought, and then another horn blew, lower in the valley. A third answered a little way up on the ridge. It sounded again, closer this time and Gruff suddenly became scared.

Surely there couldn't be more beastmen? But then another horn blew, even closer this time. He ran back to the house. 'Wake up!' he shouted as he burst into the front room. 'Get up now, for the love of Sigmar!'

He waited for a few seconds until the sound of voices and doors banging told him his daughters had woken up, then he ran back out to the stables to hitch the cart up.

Valina came out of the house in her nightgown. 'What's the matter?' she asked, shivering.

'Another beastman raid!' Gruff hissed.

'It's not possible!'

The horses shifted nervously and Gruff swore as he dropped one of the leather straps. He struggled to retrieve it, then pulled the second horse into place between the shafts.

'Father, what's the matter?' Valina asked, confused and frightened.

But before Gruff could answer the horn sounded again, even closer now, and the dogs began to whimper and growl.

'Get your sisters!' Gruff said as he dragged the horses out of the stables.

SIGMUND WAS WOKEN by a fierce banging. He rolled out of bed and pulled the door open. It was one of the spearmen. When the man raised the lantern to his face, Sigmund could see it was a boy with a scar down his cheek.

'What news?'

'Sir – there are flames in the hills.'

Sigmund frowned. 'I will come and look,' he said. He threw on his jacket, pulled on his boots and together they hurried through the empty night streets, through the old stone gateway and down Altdorf Street to the top of the rampart and the palisade.

High above the town, all along the hillsides, fires were burning. Sigmund could tell from their size and shape that these were not bonfires, but burning buildings. As he stood, shaking his head, another fire started: much closer this time, past the apple orchards on the outskirts of town. Embers spiralled up into the night sky. The low clouds glowed with reflected light, but they did not glow red, but a hellish green.

Sigmund's skin prickled.

'Run back to barracks and ask the sergeants to come,' he told the soldier.

SIGMUND STOOD AND stared at the flames for nearly half an hour. He was so immersed in the spectacle that he barely heard the footsteps of his sergeants as Gunter, Osric, Vostig and Hanz arrived, panting from the rush across the town.

They clambered up the steps and stopped when they saw the fires spreading across the hillsides. 'Sigmar!' Gunter swore, and Vostig and Hanz shook their heads in horror.

'But look at that one?' Sigmund said and he pointed towards the fire that was burning along the river.

'Is that a farm?' Gunter asked. Sigmund shook his head. There was nothing there but orchards and fields.

Osric frowned. 'Isn't there a burial mound there?'

Sigmund nodded. Something had brought the beastmen down so close to the city walls. They would not risk such a move unless the benefits were worth more than the risk. His sense of alarm grew. 'There is something afoot. We must do something to stop it!'

Gunter was adamant. 'We cannot go out into the night with beastmen around. We do not know their strength or even their location. And these creatures are wild animals – they would pick us off at their leisure. It would be suicide.'

'We cannot go out,' Hanz agreed. 'Marching out there in the dark would be suicide.'

Sigmund nodded. 'But gentlemen, we do not need to march!'

The other men gave him strange looks as he started to explain.

IN THE BARRACKS the men were sleeping soundly until the doors flew open and Gunter stormed in, lantern in hand. 'Up men!' he yelled. 'Up! Damn you all! Up!'

Elias sat bolt upright and fumbled on the ground for his clothes and his boots. He heard Edmunt cough in the bed next to him and cursed Sigmar, the Emperor Karl-Frantz and the elector count in one long expletive.

When Elias was half dressed he followed the other men outside. Osric was standing at the armoury door. Inside the lanterns had been lit and men were stumbling out, polished black breastpieces gleaming in the lamplight, tying their sword belts around their waists, halberds in hand.

'Arm yourself!' Osric shouted and Elias ran into the armoury, pulled a sword belt from the racks, and tied it around his waist. He lifted one of the cuirboili breastplates and Gaston helped him strap it on, then he took a steel cap, grabbed a halberd from the rack by the door then went to line up in the yard with the others.

Holmgar was behind Elias. He grabbed sword, powder belt and handgun. Vostig was waiting outside, and as each handgunner lined up he checked their powder flasks were full, then went from man to man, handing each twenty round lead shot that they dropped into pouches at their waists.

In twenty minutes sixty halberdiers and fifteen handgunners were lined up, ready for battle.

Gunter gave the order and Baltzer started beating the drum, and the men marched across the drill ground to the barracks gates, then turned onto the road that led to the docks.

THE HORNS WERE getting closer as Gruff Spennsweich helped his last daughter up onto the cart, and then checked the ropes that held all their possessions down. A few leaves rustled in the breeze and he turned as fast as he could – but the moonlit tree-line was silent and empty.

He shivered. The Larson farm was still burning. Olan and Dieter held the horses. They clambered up after the farmer, and clutched their pitchforks nervously.

The horn sounded again and Gertrude, the youngest, started to cry.

'Hush!' Floss hissed and put her arm around her sister.

They were all silent as the cart rumbled out of the yard onto the tree-lined road. It was uncomfortable in the back. Beatrine huffed and put her hand to stop her hair from blowing all over the place. The youngest, Gertrude, sat next to their father, her knees drawn up to her chin. The twins, Shona and Weina, sat together at the back. Valina put her arms around them. It was times like this that she felt like their mother. She brushed a lock of hair from her face. She had been born here, had grown up here, and now they were leaving. At any other time the prospect of moving to town would have filled her with excitement – but at night, like this, it was different.

On either side the trees were like silent sentinels. When she had been growing up they had seemed green and full of light and adventure. But now they were dark, sinister and frightening. Shona started to cry and Valina hugged her harder.

And the horns kept drawing closer.

* * *

WHILE THE OTHERS ran back to raise the men, Sigmund ran to Frantz's home and banged on the door until a candle was lit in an upstairs window and a woman's face peered down.

'I need Frantz!' Sigmund shouted up and the woman nodded sleepily and ducked back inside.

It took a few minutes for Frantz's face to appear, and Sigmund could barely contain his impatience.

'Sigmund?' Frantz croaked.

'Frantz,' Sigmund interrupted. 'I need boats that will carry eighty men and I need crews.'

Frantz took in one long deep breath and shook his head.

'And Frantz – I need them now!'

WHEN THEY GOT to the moonlit docks Frantz took a look at all the boats moored up along the jetties. It was a confusing tangle of masts and rigging and boats of all sizes and descriptions. Sigmund had no idea where to start.

Frantz rubbed his chin as he appraised the boats that were moored closer to the harbour entrance. When he had made up his mind he set off along the long wooden jetties. Sigmund could see the water lapping dark through the gaps between the slats. The jetty was uneven in places, and he marvelled at Frantz's and his men's ability to carry loads up and down these jetties, day in, day out.

At the end of the jetty was a thirty-foot barge called the *White Rose*. It had a single mast and a small cabin aft, where the crew ate and slept. There was a canvas stretched over the rest of the boat. Frantz lifted it and Sigmund peered down. Empty.

'We unloaded this beauty this evening,' Frantz said. 'And I know the captain. He's a good sort. I'll speak to him.'

Frantz stepped from the jetty onto the gunwale and walked quickly up the boat to the cabin. Sigmund saw him bend to knock on the cabin door and then go inside. There was a long pause. Sigmund looked to the mountains, fires slowly descending. Then he looked to the west and saw embers climbing into the sky.

It seemed like an age before Frantz came back – followed by the captain of the ship.

'Congratulations. You have your first boat! Captain Jorg,' Frantz allowed himself a little joke, 'meet Captain Ehab!'

Ehab was a short, bow-legged man with a knitted cap pulled down over his head and a grizzled grey beard that covered the lower half of his face, leaving bright eyes twinkling. His gait gave him the appearance of an ape, but he held out his hand and shook that of Sigmund.

'I need to take my men downriver,' Sigmund began and Ehab mumbled something in the broad sailor's lingo, which Frantz had to translate.

'I told him all about it,' Frantz said, and then he leant into Sigmund and whispered, 'and of course I said there would be a reward afterwards.'

EHAB'S CREW SLEPT on the boat. They got up and began to organise the boat for sailing. Frantz found two more barges, one called *Myrmidia's Grace*, which was a little larger than the *White Rose*, and one about half its size called the *Heidi*.

Their rigging had to be sorted and the sails and yardarms made ready for hoisting. It took nearly an hour to get the boats ready for sailing. Sigmund paced up and down the dock front waiting for his men. Come on, he said to himself. Come on!

But the night streets were silent and dark and empty. Just as he was beginning to think that something had gone wrong he heard the sound of a marching tune. Baltzer was bringing them on in style.

The sound of drumming and tramping feet grew louder and louder until it filled the empty streets.

It was a magnificent sight seeing the men come on through the gloomy street, like a ghostly regiment of men, repeating some final march. Edmunt was in the front rank, carrying the company's banner, Baltzer was drumming and Osric was two paces ahead of the unit. Behind them came Gunter's men and at the back were Vostig's handgunners.

The men's halberds glittered with reflected moonlight. Their steel caps shone, their black cuirboili breastplates seemed to suck in whatever light there was and throw back a distant glimmer.

Sigmund's heart swelled with pride to see his men, and to know that he was to lead them into combat.

GRUFF SPENNSWEICH'S HORSES foamed with sweat as he drove them on at a furious pace. 'We will stop at Struhelflossen,' he said, which was the nearest village, grown up around a tin mine, now long exhausted.

The cart rattled along and his girls were thrown back and forth as they prayed to Shallya and Sigmar for protection. The horns had fallen behind him now, but the night forests were no less terrifying. Valina shut her eyes and pretended to sleep – hoping this was all a dream.

Gruff didn't talk until the road started to flatten out, and he could hear the rushing water of the Struhelflossen waterfalls.

They sat up, and saw lights through the trees, and Gertrude began to clap when she thought of arriving somewhere safe.

Gruff let the reins go slack and the horses slowed down to a walk. From the windows, yellow light spilt out into the main street. Gruff said a prayer to Taal for bringing them here safely: then he saw something on top of the village sign, and realised it was a head.

The street was full of heads: impaled on stakes. The glowing windows took on a sinister air, the twins started crying. Struhelflossen had become a village of the dead.

DAWN WAS STILL a few hours off as Gunter's men made their way onto the *White Rose*. Osric's men were sent up the next jetty to the *Myrmidia's Grace*, while Vostig's men followed them and climbed aboard the *Heidi*.

'Quickly now!' Osric said as his men clambered aboard. His men sat in the waist of the boat, their heads below the gunnels, only their halberds sticking out above the water line.

Freidel was last in. He sat at the back, on top of the simple cabin where the crew usually slept. He hated boats and water and sailing and shut his eyes as the boatmen cast off, praying that he would feel dry land soon.

As the boat moved out into the middle of the river small waves began to lap against the side of it, but to Freidel they seemed like crashing breakers. He put his hands out to steady himself, a cold sweat on his forehead and upper lip.

'We're going to capsize!' he said and reached to steady himself, unable to comprehend how no one else understood this fact – but Osric laughed.

'Don't you worry! We'll have you on dry land in no time!'

IT TOOK HALF an hour to pack the men onto the barges, but the stubby thick-waisted salt barges were perfect for carrying heavy loads. The barges barely moved as the men stepped aboard. Gunter's men squatted in ranks in the *Myrmidia's Grace*, six men across, their halberds stacked against the side of the boat. In the *Heidi*, the handgunners were more cautious. Water would make their weapons useless, so they rested against the sides of the boat, keeping their handguns across their knees.

Frantz joined the boatmen poling the barges out from the jetty. As they inched towards the harbour mouth they threw ropes across to one another, and lashed the three craft into a long chain, fifty feet of rope, as thick as a man's arm, between each craft.

As they cleared the harbour mouth the current of the river took hold of the boats and began to turn them downstream. The sailors began to tug on the ropes that hoisted the sails. The broad canvas sheets flapped uselessly for a moment, then the tillers were turned and the boats turned into the wind and the sails filled.

With the current of the river and the sails full with the evening breeze they made good time. Sigmund stood on the prow, staring at the green glimmer. However fast Frantz told him they were going, they seemed to be going far too slowly.

THE BOATS STEERED to the far side of the river, and Sigmund had all the men keep their heads down. He could not be sure that there no enemy eyes watching the river.

It took an hour for them to reach the point where the mysterious fire was burning. For a long while the site was obscured by the orchard trees, but as they got closer he saw they had reached the site of an ancient burial mound. At the top a fire was burning, but unlike a normal fire the flames were green, and they seemed to coil and lick around each other, spiralling up in a column of sorcery. Silhouetted around the fire were horned figures, moving round in some macabre dance. Sigmund tried to count the numbers, but it was impossible to tell. There could be anything between fifty and a hundred.

As he watched he saw a struggling figure being dragged towards the fire. This figure did not have horns and Sigmund realised with a stab of disgust that it was the figure of a woman. He knew what was going to happen, but was unable to stop watching. He could see the woman being forced to her knees, and then she was obscured by the dancing figures. The next thing he saw was a round object being tossed into the flames.

THE WHITE ROSE sailed past the fire on the Stirland side of the river, and then when the low rise had obscured the mound, Ehab swung the tiller to the left and the barge nosed across the river. Sigmund could feel the tension in the boats rising. The sailors worked silently. Unlike the soldiers, who were deep in the boats, they too had seen the fires, and for the first time they had a sense of the real danger.

Only Ehab seemed unconcerned. He aimed his craft upstream of the jetty, and as he did so his crew dropped the yardarm and pulled down the flapping sail, then began to wrap it up and stow it amidships.

As the *White Rose* brought herself nose onto the jetty, the crew of the *Heidi* began to haul on the rope that held her to the lead craft. It took ten minutes until both boats were lashed together, and the captain of the *Myrmidia's Grace* was bringing his boat alongside.

Freidel was the first soldier from the *White Rose* to jump from the boat onto the jetty. There were many planks missing and the wood was wet and slimy with a layer of algae-green scum. His foot slipped from under him and he fell half into the water with a loud splash.

'Help him up!' Osric hissed to the next man and Baltzer put his halberd shaft down for Friedrick to grasp and then helped to haul him up. The crew of the *White Rose* were used to slippery wood and Ehab joined them on the jetty, helping the men out.

In less time than it had taken to pack the men aboard they were all ashore and ranked up. Over the rise they could see the embers circling up into the sky, but they could hear nothing. Sigmund picked out two men who knew the land, and sent them out to scout from the top of the hill.

They left their halberds and swords behind and hurried off into the gloom, keeping low to the sloping hillside. The eastern sky was beginning to pale. Sigmund went from man to man checking that they were all armed and ready. He had Gunter's men lined up with their right flank protected by the river. Next was Osric's company, and then protecting their flank were Vostig's handgunners.

Sigmund stood in front of his men, waiting for the scouts to return. The river gave off a chill damp air. He shivered.

THE FLAMES LEAPT up and lit the ancient mound with a pale green light. Red Killer personally led the last prisoner to the side of the fire. He kicked the man to the floor and then cut off his head with a single sweep of his axe. The blood splashed down onto the base of the stone, and there was a strange sucking sound as the blood flowed down into the ground.

It was done.

Suddenly the flames died down, the dying embers crackling angrily.

Red Killer roared and moved off north, into the forest. Some of his warband were unable to resist the call of the stones. He left those weak fools behind. He had business to attend to: to waylay Azgrak the Abomination and seize the leadership from him.

I⊤ TOOK HALF an hour for the scouts to come hurrying back. They were almost upon Sigmund before he saw them.

'Beastmen,' they agreed. 'Maybe fifty.'

'Any scouts?'

'We did not see any on this side. The only ones we saw were facing towards the town.'

'Did you see any prisoners?'

The men shook their heads.

Sigmund nodded. He drew his sword and the men tensed, ready to march forward.

'I want you two to keep to the left,' Sigmund told the men. 'Keep in touch with Vostig.'

The two men nodded and hurried off to the left.

Sigmund gave the signal for the men to advance and they began to tramp forward. The night dew on the long grass softened their footfall, and they left a distinct trail through the meadow.

The halberdiers carried their weapons over their shoulders. The handgunners did the same. Edmunt was at the front of the halberdiers, carrying the company banner – red and gold with the arms of Helmstrumburg. He looked up, the colours were limp in the pre-dawn gloom, but as they marched the light got brighter.

As ⊤HEY CAME up the side of the rise, Sigmund signalled a halt. He hurried up alone to the brow of the rise then lay down and peered down at the beastmen. He was familiar with the spot from his youth, but the land appeared to have changed.

Whereas before there had been a plain mound, now there was a tall circle of four standing stones, jagged splinters of black rock, at crooked angles. In the centre of the ring was the embers of the weird fire.

There were maybe fifty beastmen. Most of them were the smaller type, like the ones they had found attacking the Reikland merchants. But within this number there were maybe twenty larger ones: their heads, with their curled ram horns, standing well over the tallest halberdiers.

Sigmund shielded his eyes to see to either side, where the orchards were half-hidden in gloom. He could not see any more. The sky to the east was paling rapidly.

Sigmund scrambled down the slope until he could see his men. As they were not fighting a ranked unit of men, but what would be little more than a skirmish line of beasts, they had spread themselves out. Instead of taking up their usual deployment of twelve men across and five men deep they were now twenty men across and three men deep. The orders had been given to advance, and the men had their halberds ready, points forward.

Vostig's men were arranged on the left, the fifteen men in two ranks, their handguns loaded and shouldered. This was when the hours of training would pay off. In a normal engagement, the handgunners' role was to run alongside the halberdiers and use their guns to clear skirmish lines, or to pepper the tightly massed enemy ranks with lead shot before the halberdiers fell upon them. Now, however, in the open, the handgunners' job was to cover the flanks and the rear of the halberdiers.

Gunter and Osric stood at the front of their companies, waiting for Sigmund's sign. He gave it and the men started to march up the hill towards him. He stood and waited for them to reach him. Their approach was implacable. They kept their ranks and files in order, despite the curves of the land. All together, they crested the hill, saw the beastmen beneath them, and were half way down the slope before the cavorting beasts became aware that they had been surprised, and with a terrible speed they charged up the slope.

CHAPTER SIX

THERE WAS NO more dangerous place in battle than carrying the banner. Edmunt marched at the centre of the line, each stride bringing the enemy closer. When the first beastmen charged, Edmunt fitted the end of the banner pole into his waist belt, felt the belt take the weight, then with his right hand unhitched the hatchet from his belt.

The first beast he killed was for his mother's ghost. So was the second. He spat the excess saliva from his mouth, took in a deep breath, felt his chest stretch wide and flexed his fingers on the grip.

VOSTIG LED HIS men down the hill at a smart trot. They were about fifteen feet in front of the halberdiers when they paused and quickly ranked up in two lines.

The handgunners blew on their fuses to make them glow a dull red and then Vostig gave the order.

'Front rank, present handgun!'

Richel raised his gun and tried to slow his breathing so that the barrel would stop waving around – but it always did this when he was just going into battle. There was nothing he could do to stop the fear.

'Open your pan!' Vostig shouted and Richel flicked the powder pan open with his thumb.

The beastmen at the front were maybe thirty yards down the slope, but closing rapidly. Richel blinked his eyes to clear his vision, and made sure he was pointing his weapon at chest level.

'Give fire!'

There was a ragged splatter of shots. Each handgun threw out a funnel of smoke that cleared as the front rank stepped backwards, pulled out their scouring sticks and began to scrape blackpowder and scraps of cartridge from the barrels.

Holmgar was in the second rank. He blew on his fuse and the end glowed as he fitted the butt of the handgun into his shoulder. He could hear the men of the first rank being given their orders: 'Charge with powder. Charge with shot,' but concentrated on the orders that were being given to him.

'Open your pan!'

Holmgar lined his muzzle up at a band of ten beastmen.

'Give fire!'

There was another ragged splatter of fire and the familiar hum of spinning shot.

SIGMUND SWUNG HIS sword as he led his men down the slope. The handgunners opened up on the left and Sigmund saw one beastman hit. Its horned head was flung back and from the back of its head came a fountain of blood and gore. Within moments the creatures were ten feet away and the next rank of handgunners fired, but in the growing confusion Sigmund didn't see how many beastmen had been hit.

There were no beastmen where he was but he could hear the thud as three creatures threw themselves against Osric's men to his left. A man screamed, but the line kept advancing, trampling down the dead and dying, leaving the broken beastmen and the wounded halberdiers lying in the grass.

ELIAS WAS ON the end, his knuckles white on the halberd shaft. He could see the beastmen charging up the slope in ones and twos, and prayed that he would not get charged. Just as he had this thought, two of the smaller beastmen came sprinting out of the gloom straight towards him. As the left wing connected with the beastmen the whole line began to wheel to the right. The beastmen were a little shorter than him, but they had goats' legs and human upper bodies, man and beast blending at the waist. They carried wicker shields and had the heads of women and children slung from their belts. Short straight horns stuck straight up from their temples. The two that had singled him out had leathery brown skin all over, the only difference between them being that one had a white patch on its chest, like a farm animal.

Patch had a club and a wicker shield, No Patch a spear.

Elias felt they had singled him out from the whole line. His hands shook terribly as the screaming creatures charged straight at him.

Time seemed to warp and he could see Patch's sharp fangs as it opened its mouth and then they were upon him.

Elias thrust forward at Patch with the point of his halberd, felt it connect and realised he had shut his eyes at the last moment. He expected to be stabbed or clubbed by No Patch, but when he opened his eyes he saw Gaston delivering the coup de grace to No Patch with the point of his halberd. The creature spasmed as the foot of steel stabbed down between its ribs. A gout of fresh red blood sprayed up and Elias saw that Patch lay at his feet, the white patch now torn open with the force of his blow.

Elias laughed at the ease with which he had cheated death. He wanted to speak to Gaston but there was no time for even the briefest of comments as three more beastmen raced up towards him.

* * *

A HUGE BEASTMAN, taller than any man, was almost upon him when Richel flicked open the pan again. He didn't even wait for the order to give fire but pointed his handgun at the creature's chest and pulled the trigger, striking the pan with the glowing fuse.

The creature had its axe lifted up in the air when the blast of Richel's gun knocked it back. It regained its balance, unaware that the handgunner's shot had gone straight through its heart, and took another stride forward, roaring in fury and swinging its axe.

Richel barely had time to see it reappear through the blackpowder smoke – and cursed himself for missing at such short range – a curse that was cut abruptly short as the creature's axe caught him under the chin and split his face open in a spray of snot and blood and gore. It threw the body back into Vostig, who was desperately trying to clear his barrel.

When the body hit him and Vostig felt the warm slap which he later realised was part of Richel's scalp on his cheek, he looked up and saw the striding monster take a step towards him.

The enormous beastman opened its bloody snout and roared, and Vostig realised that there was nothing he could do to defend himself. He stood paralysed as the great axe lifted high above his head. Holmgar ran at the creature, screaming at the top of his lungs, and the creature's attention was diverted for an instant. It batted Holmgar away, and turned back to Vostig, but Richel's shot had been true – and as Vostig stared at the thing that was about to kill him, he saw some strange wave of understanding hit the maddened beast that its time had come.

The creature fell to the floor with a moan of dismay. Its horned head fell at Vostig's feet and the handgunner felt a warm sensation running down his legs.

OSRIC'S MEN TOOK the brunt of the initial beastmen attack. They came in pairs at first, but it wasn't long before a large group of fifteen warriors charged his line all together and Osric felt his men waver under the ferocity of the assault.

Kann was caught by a spear thrust and fell with a low, surprised moan. Baltzer caught the creature with the blade of his halberd and almost cut its arm from its body. Freidel stepped up into Kann's place and rammed his halberd blade down the throat of a small cream-skinned beastman.

Gunter's men continued to wheel round, sweeping up beastmen until there was fighting all along the line.

Sigmund stabbed one creature in the throat and pulled its wicker buckler from the dead fingers. As he pulled its fingers free he was struck by the warmth of its dead fingers, the rough feel of the creature's fur, and the long filthy talons. He fought until the buckler was a shredded mess of twigs, and there was beastman blood running down the blade onto his hand.

'Steady now, boys,' Gunter called out as his men wheeled round. 'Keep in rank!'

Gunter's men kept going forward, their ranks tightening as each man came closer to the other for protection.

Suddenly there was a goat-horned beast in front of Edmunt and he swung his hatchet, felt the heavy blade cut deep and snag in the creature's spine. As the beastman fell the axe was almost dragged from his hand, but Edmunt put his foot onto its chest, twisted his grip and yanked the hatchet blade free.

Fifth! Mother, another soul for you!

ON THE WING, where the handgunners stood, now twenty feet behind the advancing halberdiers, there was a fierce battle going on between the human soldiers and eight of the smaller beastmen.

The creatures had come upon them unawares, and it was only the intervention of the two halberdier scouts, who drew their swords and fell upon the rear of the beastmen, that stopped more of the handgunners being cut down.

Vostig brought the butt of his gun down on the face of the last beastman, crawling towards him. There was a sickening crunch as the half-human face shattered under the impact, but Vostig brought the gun-butt down again, driving the face of the creature back into its head, and brought it down again splattering the legs of his trews with gore.

Three of his men were dead, and another two were wounded too badly to fight. There was no time to tend to their wounds.

The last nine men ranked up.

'Prime your guns!' Vostig said, limping forward to take his place. The handgunners worked quickly and silently. When all were ready he led them down the hill, angled so that they could fire on the beastmen that were still coming up the slope.

'Blow on your coal,' Vostig ordered.

'Prepare to fire.'

All nine handguns were brought up as one.

'Give fire!'

The guns fired again, round balls of lead whizzing through the cool morning air. Three hit their mark, shattering bone and flesh and punching running beastmen back onto their backs.

Sigmund led Gunter's men round onto the flank of those attacking Osric's men. Trapped and outnumbered, the few remaining beastmen fought as if they were possessed. Elias had to stab a wounded black and white beastman, fully seven foot tall, over ten times before it finally crumpled onto the ground.

Edmunt pushed Gaston aside to get to a short brown beastman that had a band of dark fur down its back. Its vertical pupils were wide with fear and it sprayed pungent urine as Edmunt caught it by the hoof and tripped it up. The thing bleated with terror as Edmunt put a foot in the small of its back to hold it steady, and Elias looked away – heard the bleat cut short as Edmunt split its skull.

Vostig's men followed the halberdiers down the hill, their empty powder pouches flapping against their bandoliers, their handguns shouldered.

'That one's still alive!' Holmgar said, pointing. Vostig took his handgun by the barrel, swung it and caught the creature on the base of its skull, shattering the bone and snapping its neck.

The last beastmen stood their ground and fought furiously, but isolated they were cut down.

SIGMUND WAS LIMPING when Vostig found him. His sword was notched and he held a battered brass buckler in his hand that looked like it had been looted from some murdered swashbuckler years earlier.

'What happened to your leg?' Vostig asked.

'A club,' Sigmund said, by way of explanation.

Vostig nodded. There was a halberdier from Osric's company on the slope below them whose guts had spilt out over his knees. Freidel had propped the man up and was giving him water, but there was nothing to be done. He would soon be in the kingdom of Morr.

'Unlucky,' Vostig said and Sigmund nodded. Luck said that the man next to you caught the blow that should have killed you.

WHEN THE FINAL wounded beastmen had been dispatched, Sigmund posted sentries around the battlefield, and then walked down to the bottom of the hill.

The mound was a little way in front of him, but where there had once been a bare mound, now it was surrounded by a ring of standing stones.

Sigmund stopped a few yards away from the stones to examine them. They were black granite, with facets of crystal embedded in their surface that glinted wickedly. On one side they were covered with strange glyphs that seemed to shift and twist in front of his eyes, pulsing with unholy energy. Sigmund's head began to ache as if an invisible hand was slowly crushing it.

Charred bones and skulls stared out from the glowing embers. Sigmund had been too distracted to see them earlier. He started towards the ring of stone, but the closer he got the worse the pain in his head became and he began to lose his balance.

Someone caught him and dragged him back. Sigmund blinked open his eyes and saw Edmunt.

There were footsteps as someone came up, and Sigmund saw that it was Osric, staring at the pulsing stones.

'Sigmar's balls!' he swore. 'How did those get here?'

THE SUN ROSE as the halberdiers tended to the wounded. Vostig's trews were uncomfortably wet. He walked down to the river and stripped them off to wash out his urine and the gore of the enemy. Now the battle was over the shock of fighting came over him and he felt his stomach wrench, and vomited up a thin bile.

Gunter lined his men up and checked the numbers. He had lost four men.

Gaston took three men and went up to fetch the dead men and carry them down to the bottom of the slope.

'Cover their faces!' Gunter said, but there was nothing to cover them with so they stripped off the men's breastplates and put them over their staring eyes.

ELIAS SQUATTED A little way away from the main group and spat into the grass. A rivulet of blood trickled down his halberd blade and fell onto the grass in front of him. Quite suddenly he found tears on his cheeks and wiped them away before anyone could see them.

AS DAWN BROKE, the snowy crags of Frantzplinth were painted with a ruddy light. Plumes of black smoke drifted up from the upper reaches of Galten Hill, Frantzplinth and The Old Bald Man. It seemed that fell beasts were swarming through the forests: burning and pillaging.

The eastern sky was pale enough to silhouette the scattered clouds by the time the distant patter of shooting told the boat crews that the battle had begun. The sound of gunfire lasted nearly fifteen minutes, then there was silence.

'Are they dead?' one of the crewmen asked.

No one spoke.

'I'll go see,' Frantz said, and leapt onto the jetty and hurried up the slope after the soldiers. The further he went the more exposed he felt. He paused and looked round – just in case – then wiped the sweat from his hands and hurried up to the crest and topped the rise that the halberdiers had marched up, just fifteen minutes before.

The ridge sloped gently down to the old burial mound but now four standing stones thrust up from the grass: so dark they seemed to suck in the dawn light.

The slope was strewn with dead. Clawed fists and knees broke through the grass. Here and there a sword, spear or shield stood up in the air. Half way down the slope a beastman was attempting to stand up, but it was tripping over its own pink intestines, disembowelled.

The halberdiers and handgunners were ranked up at the bottom of the slope, under the scattered trees. He could see Gunter and Osric going from man to man, checking on their wounds. Behind them, fourteen men were lying in the grass, their heads and legs and arms all crooked. They lay still and Frantz realised they were dead. He looked for Sigmund and saw him, standing staring up at the ring of hills where a hundred fires burnt.

THERE WERE SEVEN men wounded. They would heal, except for Schwartz, who'd been stabbed just beneath his breastplate. The sharpened stick had gone through muscle and intestine and had punctured his liver. For him it was just a matter of time.

'I'm cold,' he said. Freidel put his flask of water for him to drink. 'I don't want water,' Schwartz said, and the colour started to drain from his face. 'I can't feel any pain. Do you think I'll make it?'

'Of course you'll make it,' Freidel said. 'We'll get you back to town and the apothecary will see you right.'

A LITTLE WAY off, standing by the Altdorf Road, Sigmund, Gunter and Osric stood and looked through the dawn

orchards. It was a three-mile march back to Helmstrumburg, along the Altdorf Road, but they had no idea whether
there were more beastmen blocking their return.

'I say we risk it!' Osric said. His men were tired and many
were wounded, but he was still fired up with the thrill of
killing.

Sigmund thought for a moment. 'I think not,' he said. If
there were more beastmen then his party, already weakened, could be decimated, even within eyeshot of
Helmstrumburg. 'We will take the boats.'

BALTZER STRUCK UP a cheerful tune and all of them were
glad to turn their backs on the pulsing stones. The healthy
men took the dead by the feet and the shoulders and the
rest helped the wounded as they climbed back up the
slopes. Freidel and Elias helped carry Schwartz. Every few
steps his breathing became ragged and they had to keep
pausing to let him recover his strength.

'My mother'll laugh when she sees men limping along,'
Schwartz said.

'That she will,' Freidel told him. Elias looked at the dying
man. His head hung forward onto his chest. The stain of
blood was spreading down his left side.

As they clambered up the slope, Elias saw Patch and No
Patch, lying about six feet from one another. They were
smaller than he had remembered. A fly crawled over the
dead face of Patch and crawled into the open mouth.

At the top of the hill Frantz had lit his pipe and gave Sigmund a fierce bear-hug. 'Well done!' he said, but Sigmund
felt tired and disturbed and empty.

Fourteen men lost in such a short time.

WHEN THEY MOUNTED the crest of the hill Elias saw the three
barges tethered to the jetty below. Mist was rising over the
river, and the scene was so still and calm that it seemed
impossible that fourteen men had died that morning.

The rest of the men tramped on down the hill to Baltzer's
jaunty tune.

The soldiers stood silently as they waited to get aboard. Dead men were passed over and laid in the waist of the boat, the water lapping over their dead hands. Schwartz's legs were useless. He groaned when they tried to lift him into the boat, and Elias's hands slipped and Schwartz half fell against the side of the boat.

'Idiot!' Osric snapped and caught the wounded man.

'It's fine,' Schwartz hissed through gritted teeth.

ONE BY ONE the boats cast off and floated downstream until the sails were hoisted, and they began to tack back upstream. The going was painfully slow. The men huddled in the damp bellies of the barges, the dead men were laid out in the bows. Osric's men were laughing and joking, even though they had suffered most. Osric re-enacted beheading a beastman. He could still see the expression of snarling hatred change to shock and then pain as its head flew up from the neck. Freidel was laughing that he still had nine fingers and Schwartz laughed because, although he was wounded, he was relieved that the battle was over.

Gunter's men were strangely quiet. Elias was still shocked – the battle felt like it had lasted mere seconds, but fourteen men were dead, and he couldn't believe he had survived.

Edmunt used the water in the boat to wash the blood off his hands and axe-head.

Seven beastmen, he told himself with a grim satisfaction.

His breastplate was uncomfortable. He undid the buckles and pulled it off and saw three deep gouges in the polished leather surface. The deepest had gone through all but the last few layers of leather. It looked like a spear thrust that had been turned aside, but he had no idea where it had come from. He felt the bottom of his ribs on the left side and found a lump that had swelled up. He laughed to think that he had never felt the blow or the bruise until now.

SIGMUND COUNTED THE dead men again. Fourteen – and from the look of Schwartz, bent double between Freidel and Elias, he would soon be joining them. And six wounded.

In truth, for sixty dead beastmen, fourteen dead men was not bad. If the beastmen had attacked together then the result could have been very different, but the halberdiers' discipline had paid off. Sigmund was overcome with pride in his men, he bent over the side of the barge so that no one could see how emotional he felt.

EHAB KEPT THEM well to the side of the river, where the current was weakest. Sigmund took a deep breath and then it struck him what they had achieved and was eager to return to the town and spread news of their win. If the journey downstream was slow then the trip upstream was much slower. It took them three hours to tack back. They didn't see anyone on the bank – man or beastman. The orchards were empty. But as the sun rose higher and lit the hillsides, Sigmund's emotions turned from excitement to foreboding. From Galten Hill to Forester's Peak a hundred fires burnt – the long plumes of black smoke curling up into the morning sky, each a sign of death and destruction. In the valley where the village of Burhens sheltered, a huge cloud rose into the morning.

On the hillside smoke from burning farmsteads crept inexorably to town. Village by village, the beastmen were purging the forests of human-kind. An army of nightmare creatures that had risen from fables and legends to terrify their daylight and conscious hours.

Sigmund shook his head. He would have to prepare the town against this onslaught. Even if he had started to bring the people in he could never have managed to clear such a huge area, and if his men had been caught by such a large force then they would have been decimated.

'Faster!' Sigmund urged, but there was nothing Ehab could do.

For two hours they slowly tacked upstream, but then the wind changed and his crew hoisted a spinnaker and the prow began to cut through the river water.

Viewed from the river, Helmstrumburg looked small and vulnerable, perched on the river banks, its stone walls and tightly packed houses dwarfed by the looming hills and forests. As they turned into the harbour it seemed that the town was in a pitiful state.

Without leadership people were concerned about one thing only: saving themselves.

THE WHITE ROSE tacked in through the harbour entrance then the sailors hurried to furl the sails and lower the yardarm.

Sigmund was horrified at the sight that awaited them. Gone was the usual frenetic hurrying of dockers with sacks on their backs and the bartering of merchants. Instead, it was a scene of chaos. Crowds of desperate people were rushing up and down the docks and jetties. Half-filled barges were casting off, and there were merchant families hurrying to clamber aboard, stacks of possessions piled up on the docks. White-faced wives and daughters of the rich stood amidships as the poor looked on.

The door of the guild hall was shut and the town watch were nowhere to be seen. A mob heaved back and forth as townspeople attempted to find passage on any boat that was going. At the end of the jetty, they saw an undefended boat and stormed towards it, but the crew clambered for their bill hooks and fended them off. There were screams of pain and horror and Sigmund saw one man who had scrambled aboard getting beaten down with a club. He shouted to the men to stop, but the din of panic drowned out his voice.

Blood spurted out from the back of the man's head and then he crashed down into the water, and lay there face down in the ripples.

Sigmund shook his head. The town seemed to be floundering in a leaderless panic. Ehab steered them towards the nearest berth and the mob surged towards the barges, until they saw that the boat was full of halberdiers. For a moment they thought it was a new unit of men sent from

Kemperbad, but then they recognised the ill-matched uniforms of the Helmstrumburg Halberdiers and their hearts sank.

As the halberdiers began to lift their dead off the boats then the panic only increased.

'We're in town now!' Freidel shouted to Schwartz, but he remained slumped over. Freidel lifted the man's head, but his eyes were glassy.

'He's gone,' Freidel said to Elias, and dragged him to the side of the boat.

Elias watched in horror. A man had just died next to him: silently and without a murmur. He saw the crowd and the panic and did not know what the halberdiers could possibly do to save Helmstrumburg.

CHAPTER SEVEN

FARMER SPENNSWEICH HAD driven by moonlight, all the while praying fervently for Taal to shield him and his family. When dawn came it seemed that the god of the forest had heard their pleas. The mare was foaming at the mouth, her flanks were dripping with sweat, but they were only two miles north of Helmstrumburg. Farmer Spennsweich flicked the reins and drove the mare onwards. He knew he wouldn't feel safe until they were inside the town walls.

RODERICK WAS ON duty on the west gate, on the Altdorf Road, when he saw the cart came clattering down the road, piled up with possessions and frightened children. He put his hand out to stop it. The last thing the town needed was frightened country folk spreading panic and rumours in town.

'What's your business here?' he demanded.

Gruff Spennsweich was white with fear. He pointed up to the forests on the hills. 'Look! Can't you see the smoke!'

Roderick refused to be alarmed. It was probably some hayrick that had caught fire. He cleared his throat and spoke with mock politeness. 'What is your name, good sir?'

'Gruff Spennsweich.'

'Well, Gruff Spennsweich,' Roderick said, putting his hands inside the tails of his blue velvet coat and resting them on his hips. 'I don't know what rumours and scare-mongering have led you to bring your family into town, but I assure you it is safe to return home and your hon-ourable occupation! Is spring not the time to sow your crops?'

Roderick expected the man to doff his cap and give in to good sense, but the farmer refused to back down.

'The whole village of Stuhelflossen has been butchered! We saw it with our own eyes!' he said. All his daughters and the two farm hands nodded mute agreement, but Roderick was not to be dissuaded and refused to let them in.

'There is no room for rumour-mongers in town!' he snapped and took the horse's bridle to turn it away from the gate, but Gruff flicked the reins and drove the horse straight at the officer.

Roderick leapt to the side and the four watchmen at the gate jumped up, grabbed the horse, and manhandled the burly old farmer off his wagon. Valina tried to pull the watchmen off, but her screams were ignored and she turned to Roderick for help, who was dusting his coat down.

'In Helmstrumburg we have laws,' he spat when his watchmen had finished with Farmer Spennsweich and left him lying outside the walls, next to the wheels of his cart. 'I suggest you remember that!'

THE BURGOMEISTER SENT word that all refugees were to be denied entrance into the town and ordered to return home, but within the hour there were already fifteen carts outside the west gate, and at least as many more at the east and north gates.

Roderick climbed up onto the gatehouse and held out his arms for silence. Gruff and the other farmers shook their fists at him. Roderick's face reddened in anger. He gestured to his badge of office as if that would still their protests.

'Good people!' Roderick started. 'I implore you to ignore the rumours and superstition that have driven you from your homes! If we are to flee in the face of the smallest threats, then how can we hope to build a prosperous and wealthy community?'

The people booed and the Roderick opened his hands and tried to quieten them down.

'Why blame me for your plight? If you have not been protected then you should take your complaints to the barracks and Captain Jorg!'

The jeering relented for a moment as another target of their anger was presented. 'I assure you it is safe to return home!' Roderick said earnestly – then a fresh lump of horse manure flew up and splattered against his blue coat. At the same moment a stone hit the man next to him and within seconds there was a hail of missiles flying through the air. The farmers surged up to the wall, hurling stones and abuse, but the gates were shut and instead of offering them shelter, the city walls left them locked out.

AT THE JORG family mill, Andres Jorg got up early to see his wife and son to town. The upper slopes of Galten Hill all the way across to The Old Bald Man were shrouded in smoke.

'Please come with us!' his wife begged one last time, but he shook his head and scowled. He refused to flee before beastmen.

His wife wiped the tears from her cheeks and Andres helped him up onto the cart, and nodded to his son. Look after your mother, the nod said.

His mill-hands stood behind him, watching the cart head down the slope and over the bridge towards town. Their master was the most famous soldier for fifty miles.

He had served the count's father himself in his personal bodyguard. They would stay as long as their master did. Andres spat and then turned towards his men, and gave them a look as if they were soldiers waiting for orders.

'Right men! Back to work!'

THE WHEEL OF the watermill turned all morning. Andres stumped under the rafters, listening to the hypnotic sound of the water splashing through the mill mechanism. The huge grind stone turned slowly and ponderously: one man fed grain into the hole in the centre, coming out from the outside edges in a fine white powder.

The others sacked it up and piled the sacks against the far wall. All the men were dusted with flour. Even Andres had started to take on the ghostly white; he brushed the flour from his shoulders and went back outside, for the tenth time that morning.

The smoke from the high forest fires crept steadily downhill.

What was that son of his up to, skulking in town when raiders were terrorising the higher settlements? If only he had his leg back. If only he were Marshal of Helmstrumburg. He would march out and destroy those cursed goat-men!

THE MORNING WAS well underway when the halberdiers clambered out of the *White Rose* and lined up on the dockside. The scene around them was one of pure panic. People streamed from the town and there was a terrible crush on the docks as they tried to find safe passage away from Helmstrumburg. Fighting erupted over another boat and Sigmund barked an order and drew up his men in rank, Osric's men at the front, Gunter's men behind, Edmunt standing with the colours of the Helmstrumburg Halberdiers hanging from the banner pole.

The mob shrank into itself, but pushed from behind by terrified people the crowd surged forward again.

'Back!' Sigmund shouted to the terrified people, but they were too frightened to listen. 'Back to your homes!'

'So we can be torn apart by beastmen?' one man shouted, but Sigmund could not see who.

'I am the Marshal of Helmstrumburg!' he shouted, trying to find a way through to the people in the mob. 'This morning we killed sixty beastmen!'

People jeered him and someone shouted something about refugees being shut out of town to stop the truth spreading about the numbers of beastmen.

'You may have killed sixty but there are hundreds more!' another voice shouted.

Sigmund saw the man who spoke and addressed him by name. 'Master Ekker! I thought you were a man who held his head up with pride – not abandoned ship at the first sign of trouble!'

The man stopped. Sigmund pointed to another man. 'Gurge Svenson! I would never have thought you would be here – with this rabble!'

The mob paused for a moment and lost it coherency. Sigmund seized the opportunity. 'My men are the match for any beastmen! Does the town not have strong walls? What is there to fear? Why leave all that you have here to be wandering beggars in a foreign land? Go back to your homes. If there is any news, you will be informed!'

The mob dissolved into clumps, but many people saw the sense of what he was saying and began to drift back to their homes.

Sigmund set Osric's men on guard until he could send relief from the barracks, then left Gunter and Vostig in charge of taking the men and the dead back to the barracks. When all was set, Sigmund straightened his uniform, cleaned his face and hands then pushed his way through the crowds to the guild hall. There were more and more people hurrying over the cobbles, sacks and bags on their backs containing all that they could carry with them. There was a number of rich tradesmen and artisans who had servants or ponies to carry crates – or coins no doubt – but all their progress was slowed by the people who were making their way back home, for there were no more boats to be had for blood nor money.

Sigmund shook his head. There was no point in telling them to return home. When they saw that all the boats were full or had left then they would leave. There was no choice.

Sigmund hurried up the steps of the guild hall. There were four town watchmen at the door. They looked as nervous as everyone else, truncheons in their hands. They stood well back in the doorway, as if the crowds of frightened people might turn on them. When they saw Sigmund stride up the steps relief washed over their faces.

'Captain Sigmund!' said one of the men. 'We heard you had fled!'

'Who told you that?' Sigmund demanded.

The man shook under Sigmund's glare. 'Why – Master Roderick,'

'My men were fighting,' he snapped. 'Tell Master Roderick that the Helmstrumburg Halberdiers killed sixty beastmen last night!'

The men nodded fearfully, and Sigmund strode inside and pushed the door to the burgomeister's hall open. The room was empty except for the burgomeister and a smartly dressed merchant. They were standing by the tall windows, peering down into the river that ran along the side of the guild hall, deep in conversation.

The merchant turned and Sigmund was surprised to see it was Eugen, the Reiklander he had rescued three nights earlier.

The two men seemed just as surprised to see Sigmund as he was to see them.

'I see you have returned,' the burgomeister said. 'Although you seem to have forgotten to knock before you enter my chambers.'

Sigmund could not believe what he was hearing. 'Sir,' he said, holding back his impatience. 'I do not believe you understand that Helmstrumburg is in terrible danger. My men killed sixty beastmen last night and yet there are a hundred more fires burning in the hills.'

'Please captain – I have heard enough of this scaremongering this morning!'

'If you cared to step outside these four walls then you would see that those fires span from Galten Hill all the way across to The Old Bald Man! Do you think they will ravage the land and then return to their caves, like obedient school-children? No – they are making their way here! For what reason I cannot guess, but one thing is certain. The numbers of the beastmen must surely outnumber my men ten to one. Unless we take urgent action I am certain that the town will be overwhelmed!'

Eugen put his hand out to the burgomeister and the master of the city stepped back, as if this was not a matter for him to be concerned with.

'I do not think the town needs your hysterical rumours,' Eugen spoke slowly.

Sigmund tried to look past him to the burgomeister. 'Sir! We should raise free companies at once!'

The burgomeister seemed hesitant. He glanced towards Eugen and the Reiklander stepped back and gave the burgomeister a barely perceptible shake of his head.

'The town cannot afford such expenditure!' the burgomeister said.

Sigmund could scarcely believe what he was hearing. 'Sir – have you stepped outside these walls to look for yourself?'

The burgomeister did not reply.

Sigmund stepped forward. 'People are saying that the country refugees have been locked out of the town? Why have they not been let in?'

'I will not be spoken to by a mere sell-sword!' the burgomeister snapped. 'I run Helmstrumburg, Captain Jorg, and I will not have cowards and beggars littering my town!'

Sigmund shook his head, but held back his frustration. 'Sir – I beg you to come and look for yourself!'

'In my own time,' the burgomeister snapped and turned his back.

Sigmund slammed his palm onto the table and glared at the lord of the town. 'Master burgomeister – your position is given to you by the Elector Count of Talabecland. It is your job to govern in his name. It is your job to protect the people! I insist that you call for all men who can bear arms! There is an army of beastmen in the hills and if we do not mobilise all who can fight then we will surely be overwhelmed!'

Sigmund was about to mention the standing stones that he'd found when he caught a slight shake of the head that Eugen gave to the burgomeister and felt his skin prickle. What games were these men playing? He had no intention of bringing them up now. He took a deep breath. 'Sir! If you deigned to look out from this hall then you would see that the whole of Helmstrumburg is in a state of near riot. Even though you are convinced that there is nothing to fear, then perhaps you would share that sentiment with the townsfolk.'

'Captain Jorg, I do not know what has possessed you. Am I to jump each time a rat farts? The people live on rumours! I can scarcely credit that you expect me to concern myself with each panic that grips the fools! I can hardly believe that you are so giddy as to be swayed by them – or is this a case of you promoting these fears?'

Sigmund bristled at the implication. 'I returned to the docks this morning to find the area in a state of near riot. The town watch are too frightened to go onto the streets. I have stationed a company of men on the docks to restore order.'

'Good. When the rabble have returned home then please return your men to their barracks. I am sure they need a good rest.'

Sigmund bowed politely. 'If you'll excuse me, I am tired. I will return to barracks. If the situation changes then I am at your command!'

Sigmund shut the door behind him, but instead of leaving, he hurried down the stairs to the stone vaults, where Maximillian, the town treasurer worked in the inner vault. The stone walls arched over his head, the walls glistened with river-damp. Between the thick columns that supported the ceiling was set his desk, made from slabs of Talabheim oak. There were ledgers spread all around him, and a number of candles cast puddles of flickering yellow light over their intricately-inscribed pages, tithes received and monies spent. When the treasurer heard footsteps on the stone stairs he dipped his quill in the ink pot and finished the line he was inscribing then sighed and looked up.

'Maximillian!' Sigmund whispered, and the man looked up from the vellum page he was working on and gave a weak smile.

'Captain Jorg!' he said, and then in a voice that betrayed no sense of irony. 'This is a pleasant surprise. Please tell me that you have lost no more men?'

Sigmund had no intention of wasting time. 'I need your help finding out a piece of information,' he said.

Maximillian laughed for a moment – a dry, humourless laugh. 'I don't know if I can help. All I do is add and subtract all day.'

Sigmund smiled, but his heart was racing. If the burgomeister had any idea that he was still in the building then he was sure he would hunt him down, and he needed to be discreet.

Sigmund wasn't in a mood to play games. 'I need to find out about that burial mound south of town.'

'Where that fire was last night?' Maximillian said and there was a mischievous twinkle in his eye.

'Yes,' Sigmund said.

'Come now, Captain Jorg, don't play the fool with your old friend Maximillian. I saw that fire last night. And I heard the boats sailing out of the harbour in the middle of the night. This morning I hear that you have fled the town, but now you come back, and if I have heard true then there are fourteen of the count's soldiers dead this morning. That makes fifty-two pennies, if I am not mistaken. I have already written it in this column, here. See!' Maximillian smiled. 'Now what is you want to know?'

'Are there any old records about that burial mound?' Sigmund said.

Maximillian pushed his chair back and stood up. He took the candle and moved deeper into the dark vaults, his keys jangling at his waist. As he moved forward into the dark chambers, Sigmund's breath began to steam in front of his face. He had the feeling of many vaulted chambers to either side, and remembered with a shiver how it was rumoured that the burgomeister had imprisoned a few notable enemies here, locked up in one of the many rooms, and left to die in the pitch black.

Sigmund looked back over his shoulder and saw the desk, with its flickering candles thirty feet behind, and the dimly illuminated staircase that led back to daylight. Maximillian stopped and Sigmund could see that he had paused at a heavy oaken door.

'This room contains all the old records,' Maximillian said. He took a set of keys from his belt and chose a large brass key, worn with many years of use, blackened with age, slipped it into the lock and turned. 'After you!' he said.

Sigmund stepped inside and remembered the men who were rumoured to have been locked up here. He turned in a moment's panic but Maximillian had shuffled inside after him. The scribe held up his candle and illuminated a low-ceilinged room whose walls were covered by wooden racks. Arranged in niches there were hundreds of tomes, scrolls and thick scraps of vellum, some of them so old that they were deep in dust, their edges worn smooth with years of thumbing.

Sigmund peered at the spines, but most of the books were worn and the lettering was indistinct. One caught his eye: an ancient copy of *The Life of Sigmar*. It was almost impossible to believe that Sigmar had once been a man – a soldier – like him who had carved eternal glory for himself by saving his people. Sigmund felt the same responsibility for Helmstrumburg, and for a moment he feared failing.

Maximillian held up the candle and in one of the top niches they saw a huge tome with gilt fittings.

'The Life of Johann Helmstrum!' Maximillian said.

Sigmund pulled a chest over to the wall and stood on top of it to get the tome. There was a cloud of dust as he pulled it down. It was heavier than he had imagined, but the leaves were leather, not paper, and the book ends were made of wood bound with leather and gilt set with semi precious stones.

He hurried out of the room and Maximillian followed him out and locked the door after them. Sigmund put the book down on top of the ledger that Maximillian had been working on, and slowly opened the pages. The writing was of a style that was difficult to read, with fantastically illuminated letters – incomprehensible to Sigmund.

Maximillian began to read hesitantly, his finger following the arcane lettering and language. 'Herein is told the life of the most illustrious and noble Johann Helmstrum, First Grand Theogonist, Friend to our Precious Lord Sigmar, and Hammer of the Beasts…'

'Find out what it says about the tomb,' Sigmund said. Maximillian carefully turned the pages, but the story was still talking about the first Grand Theogonist's childhood.

He opened the book half way.

'The Lord Sigmar said unto Johann…'

Maximillian turned the thick pages two at a time. Legends said that it was after the death of Sigmar that Johann led the crusade to clear the Stir River Valley.

It took half an hour to find the chapter they wanted. It told how the Grand Theogonist killed the great beastman warlord in a great battle at the very centre of the beastmen's sacred land – which was marked by a circle of stones. The narrator told how the stones were shattered with fire and water.

There was no description of the stones, but surely they were the same. Sigmund shivered. There was some power in those stones that remained after two thousand years.

'Over their ruins holy water was sprinkled and then the warriors who had fallen in the battle were laid there. Chief amongst them was Ortulf and Vranulf Jorg, who were the bravest among warriors.'

It took Sigmund a moment, then he frowned and put his finger to read the names again. 'Ortulf and Vranulf Jorg…?'

There was only one family of Jorgs in Helmstrumburg. Could it be that this was his ancestor?

Sigmund hardly dared to believe that the blood of heroes flowed in his veins, and quickly shut the book and thrust it into Maximillian's hands. The knowledge of this possibility gave him a sudden rush of confidence. The stones had to be the reason that the beastmen were attacking. He couldn't be sure yet, but he had a hunch and clapped Maximillian on the back. 'I think you have helped to save the town of Helmstrumburg!' Sigmund said. Maximillian seemed confused, but Sigmund was gone, running up the stairs and out of the burgomeister's hall, and out into the streets.

WHEN SIGMUND RETURNED to the barracks, Gaston and Edmunt were leading a team of men towards the Garden of Morr on Altdorf Street, where there was a small chapel and an old priest.

Sigmund called to Edmunt. The woodsman stopped and he rested his hands on the pick. Sigmund waited until the men had moved off before he spoke. 'Those merchants we saved…'

'The Reiklanders?'

Sigmund nodded. 'Did anything strike you as strange about them?'

Edmunt thought, but he shook his head.

'I think they have some control over the burgomeister,' Sigmund said. 'What, I have no idea – but I am sure he has abandoned the town to its fate.'

'What are you going to do?' Edmunt asked.

Sigmund may have only been a captain, but he was the only person in a position to save the town. 'Bring the sergeants to my room. I have a plan.'

ALL MORNING THE smoke continued to plume into the sky, a constant reminder of the gathering danger. The numbers of people locked outside the walls of Helmstrumburg grew steadily, until it seemed an army was camped at the walls: an army of the desperate and the terrified. But the burgomeister had spoken. The town watchmen looked to Roderick and he bristled inside his blue velvet jacket and set his jaw firmly. Orders had been given. The refugees must return home.

In the Jorg family mill, the mill-hands worked hard, but even though they had promised to stay with their master, as the fires came further down the mountain, and the procession of terrified country-folk hurried past, their morning resolution began to fade.

They were not paid to risk their lives like this.

After a lunch of fresh bread, cheese and salami sausage, the men did not get up to leave. Andres heard the silence and looked up and found the men staring at him. He stared at them in turn as if they were deserters. Their faces reddened. Andres took a bottle of kirsch and poured himself another cup, drank it down.

'What is it?' he demanded.

The men shuffled uncomfortably. None of them wanted to say what had been agreed among them.

'Speak up!'

'We want to go to town,' one of the men said nervously. 'Just for a day or so. Until the danger has passed. We heard that there was a fight on the other side of town last night. Eighty beastmen were killed. It's said that there are free companies being raised.'

'Free companies!' Andres laughed and put his hands on the tabletop and pushed himself up. 'Apprentices, greybeards and fat-guts! Do you think free companies will do anything to stop the goat-men?'

The men didn't know what to say.

'Flee if you will – I'll not stop you! I will not call you cowards, but I tell you those beasts will never dare come here to the riverside. And if they do,' Andres stumped across to pull the zweihander down. 'If those beasts dare come to this mill then we will meet them with cold steel!'

Two of the men left immediately, but the other four stayed on, their resolution shored up by Andres's conviction. If their master said it was safe then they would not leave him.

As THE TOWN bells rung three in the afternoon, Theodor wrote a message on a piece of paper and summoned Josh to his room.

'Take this to Captain Sigmund at the barracks!' he ordered and flipped the boy a penny for his trouble.

At the same time the barrack gates swung open and two units of ten spearmen marched out. They wore steel caps, cuirboili breastplates and carried their weapons in their hands. Behind them were ten halberdiers, led by Edmunt. There was a grim purpose about the three units, and people stepped well back to let them pass.

Hanz led one squad, Stephan, a scar-faced young Vorrsheimer led another, and Edmunt led the last. Hanz's men set off towards the east gate, Edmunt the north and Stephan to the west gate.

At THE EAST gate the town watchmen watched Hanz's spearmen approach, but the soldiers did not smile or nod. Hanz marched up to the four watchmen standing at the bottom of the gate. Without speaking the spearmen rushed the guards and wrestled the batons from their hands. The town watchmen were too surprised to speak or protest as they were pushed flat against the wall, cold knife blades held up against their throats.

At THE WEST gate Stephan's men took the gate in a similar way, without violence, but as Edmunt approached the north gate a man stepped out from the guardroom and stared at their approach.

'Welcome Edmunt,' Roderick smiled. 'How can we help you?'

Edmunt halted his men just in front of the blue-jacketed officer of the watch. Roderick smiled coldly. His men stood behind him, their batons ready.

'We're taking control of this gate,' Edmunt told him.

Roderick started to protest, but the halberdiers shoved his men back and soon they were up against the wall, the points of the halberds sticking into their chests.

Roderick told his men to drop their batons.

'Thank you,' Edmunt smiled, 'for your peaceful coopera-tion.'

WHEN THE GATEHOUSES had been secured, the soldiers lifted the heavy oak crossbars from the iron braces and drew the bolts that held the gates in place.

When all was done, the soldiers pushed on the gates and they swung open easily on the massive iron hinges. The refugees panicked, fearful that the gates might be shut at any moment. Some left all their belongings outside, others hitched their horses to their carts and lashed at them with their whips. The carts lurched forward as the whips cracked. They pushed and shoved, and now each family fought the others in their desperation – until the soldiers came out and organised the people into orderly queues.

AT THE SAME time that the gates were being taken over, Osric took twelve men and marched to the marketplace. They found Fat Gulpen, the town crier, in the Crooked Dwarf. There was a cloud of pipe smoke in the air, a few old drinkers were sitting with their steins, and Josh, Guthrie's young lad, was carrying a platter of beef stew out to the town crier, whose rotund form was squeezed into the red velvet jacket that marked his office. His chins pressed up against the high collar as he turned to glare at Osric. There was a long-standing animosity between the two men that dated back to Osric's time as officer of the watch.

'Gulpen!' Osric said.

Fat Gulpen took a long swig of his stein and refused to look up.

Osric took the piece of paper that Sigmund had given him and slammed it on the table in front of him.

Fat Gulpen wiped the foam from his upper lip and glanced towards it, and started to read. It took a few seconds.

'You want me to read this?' he said.

Osric nodded.

'Now?'

Osric put his thumbs in his sword belt and smiled.

'Yes, now,' he said.

As soon as Roderick was out of sight of the halberdiers at the north gate he slowed down, but kept walking quickly, looking over his shoulder.

The streets were full of nervous people, hurrying back and forth in their panic. Roderick passed a couple of town watchmen and ordered them to gather all his men and meet him back in the marketplace in half an hour.

Roderick kept hurrying along until he reached the docks, where the guild hall stood. He was relieved to see that there were no soldiers standing on the steps of the hall, and nodded to his men as he hurried inside.

Roderick crossed the inner courtyard and hurried up the steps to the burgomeister's chambers. He knocked and then tried the handle, but the door was locked. Roderick knocked again. He could hear voices inside.

'Lord burgomeister!' Roderick shouted.

'Wait outside!' the shout came back, but the burgomeister's voice sounded strange.

Roderick stepped back from the door and waited. He had a strong feeling that something was not right. When at last the door opened it was not the burgomeister who came to see him to ask him what he wanted, but the Reikland merchant that Sigmund had brought in a few days earlier.

'Yes?' Eugen snapped.

'I need to talk to the burgomeister,' Roderick began. 'The soldiers have broken his official decree and opened the town gates!'

Eugen frowned. 'And this is the news with which you disturb your master?'

Roderick opened his mouth but didn't know what to say.

Eugen shut the door again, and Roderick stepped back in shock. He hurried out to the steps of the guild hall.

'You two,' Roderick said, to the guards. 'Wait here! You two come with me.'

And then they hurried towards the marketplace.

SIGMUND ARRIVED IN the marketplace in time to see Fat Gulpen come out of the Crooked Dwarf, ringing his bell as he made his way to the centre of the marketplace.

'Hear ye! Hear ye!' he called. 'Hear ye! Hear ye!'

A crowd gathered, desperate for news of relief or reinforcements.

'All men of fighting age are asked to join in free companies for the protection of Helmstrumburg! Assemble at the barracks for free companies!'

There was an excited buzz as Fat Gulpen rang his bell again.

'Hear ye! Hear ye! Free companies to assemble at the barracks!'

IT WAS SOME time after lunch when the door to the burgomeister's office opened and Eugen stalked out. He ignored the watchmen on the door and strode through the streets to the market.

People were running back and forth. He could smell their fear and the scent made him smile. They would all have reason to fear soon enough.

In the marketplace there were a number of crude banners raised on poles, acting as rallying points for the young men of Helmstrumburg. The inn signs had been nailed to the end of long poles and the regulars of each establishment were coming together, ready to march to the barracks to be given weapons.

The Crooked Dwarf sign had been nailed to a pole, and Guthrie was there handing out free ale to all who enlisted. There was also a band of men at the White Unicorn, and another at the Drayman's Rest.

Free companies! Eugen snorted with derision. It was too late to try and dam the flood that was coming. They would all be washed away in a river of blood.

He hurried up the steps and ducked inside the Crooked Dwarf. The bar was unnaturally empty. Eugen hurried across it and took the steps two at a time. He turned right down the corridor and opened the door to their room.

Theodor was sitting on the bed, waiting. He had the window open and was watching the commotion in the market square with interest.

'The fools are too late!' Eugen said with obvious delight.

'Have you heard?' Theodor said. 'There were a hundred beastmen killed last night at the sacred site!'

'Of course I heard!' Eugen spat. 'But this will not stop our plans. They disobeyed the orders. None were to come near the town until tonight. For their impatience they will never see Helmstrumburg burn!'

'Do you think that there will there still be enough?'

Eugen laughed at his acolyte's naivety. 'There are more beastmen in the woods than there are people in Helmstrumburg! Each one of them is bound to this task by a force stronger than force – hatred! They have waited so long for revenge. Nothing will stop that now!

'Now,' Eugen said after a deep breath. 'We have important business to attend to.

HELMSTRUMBURG WAS FULL of frenetic activity all that afternoon. As soon as they heard that free companies were being raised, men hurried to fetch whatever weapons they had. In the Crooked Dwarf band, there were a number of old soldiers who bantered back and forth as if they were still in the count's pay, drew their sword and gave their sword arms another feel of the weight of their swords.

There were farm lads who had kitchen knives strapped to their belts, and pitchforks or blacksmith's hammers in their hands. Whatever weapons they could find they brought with them, and they stood feeling responsible and nervous, looking at the other men's faces, thinking that they would soon be fighting shoulder to shoulder with these men.

Josh had been to the barracks but Captain Jorg was not there. He had waited for a while and then he had got caught up in all the excitement and had almost forgotten the note he had been paid to take. When he returned to the barracks there were a couple of soldiers on duty.

'What, boy?' Baltzer demanded.

'I have a note, sir!' Josh said. 'For Captain Jorg.'

'He's busy.'

Josh looked frustrated. Guthrie would be wanting him back at the Crooked Dwarf. He took out the note and held it in his hands, unsure what to do. 'It's from the Reiklander merchants,' he said, as if that might gain him entrance. 'For Captain Jorg especial.'

Baltzer smiled. 'Is it now? Then you give it to me and I'll make sure it reaches him!'

Eugen and Theodor made their way through the streets to the western gate, where Stephan's men were still on duty. As they walked up to the gate two spearmen stopped them.

'You cannot go out,' they said.

'Why?' Eugen said innocently.

The soldiers laughed. 'Have you seen what is happening?' They gestured to the long plumes of black smoke that now reached as high as the clouds.

'My mother is frail, she lives just a little way up the river,' Eugen said. 'We will fetch her and then come back. I assure you we have no intention of putting our own lives in danger.'

The soldiers relented and Eugen and Theodor hurried along the Kemperbad Road. The mill was a few miles outside of the west gate. They came off the road a little way before it and spied out the land. There was a boat at the mill, loading up with grain. They could see the men carrying sacks down to the waterside and stacking them inside.

A one-legged man stepped out of the mill.

'That's him!' Eugen whispered with relish.

SIGMUND WAS BUSY all afternoon meeting the self-appointed captains of the free companies. Of all his men, only he and Gaston were able to read and write to any standard, so Gaston sat and recorded all the information about the various bands.

At times Gaston was barely able to keep his eyes open as he dipped the quill into the ink and scratched it across the page.

Each company's name was listed, with the name of their captain and the number of men they led.

The Crooked Dwarf Volunteers. Guthrie Black. Thirty-four brave men.

The Guild of Blacksmith's Hammerers. Strong-arm Benjamin. Twenty brave souls.

The Old Unbreakables. Blik Short (retired marshal). Fifteen former soldiers. Each man bears his old armour and equipment.

Squire Becker's Helmstrumburg Guard. Squire Becker. Shields and spears. Twenty men (not including Squire Becker).

As evening began to fall, Sigmund thanked all the remaining men and sent them away.

'Get some sleep, men!' he told them. 'If anything happens then we will notify you!'

The men left reluctantly, heading either to their homes or rented rooms, or went to the bars and shared a stein or two, while they laughed about how they would send the beast-men back to their forests.

WHEN ALL THE volunteers had left, Sigmund let out a long sigh. He had not slept for two days, and the frenetic activity of the day had left him utterly exhausted.

He lay back on his bed, and put his feet up. He should go and see his mother, he thought. He shut his eyes, thinking that he would just rest them for five minutes – but he fell deeply asleep.

* * *

As MORRSLIEB ROSE, the guards looked out from the walls, and wondered how long until the beastmen swept down from the forests.

And then in the darkness a fire appeared – and another!

Soon a circle of fire was burning. A ring of torches that encircled the Jorg family mill.

CHAPTER EIGHT

THE SUN SET through the haze of smoke like a ruddy ball of blood.

Andres let the dogs out for the night, then he shut the house door and sat down. The remaining four mill-hands watched as he poured himself a cup of kirsch and began to recount stories of past battles.

The first battle he fought was against the Count of Ostland. The Talabec army was outnumbered two to one, and they had lined up on the upper slopes of a broad hill: infantry in the centre and cavalry on the wings. He told how the Ostlanders had crossed the ford and lined up with the river at their backs. They'd looked garish and extravagantly dressed in their fine uniforms and feathers. They were so close that he could make out the gilt touches on the armour of the Ostland pistoliers who had pushed up to test the Talabecland right wing.

For a number of hours the armies traded cannon and musket shot. The Ostland cavalry swept the Talabec right from the field and then the Ostland infantry had struck up their marching tunes and advanced.

His memories were blurred from then. While the Ostland cavalry was looting their baggage train, the Talabec cavalry had broken the Ostland right and fallen upon the Ostland rear, which had panicked and fled. It seemed like half an hour had gone by – but when the battle ended the sun was setting and hours must have passed. How they had drunk that night!

He told them of another time when he had faced a rabble of revolting peasants from south-west Talabecland. They had formed themselves into a mock army: shoe lasts or buckets atop their banner poles. They gave themselves grand titles such as the Grand Army of Rustic Unity or the Brothers of Branbeck. They had hired the help of Tilean mercenaries and the Tilean pikemen were the only ones who put up a fight. They repulsed three attacks from the halberdiers and handgunner columns before the greatswords were sent in. Andres looked up at his zweihander and laughed as he remembered how they had cut through the thicket of pike shafts and then closed in on the startled Tileans and set to in a ferocious hand to hand struggle. The Tileans fought well, but they were surrounded and beaten and after an hour their leader limped out from their lines to surrender.

Andres spat. The fleeing peasants had looted the mercenaries' camp during the fighting and the next day the Tileans joined in the hunt. They hung hundreds of rebels, . he remembered. Taught those men a lesson they would never forget.

As the night went on and Andres drank more his memories turned maudlin. As common as the victories were battles that neither side won outright. The time his best friend, fellow Helmstrumburger, Johann Kilmar, was killed. The last story was the one in which he lost the lower half of his leg: not to an enemy's sword, but to the surgeon's knife and saw. There had been nothing to still the pain as the surgeon made a neat cut through the flesh, and then took his saw to the living bone. Not even a drop of kirsch, Andres thought with a sigh and poured himself another cup.

The men listened silently. Andres realised how young and naïve they were. Soldiering aged a man quickly, if he lived.

'Now, bed!' Andres said and the men lay down on the makeshift beds of sacks and old rugs from the mill. 'Sleep well! I'll keep watch tonight.'

The men shuffled until they were comfortable, then went to sleep. Andres sipped his cup slowly. Outside the wind had picked up and the drafts made the candle flames flicker back and forth.

Every once in a while one of the mill-hands turned in his sleep. Andres finished his cup. He took the bottle tipped it up again, the last drops dribbled out into the cup.

His supply of Averland kirsch was out in the woodshed. He pushed himself up, unbolted the door and braced himself to the outside chill. There were packs of clouds racing over the sky. He turned towards the hills, to see if there were any more fires. If there were, they were hidden by the landscape, but he thought he saw a torch a little down the hill, through a patch of trees.

Andres stumped down the slope towards the mill to get a better view. It looked like a bonfire. There was another fire to the east just a hundred yards away.

One of the dogs started barking frantically.

Just the breeze he told himself, but he shivered, stopped and looked over his shoulder. There was something on the slope by the river. The barking stopped in a whimper, then there was the sound of flesh being hacked. Andres called out the dog's name but there was no answer. A figure crossed in front of one of the fires.

Andres saw another figure pass in front of the fire and recognised the silhouette: it was a beastman!

Andres rushed back up the slope. He could hear the panting breaths of his pursuers as they gained on him. The doorway seemed impossibly far away – but he reached it just ahead of them and slammed the door shut and threw the bolts.

'Up men! Up!' Andres roared.

A body crashed against the door. And another. The mill-hands scrambled from their make-shift beds and reached for weapons: a club, a kitchen knife, two of them grabbed pitchforks as Andres yanked his greatsword from the mantelpiece. One of the shutters on the other side of the room exploded in splinters of wood. A horned head thrust through the hole, and the creature roared.

The beastman started to drag itself through the smashed shutters. The mill-hands panicked.

'Fight, lads!' Andres bellowed. He pointed towards the rack of kitchen knives and the men with pitchforks scrambled to arm themselves with something less cumbersome.

Andres brought his sword down onto the beastman and cut it clean in half, the upper body falling in through the window with a great gout of gore.

For a few minutes there was a terrible stand-off. Any beastmen that tried to clamber inside were dealt with savage ruthlessness – but there was no way Andres and his men could escape.

From the sounds on the kitchen roof, it seemed that a number of beastmen climbed up there and were beginning to smash and tear away the tiles. At the same time it sounded as if they had found something to ram the door. The planks began to shudder and crack as holes began to appear in the kitchen roof. Andres smelled smoke, and the brief glimmer of hope that they could hold out was gone. This was a trap from which he would never escape. They would all burn.

A fell bravery came over Andres. He would soon be in the Halls of Morr, and he would see his long-dead brothers again: and with him he would take a heap of beastmen heads.

A beastman dropped through the ruin of the kitchen roof. It bellowed as it fell onto the floor, but Andres caught it with an upper-cut in the ribs, and the power of his blade tore through the ribs, and splattered the wall with shreds of lung and blood.

A second beastman hesitated to follow the fate of the first, and Andres threw back the bolts on the doorway.

'Come and meet me!' he bellowed and three beastmen charged inside as another dropped onto the kitchen table. They would all die together.

WHEN NIGHT FELL, Baltzer and Osric slipped out of the barracks and made their way along the eastern wall, looking for the hut that had been described to them. Osric had a lantern in his hand, but it was hooded so as to allow them to move stealthily.

'What did that note say?' Osric hissed and Baltzer repeated it verbatim.

'A ramshackle shack. Within which you will find something of great value for Helmstrumburg.'

Osric nodded and they made their way along the wall. The round water tower, which marked the spot where wall and river met, loomed over them. They could see a couple of spearmen sentries in the tower, but they were looking out of town.

The two men crept forward and in the crook of the shed, where a large crack in the base of the water tower had begun to inch its way up the tower, there indeed was the 'ramshackle shack.'

A rat skittered by and Osric jumped. 'I hate those things,' he hissed, but he could see Baltzer laughing and pointed at the door. 'Right – you open that thing!'

Baltzer felt for a lock, but there was none. He pulled the doors open and there was a familiar smell that made him smile.

'Blackpowder!' he grinned and Osric stepped forward to see for himself.

Four firkins of blackpowder. From his time as officer of the watch, Osric knew all the smugglers in town. Knew who would be looking to shift something as valuable as blackpowder. Just one of these beauties would make them a handsome profit. All they had to do was to get through this chaos alive!

* * *

SIGMUND DREAMED HE was in a room full of flames and screaming voices. The sounds of running footsteps startled him from his sleep and he sat up in his bed. His lamp was still burning, but the flame was weak and the oil was almost out. He realised he must have fallen asleep without meaning to, and hadn't turned it out. He shook his head to clear his head.

He felt a terrible sense of imminent danger. He stood up and threw back his door. There was a wind blowing and someone was running past.

'Ho there!' Sigmund shouted.

The man stopped.

'What news?'

'Sir! There are fires just outside town.'

'Which way?'

'To the east,' the man said. 'Along the Kemperbad Road.'

'How far?'

'About three miles.'

Three miles would set it at his family's mill. Sigmund had forgotten his father. Damn! Something told him that the dream and the fires were connected. He ran to the room where the sergeants slept, but there was no time to raise his men. He considered taking a boat, but there was no way to go upstream. He had to do something – but there was no way he could explain this to his sergeants. The fires and the stones and the knowledge of his ancestry were somehow linked, of that he was sure.

Sigmund paused for a moment then turned and sprinted to the stables. There were a couple of old horses kept here for pulling the barrack's supply carts. He dragged an old cavalry saddle off a rack, and brushed off the cobwebs. He selected one of the horses, threw a blanket over its back, then saddled and bridled it.

The horse stamped a front hoof, uncomfortable at the almost forgotten feel of a saddle, but Sigmund led it out of the stables and into the dark drill yard. He mounted and spurred the horse out of the barrack gates and into the quiet streets. The horse's hooves were loud on the cobble stones.

'Open the gates!' he shouted and the spearmen hurried to obey, despite their confusion.

Sigmund spurred the horse out along the Kemperbad Road. The horse whinnied as it started to trot. Here and there, when there was a break in the trees, he caught glimpses of the flames. It looked as if the mill building was on fire, and he could make out flames on the east side of the house.

Sigmund felt the wind sweep his hair back from his face. He spurred the horse on, felt the old horse begin to remember its days as a cavalry mount – and stretch its stride. The nightmare stayed with him as the horse galloped on: he had a strong premonition that there was some sinister link between the stones and the beastmen and the attack on the mill: but what it was exactly, he had no idea.

THE JORG FAMILY mill was set atop a long ridge, two and a half miles along the Kemperbad Road, that lifted it above the surrounding forests and water-meadows and made it clearly visible from the east gate.

The news that the mill was on fire spread through town like the plague. The bells of the Chapel of Sigmar began to ring and in the Crooked Dwarf inn, Guthrie Black sat up in alarm.

He had no idea if this meant that the beastmen were attacking.

'Josh!' he called and the young lad sat up from the mattress where all Guthrie's sons slept.

'I have to go out,' Guthrie said, but his stomach felt hollow as he pulled on his boots and fastened his belt around his expansive waist. It was easy to decide to join the free companies in the light of day: but now, at night, when the bells were ringing, it was a different matter entirely.

'If something happens to me then you will have to look after the inn and the other boys.'

Josh nodded. He leant against the doorframe and then pushed off and walked towards the only parent he had ever known. Josh put his arms around Guthrie's waist, and

Guthrie put his arms around the boy – overcome by the sudden display of emotion.

Neither of them wanted Guthrie to go, but the bells were ringing frantically.

Guthrie felt strange as he descended the staircase, thinking it might be for the last time. He stopped in his bar for a moment and had a good look round. He didn't know what he was doing with a sword at his waist, going to fight like this. He was a barman not a soldier. But there were things that a man could not run from. And this was one, he thought as he unbolted the front door and let himself out. He had not asked the beastmen to come – but they had come regardless and, he told himself as he closed the inn door behind him, he would fight.

FLAMES LICKED UP the side of the house, and smoke swirled under the rafters and billowed inside.

Andres wiped the tears from his eyes and rested the zweihander on his shoulder to get a moment's rest, coughing with the smoke and the sudden exertion. At least the smoke affected the beastmen as much as the men.

To his left one of the mill-hands, a boy from Burhens called Gunner, was keeping the beastmen at bay with a table leg. As far as he knew, the other mill-hands were dead.

'Keep them back!' Andres shouted, and he felt that he was a young man again, back to back with his brothers. His forehead dripped seat, his arms ached and he had not realised how unfit he had become. He prepared himself for more exertion, braced his wooden foot, and caught a small beastman on the arm, shattering the bone. A beastman tried to duck in under the swing, but Gunner drove it back and Andres recovered his balance. He was about to thank Gunner when he saw the young lad double over and stagger forward.

Flames were leaping up the inside of the walls, and they lapped along the rafters. The noise was deafening and the heat became stifling. Andres coughed and swung his sword blindly into the smoke. On the third swing he caught something. There was a satisfying roar of pain. Andres pushed the tumbled kitchen table out of his way and backed across the living room.

He stumbled on a dead body and saw Josen, his throat torn out, a bloody kitchen knife still clutched in his hand and then a beastman leapt the kitchen table and drove straight at him.

Andres executed the creature and then swung the greatsword in a wide arc, driving the beastmen back over the fallen chairs. Outside there was a inarticulate scream of agony. The voice was unmistakably human.

Maybe his men were not all dead, after all.

His sword felt light and easy in his hand. He laughed as he slashed out and felt the blade strike home. One of the beastmen dropped its spear and lowered its head to gore him, but he twisted his wrist so that the sword was vertical and stabbed it through the back of the neck. An untrained man might have aimed for the spine, but Andres aimed well to the side – where the arteries connected neck and head and opened them up in a spray of blood that made the other beasts snort with bloodlust – even though it was one of their own.

No goat-beast was going to take him alive, Andres thought, and stabbed another foul creature in the windpipe.

The smoke was almost impenetrable, and the heat in the main room was unbearable. Andres crouched low under the smoke and backed into his bedroom, hearing the snorts and grunts as the beastmen followed.

Andres kicked a chair out of the way and backed into a corner, the greatsword stretched in front of him. There was a moment's pause before the beastmen dared to step into the room and Andres wiped the sweat from his forehead and his hands, then braced himself, his greatsword thirsty for more blood.

He had chosen, and here – unseen and unremembered – would be where he would die.

* * *

ON THE EASTERN wall of Helmstrumburg a crowd gathered to watch Andres Jorg's mill burn. The flames reached a hundred feet into the air, lighting the waters of the Stir with a thousand tiny sparks.

Hengle joined the crowd then ran through the streets back to the marketplace. He slipped on the cobblestones and scrambled up the steps and up the narrow staircase to the back room he shared with his mother.

'The mill's burning!' he said.

'And your father?'

Hengle didn't know. 'No one has seen him,' he said.

'What about Gunner and the others?'

Hengle shook his head. His mother bit back her tears, determined not to cry. Andres would have escaped, she told herself, even though she doubted the truth of the words. He wouldn't have stayed to fight, would he, she asked herself – even though, in her heart, she knew the answer. He would die rather than let beastmen drive him from his mill.

SIGMUND RODE HARD along the Kemperbad Road, foam splattering down the horse's flanks as he drove it on. Half a mile from town there was a low defile to the left, and on the right a patch of trees grew close to the road. As Sigmund approached, five beastmen ran out of the copse, attempting to intercept him. He used the ends of the reins to swat the flanks of his mount. They outpaced the beastmen, but behind him a crude horn sounded and Sigmund felt trapped, as if the alarm had been sounded and the whole forest would now be ready for him.

As he passed through a dense patch of forest the bank where his father's mill stood came into view. It was clearly visible in the darkness, flames reaching a hundred feet into the night air.

A hundred yards off he drew his horse to a halt. Both the mill and the house were ablaze: flames leaping hundreds of feet into the air. Sigmund could see figures outside – horned figures – illuminated by the conflagration running away from the heat. He could feel the warmth on his cheek: it bathed the forests with a ruddy light. Roof timbers crashed down in the house. The mill wheel kept slowly revolving as the rest of the building began to collapse.

There was no way anything was still alive in there. His father must be dead, Sigmund realised – but there was no time to grieve. His mount seemed ready to collapse with exhaustion and it snorted with alarm at the scent of smoke. Sigmund looked away from the flames into the dark shade of the trees. He was sure that he saw two horned figures detach themselves from the shadows and start silently towards him. The horse stamped with alarm and Sigmund turned it round. He'd never trained in fighting from horseback, but to dismount would be suicide in the forests at night. He felt the nag stumble in the darkness and cursed the creature's age. He had pushed it too hard. If it died here he would never make it back to Helmstrumburg. The horse pulled down on the reins as if it was trying to lie down. Sigmund suspected that if it fell then it would never stand again. He had to keep the creature moving.

Sigmund spurred the horse towards the creatures – their horned heads becoming visible as he got closer. Their eyes were fierce and their crude lips were curled with ferocious snarls. The nearest had long fangs that overlapped the bottom lip, the other's teeth were blunt and yellowed, standing out in irregular angles from enflamed red gums. Both had fetid breath that Sigmund smelled as he rode past, parrying desperately.

There was nothing he could do here. It was stupid and dangerous for him to come out at all. His father was dead. But there were thousands of people in Helmstrumburg who needed him. Sigmund cursed his rashness and spurred his horse forward. There was nothing more he could do to help his father. His duty was with the town and his men.

OSRIC AND BALTZER took a barrel each and hefted them onto their shoulders.

'Where are we going to put these things?' Baltzer hissed.

Osric thought for a moment. 'I know the perfect place!' he grinned and set off towards the centre of town.

THERE WAS A crash as the roof of the main room fell in. Scorching air blasted into the bedroom, and with it came a thick chocking smoke.

Andres choked and tried to blink away the stinging tears in his eyes. There was a pile of dead beastmen at his feet, but he was almost spent.

'Come on spawn of the Dark Gods!' Andres Jorg spat as he heard the unmistakable tap of hoofed feet move towards him.

There was another crash as the kitchen roof collapsed. It wouldn't be long until the bedroom was an inferno too. Hooves tapped on the floorboards as the beastmen inched forward. A thrust caught Andres on the thigh and he gasped with pain and swung the greatsword – but his arms were now so weak that there was no strength in the blow and it did little more than stun one of the attackers.

Andres threw the greatsword away and drew his short sword. It felt light as he parried another spear thrust and another. But this was an impossible battle. Another jab caught him on the arm and he dropped the sword.

This was it. The beastmen dropped their spears, took out long knives and moved in for the kill. There was a moment before Andres realised what the beastmen intended and he promised himself that they would never take him alive.

In the confined space there was a thunderous explosion and one of the beastmen's head exploded in a shower of brains and skull fragments.

Andres ducked and there was a flash and another explosion – but this time he could see what had caused it. A silver pistol appeared from the smoke and rested against the temple of his last attacker. The beastman paused – confused that there should be anything behind it – then the trigger was pulled and the round shot exploded from the other side of the creature's head in a shower of gore and imbedded itself in the wall.

'Here!' a voice shouted, but Andres had collapsed onto the floor and all he saw was a hand. He felt himself being dragged up from the floor then tipped through an open window, onto the slope at the back of the house.

Andres sucked in lungfuls of air – and then he saw his saviour, a tall, thick man, with two pistol holsters at his waist and a few singe marks on his fine jacket.

'Take this!' the man said. He took the cutlass from his waist and handed it to Andres – then he fumbled to reload his pistols.

Andres shoved himself up. The wind was blowing the flames and smoke away from the bedroom towards town, and Andres understood why it had taken so long for the flames to spread to the bedroom. His head was clearing with each breath of clean air. He felt the cutlass for balance for a moment before more horned shapes appeared through the smoke. A pistol shot felled one and Andres disembowelled the other.

'Run!' the man said, leading the way away from the house and Andres stumped along on his peg leg with the speed of a two-legged man. His saviour fumbled with his pistols, but he did not have time to reload before a huge maddened beast charged down the slope.

The man threw a pistol into its face and it distracted the animal long enough for Andres to hobble up and dispatch the creature with a well-aimed slash across the throat.

They kept hurrying down the slope behind the mill and towards the sluice that fed the water mill. The beastmen seemed so maddened with blood-lust that they had forgotten the purpose of their attack. Andres and the man hurried out of the circle of light around the blazing mill and along the path of the water sluice.

There were two horses tethered to a tree and the man untied the reins of one and thrust them towards Andres. It was a long time since Andres had ridden a horse, but he set his good foot in the stirrup and pulled himself up, managing to fit his peg into the other.

The man leapt into the saddle and moved his horse between Andres and the mill.

'Ride!' the man shouted. 'If you stay close to the river you should be safe. Do not head into the hills!'

Andres's horse shied for a moment, but he wrestled the creature back under control and brought it round next to the man's.

'Go!' the man shouted. 'Please go! There's no time to explain! This is too important! Ride to Talabheim! Ask for Hoffman! The Black Goat inn in Talabheim!'

The stranger seized the bridle of Andres's horse and turned its head away from the blazing buildings and out over the dark meadow towards the road.

'Go!' he shouted. 'Just go!'

Andres kicked his peg leg into the flank of his mount and it jumped forward, eager to be away from the flames. He paused for a moment and turned to watch the mill collapse in a shower of sparks. It was a beautiful sight, but best of all, he was still alive.

As SIGMUND DROVE his exhausted horse back to the city, he could see a crowd of people standing on the eastern wall. The gates opened as he approached, and a mob of forty armed men surged forward with a great roar – led by Squire Becker's Helmstrumburg Guard, with spears and shields, as he had promised, and at the front the squire himself with an inherited breastplate, brass buckler and rapier.

Sigmund almost smiled at the sight of the pompous aristocrat and his motley band of soldiers, but he was exhausted by shock and grief and, worst of all, failure.

'Captain Jorg!' Squire Becker said. He was a short plump man, who seemed more suited to horseback hunts than armed service. 'I have assembled my men. Let's march forth and punish these filthy animals!'

Sigmund glared down at him. He had wanted glory as much as any man, but glory would not save the people of Helmstrumburg. And the care of the whole town was his responsibility as captain of the army here.

'Squire Becker,' he spoke in a cold and clear voice. 'You will take your men back to town and await my orders. There is an army of beastmen in the hills, and we will need each man we have. I will not have you sally out and waste a single life – not even your own!'

The squire opened his mouth to argue but Sigmund cut him off. 'Do I make myself clear?'

Squire Becker's cheeks reddened. He was not used to being spoken to like this. His mouth opened but nothing came out.

'Good!' Sigmund said, and kicked his horse through the deflated crowd. There will be enough time to fight, Sigmund knew. And then Squire Becker and his rabble could have all the glory they wanted.

SIGMUND'S HORSE WAS too exhausted to carry him back to the barracks. He had to dismount and lead it slowly back through the streets, and as he went he felt the eyes of all the people on him. Riding out had been the stupidest thing he could ever had done. He was Captain Jorg of the Talabecland army. The army was his family. He had responsibilities to the whole town.

But however much he told himself this, Sigmund couldn't help thinking that he might have been able to save his father. He imagined his father's screams as he was flayed alive – and had to struggle to fight back a wrenching sob.

WHEN SIGMUND REACHED the barracks he could see from the men's faces that they had heard what had happened, but he couldn't bring himself to speak to them.

He led the horse back to the stables, took off the saddle and rubbed it down. He washed the smell of horse sweat from his hands and crossed the yard to the barracks.

Sigmund fell onto his bed, kicked off his boots and then pulled the sheets over his head and bit back his grief.

THE FLAMES AT the mill burned all night. People were still standing on the city walls as Sigmund's men came home, watching the spectacle.

Dawn came early and only a thin trickle of smoke climbed into the sky. The sentries on the walls looked for flames in the hills, but the air was clear. Not a single fire burned – but the very absence of flames was ominous. The forests and hills: for so long home to so many of them had become suddenly evil and threatening. No one knew what the forests held: but all were clear – whatever it was it was now very close.

In the barracks Sigmund had barely slept. The whole night had been a torment. If he had not gotten so angry with his father he might have persuaded him to come to town. If he had not been so busy with the free companies he might have sent men out to bring his father home. Not only had his father died, but also the six men at the mill. All of their deaths weighed upon him.

And on top of all his worries, there were the beastmen moving inexorably towards town. When the dawn reveille sounded, Sigmund was glad to roll out of bed and dress for parade. Anything was better than being alone with the endless and revolving list of 'what ifs'. There was work to be done, and he was in charge.

CHAPTER NINE

THE BEASTMEN CAME face to face in a clearing at the foot of Galten Hill. The forest was silent as Red Killer waited. The scent of musk hung in the air, an unmistakable challenge to the white figure that stepped into the clearing.

A fallen branch snapped beneath Azgrak's hoof. The pink eyes focussed on the challenger and blinked with recognition and fury.

The animal lips formed crude, bestial words: a challenge. The sound of Dark Tongue was harsh in the stillness.

Red Killer did not respond, but hefted his axe and charged.

SOLDIERS AND CIVILIANS alike stood on the eastern wall and watched the sun rise over the ridge, silhouetting the smouldering ruins of the Jorg family mill. The most long-sighted among them could make out lone timbers thrust up from the ruins, blackened and charred. The waterwheel was a half-burnt skeleton, the machinery that had been the wonder of Helmstrumburg had devoured by the rapacious flames.

Unseen at such a distance was the gruesome fate of the mill-hands who had stayed with Andres. Nailed to an apple tree in front of the house were four flayed human skins. The skinless bodies lay abandoned in the grass not far off, crude runes carved into their flesh. Their eyes and tongues had been ripped out.

DESPITE THE PROXIMITY of the mill, no one dared to venture out to see for themselves. People looked to the hills with a sense of dread, but this morning there were no fires. A few people began to celebrate, but most saw the stillness with dread. The silence seemed to grow ominously. No one seriously believed that the beastmen had retreated into the hills. They felt that they were being watched.

The free companies – the Old Unbreakables, Squire Becker's Helmstrumburg Guard and the Crooked Dwarf Volunteers – assembled at their meeting points, the men edgy and eager in the early morning chill. If there had to be a fight they would rather get it over with. The long wait was a trial of courage.

Blik Short, Squire Becker, Guthrie Black and Strong-arm Benjamin reported to the barracks to receive their orders. Sigmund assigned each of them stations of duty along the walls or in the marketplace, from where they could be rushed to any point along the walls. Each gatehouse also had a unit of Sigmund's own men, and one of his sergeants.

Squire Becker wasn't comfortable taking orders from a miller's son. 'My men want to be at a gateway,' he declared in his aristocratic accent. 'Where they can be of most use.'

Sigmund gave the plump noble a hard stare. He was surprised the man had not fled town. 'I am in charge of the defence of Helmstrumburg, Master Becker. And when I am not around you will all take orders from my sergeants! Do I make myself understood?'

The squire's face reddened. Sigmund smiled. 'Good. It will be a hard fight, but with good men like you, and with the strength and courage and determination of the Helden-hammer we will prevail.'

The men around were heartened by his businesslike speech and there were nervous smiles. Last week they had just been simple farmers and merchants and artisans; this morning they were kitted out in all the accoutrements of war. Sigmund looked from man to man, and there was something in his fierce stare that made them feel that they could fight and that they could win.

'Good,' Sigmund said. 'When the beastmen are sighted then the bells of the chapel will ring. Until then I want you and your men to stand to.'

THE FIRST NIGHT in Helstrumburg Gruff and his daughters had slept in their cart, but in the morning he set off to find proper lodgings. There were so many refugees in town it wouldn't be easy, and any rooms that were still available were way overpriced. In the end Gruff managed to find a place in the new town.

The house was a part of a rickety row of timber-framed houses that seemed to lean on each other for support. The street was called Tanner Lane, and the stink of ammonia from the tanners' vats was so strong it made the twin's eyes water.

'We cannot stay here!' Beatrine declared, but they were tired and hungry and there was nowhere else.

Beatrine started to cry but still no one took any notice. 'I refuse to stay here!' she said, at which point Farmer Spennsweich turned to her and spoke in a low hard voice.

'You will stay here, young lady, or I will put you over my knee and thrash you like the insolent brat you are!'

Beatrine blushed and bit her lip, but Farmer Spennsweich took no notice. He conversed with the landlady, an old widow with a hairy mole on her cheek and agreed a price.

'Valina!' their father called. 'Get everyone inside. Organise the rooms, and when you have made everything comfortable then look after your sisters. Keep them inside and safe! You are in charge!'

Valina nodded. 'Quickly now!' he shouted and the twins hurried to grab their packs and cases and climb down from the back of the wagon.

They helped Gertrude down and then followed Valina inside. Beatrine made a show of holding her nose, but the landlady didn't speak as she showed them into the room that their father had rented. Their father took the cart down the road to an inn, where there was room to stable his horse.

It was a ground floor room that appeared to have been used for storage and keeping domestic animals. It stank of the tanneries, and the corner of the room smelled as if a tomcat had sprayed all over the straw. The floor was packed dirt. Foul-smelling straw was piled up against the front wall. The only hint of luxury or former opulence were the two glass windows. One looked out into the street, the other looked into the backyard where the girls could hear a pig rooting round. Both windows had been paned with thick bull's-eye glass that distorted the world outside.

The twins didn't appear to notice the smells or the dirt, but ran to the windows. 'Is this glass?' they asked. Gertrude ran after them and they tapped the strange substance, laughing at how it distorted the world outside with its swirls.

Valina put the bags down, pushed the hair back behind her ears and tried to smile, but Beatrine slammed the shutters to the rear and then glared. She didn't think it was any better than a stable.

'Come, sister,' Valina encouraged. 'We will make it better,' but Beatrine did not move.

'Valina – tell father we cannot stay here!' Beatrine said but Valina grabbed a hazel-twig broom and thrust it towards her sister. 'Here!' she said. 'Start cleaning!'

THE MORNING WAS taken up with work preparing Helmstrumburg for attack. Osric's men manned the palisade, while he personally supervised work-parties that replaced rotting timbers and repaired those that would last. Once, the moat had been filled with river water, but the mechanism had long since fallen into disrepair, and the water had dried up long ago.

The people had used the dry moat as a dump. The common practice with chamber pots was to toss the contents from the wall or the palisade down into the ditch. The ditch was almost full of a thick, foul-smelling black sludge, that he had the work parties scrape and dig out and pile up outside.

Osric spat as he went along, exhorting the men to dig faster and deeper. Friedel stopped to rest on the spade shaft. 'You don't think these beastmen really will attack, do you?'

Osric didn't like anyone slacking on his watch. 'I don't care whether they attack or not – I want this ditch dug so deep that you could take a bath in it!'

Baltzer winked at Friedel. 'I joined up to have an easy life at the count's expense. Not to dig holes!' he cursed.

Osric span around so he could see all his men. 'This is meant to be a barricade!' he spat. 'This ditch wouldn't stop my grandmother from storming the walls! Now quit talking like a bunch of old women and get digging!'

HANZ'S SPEARMEN AND Vostig's handgunners took over control of the north and the west gates and walls. The handgunners spent the morning loading the barrack cart up with their small barrels of blackpowder and shot that had been stored in the stables, and transporting them to the various strong points along the walls.

Vostig took Holmgar along the walls, checking the loopholes that had been cut into them. They had been poorly thought out, offering limited fields of fire to the defenders.

At one point there was a loop-hole low in the wall set at an angle to the main gate.

'See here!' Vostig said, and he and Holmgar scrambled down the well-worn steps to the inside of the loop-hole. There was a hole, maybe a foot square, that fanned out to create a funnel that covered the approach to the northern gate. There were metal fittings embedded into the stonework, which were well rusted.

Holmgar frowned. 'It's too large for a handgun,' he observed. 'And too small for a cannon.'

Vostig nodded. He had seen similar constructions on the walls of Kemperbad and Talabheim.

'It's for a swivel gun!' he said, and described a short barrelled gun that resembled a miniature cannon. 'If anyone knew where one was then we could cover this gate easily.' He peered through the loop-hole and saw it panned a few inches left and right – but a wide enough arc to ensure that nothing could approach the gate without being subjected to a withering hail of grapeshot.

'Not much good it'll do us without a gun,' Holmgar said.

Vostig nodded sadly. Then he clapped Holmgar on the back. The day they had cleared out the stables, he had seen something that might just be the missing gun...

A ROAD RAN directly behind the palisade all the way from the old stone wall to the river, and from that three main roads ran in parallel through the new town into the old town: Altdorf Street was wide enough for three carts abreast; Eel Street was the next largest, with tall houses overhanging the cobblestones; while the third and last was Tanner Lane, where Gruff Spennsweich had found lodgings, from which a number of small lanes led down to the river.

Sigmund and Gunter walked these streets looking for good place to set up a barricade should the outer defences fall. The old stone wall had only been breached to allow traffic through Eel Street, Tanner Lane and Altdorf Street.

'Let us build barricades here,' Gunter said, but Sigmund shook his head and moved a little way down Altdorf Street, thinking that its line would provide an admirable line of defence.

'We will hold the first line at the walls. If that line should fail, then the enemy will be inside the old town and there will be no way to stop them.'

Sigmund paced a little further up Altdorf Street, where the houses jutted out into the road.

'Here!' he said. 'We will build the first barricade. If we have to we can fall back to the stone wall.'

Gunter didn't seem impressed but Sigmund pointed up to the stone wall, the parapet of which would still allow men to move unhindered between the three main streets. 'We can use the stone wall to reinforce each other. Besides, this is the narrowest point.'

Gunter nodded and his men started to go into the houses on either side of the street and carry pieces of furniture out.

Edmunt nodded to the family sitting at the dinner table as he came in and started to drag a heavy oak cupboard towards the door.

'Not my cupboard!' the woman of the house said, her pink cheeks flushing, but Edmunt took no notice. The choice was simple: her oak cupboard or the future of Helmstrumburg.

As SIGMUND RETURNED to the barracks he walked into the marketplace to check on the various bands of free companies who were training there.

Blik Short and the retired soldiers of the Old Unbreakables had taken it upon themselves to drill the other companies, and now they were marching up and down, or duelling with each other.

The men marched out of step. Half of them turned to the left when ordered to right turn, and when they wheeled round the bottom of the market square they lost their ranks and ended up a jumbled mess of men.

Blik Short smoothed down his waxed moustache.

'No! You three-legged bunch of apes!' he bellowed. He reminded Sigmund of the drill sergeant who had trained them when they were first enlisted; he and his friends hadn't known their right foot from their left. Until this point he hadn't realised how used to army life he had become, and how much he had learned, but now he and his men marched in their dreams.

Marching did more than teach men how to walk in step: it trained them to accept orders and most importantly – it built up the unit spirit. A unit couldn't march if one man was out of step. When all the men could walk together, then there was a hope that they could fight together too.

Sigmund left Blik to his business and started to cross the marketplace to the Crooked Dwarf inn. The pub sign had been taken down and the place looked odd without it. His heart was racing, and his mouth was dry. He had not seen his mother and brother since they had come to town. Now his father was dead and he felt it was his fault and he dreaded seeing them.

'Captain Jorg!' Sigmund heard his name called and stopped.

Vasir, the trapper was running up to him. 'Captain, sir!' the man said. 'I wanted to talk to you.'

Sigmund paused for a moment.

'Captain – when you called for free companies to be raised, I brought together a few trappers and hunters I knew,' he nodded in the direction of a motley collection of fifteen skinny, bearded men in simple jackets and trews of crudely stitched leather and fur, squatting in the shade of an abandoned cart. All of them had large skinning knives at their belts, short hunting bows and quivers of arrows at their sides. A disgruntled member of the Old Unbreakables had given up trying to drill them. 'We wanted to be given a spot to defend, sir!' Vasir said hopefully.

'I do have a job,' Sigmund said. 'But it is more important than defence. I need you to go out and find out where the beastman are and what their numbers are.'

Vasir grinned his gap-toothed grin.

'Oh – and Vasir,' Sigmund said and he spoke more quietly now. 'I want you to go to my father's mill. I want you to…' he started but he didn't know how to finish the sentence. They both knew what happened to those that the beastmen took alive.

Vasir nodded. 'I will look,' he said.

SIGMUND'S HEART WAS pounding as he pushed open the bar door. The place was empty except for a boy who was sweeping the floor.

It was Josh.

'Captain Sigmund!' Josh said. 'Are you looking for your mother?'

Sigmund nodded.

'They're in the back room!'

Sigmund nodded.

'And Captain Sigmund!' Josh said as he put down his broom and hurried around the tables. 'I want to fight!' he said, 'but Guthrie says I'm too young! Please will you talk to…'

'Josh,' he said. 'You must listen to Guthrie and stay here and look after the other boys. If the fight comes to you then strike with all your courage. Until then, do what Guthrie says.'

Josh nodded. He turned away and went back to his broom and swept slowly.

As HE CLIMBED up the stairs, Sigmund kept thinking how he should have forced his father into town.

He paused on the fourth stair, remembering the time he had gone to tell Arneld's mother that her son had been cut down in the defence of Blade's Reach. He had stopped at the gateway and had not gone in. The old lady had faced him down and he had turned away and walked home. It was not enough for a captain to be brave in the face of the enemy, he also had to be brave in harder situations like this when the sense of failure was almost overwhelming.

Sigmund pulled himself up, the stairs creaked as he climbed the stairs. This was not only his job but also his family. He turned right at the top and followed the corridor to the rear room, but paused at the doorway. He could hear the muffled sound of people talking. Yellow candlelight flickered under the door.

Sigmund took a deep breath and turned the handle. His mother was sitting on the bed knitting, Hengle sat next to her. As Sigmund came in, his mother looked up. Her eyes were dry, but her lower lip was trembling. She looked for Sigmund to give her good news, but he slowly shook his head. She put her knitting down and put her hand to her mouth.

'I tried to help,' he said, and put his arms around his mother and brother together. 'I'm sorry. But I was too late.'

Sigmund's shoulders started to shake and the three of them held each other tight, as if it were some protection from the loss they all felt.

RODERICK HAD REFUSED to leave his house since Sigmund's men had taken control of the gates but at last he set off to the guild hall to talk to the burgomeister and plan to return the power to themselves.

The docks were strangely empty. All the boats had left. A few dockers stood around, but most of them had enlisted in the free companies and were marching up and down the market square.

Roderick's blue coat was unmistakable – the dockers laughed as he passed. No one listened to the town watch any more.

He strode towards the guild hall, but the front door was shut.

He shouted up to the windows but there was no answer. His skin prickled: it was strange seeing the centre of the elector count's authority in Helmstrumburg locked up and deserted. Where could the burgomeister have gone?

From the side of the guild hall to the banks of the river ran a short wall, seven feet tall and made of red brick.

Roderick jumped and caught the top of the wall and hauled himself up then dropped down onto the other side. The guild hall's private jetty was twenty yards away, jutting out into the river water. The burgomeister's ceremonial barge was still moored there, bobbing violently. Roderick waded through the deep mud, heard voices and ducked down against the side of the guild hall, even though it offered him no cover.

Despite the danger of discovery, Roderick crouched down and edged forward. He could hear footsteps and the scrape of boxes being dragged over wooden planks. He tried to move silently through the mud, but it was so thick as to be impossible, so he stopped and peered up.

It was the burgomeister, pulling crates onto his barge. There was a man with him – and Roderick peered up to see who it was. Of course, he thought, who else! He was about to stand and make his presence known, when he heard the two men exchange a joke and the note of their laughter made his skin shiver. Instead, he huddled low until it was safe to flee.

SIGMUND'S MOTHER HAD brought all kinds of supplies with her: a ham, a sack of flour and a couple of large cottage loaves with a freshly hung cheese. She insisted that she did not need anything, but Sigmund gave her a purse full of coins. At last his mother accepted the money.

'I will be back as soon as I can,' Sigmund said, and his mother forced a smile.

'Son, your job is with the town. If the town falls then we will all die. If you save it then we will also be saved,' she said and fumbled for a chain that her husband had given her, years before. It was a silver hammer of Sigmar, strung on a steel chain. She held it out and the hammer swung back and forth. 'Your father gave me this when we were betrothed,' she said. 'And now I give it to you. Sigmar be with you, my son!'

The hammer was worn with age. Sigmund imagined it coming all the way from Ortulf Jorg, the man who slew the beastman lord a thousand years earlier. He had tears on his cheeks as he took the amulet from his mother and fastened it round his neck. Then he kissed his mother and brother, and hurried from the room.

IN THE BARRACKS there was a long queue of volunteers trailing all the way across the drill yard. The queue ended in the 'U' of buildings, where Edmunt stood at the doorway of the armoury as each man came up to be equipped with old weapons and armour that had been stored there. Much of the equipment was broken or simply forgotten by the many units that had been stationed here: but broken straps could be repaired, rivets could be fixed and sword and spear handles could be re-strapped. Old spearheads were mounted on freshly cut shafts.

'Sword and cap!' he called and Gaston and Elias tried to find something suitable from all the old weaponry stored there.

Gaston found a sword, with no scabbard, that the volunteer thrust through his belt.

'You'll need to sharpen that thing,' Edmunt told him and the man's cheeks reddened as if he had not realised.

'It's for killing,' Edmunt said. 'Not for impressing the girls!'

'Don't listen to him,' Gaston said. 'It's just that he doesn't have a girl!'

The men who were queuing laughed, but not too loudly. Edmunt was bigger than all of them.

'Next!' he scowled and the next man stepped up.

'Did you think that was funny?' Edmunt demanded.

'No,' the man said.

'Good.' Edmunt looked the man up and down. He had a sword of his own: a machete blade such as some of the farmers used to clear scrubland. 'Cap!' Edmunt shouted and Elias brought out a plain steel cap, rusted in a number of spots. Edmunt tried it onto the man for size. 'There you go!' he said. 'Next!'

WHEN SIGMUND GOT back to the barracks there was still a queue of men waiting to be armed.

There was a group of men standing together who were short and thick-looking. Their banner was the sign from a tavern that was frequented by dockers, and supervising their arming was a man with a short stabbing sword at his belt and a leather jerkin with metal plates stitched on. He had a stiff leather cap on his head, metal bands riveted onto it, but he was smoking a clay pipe and under the martial exterior Sigmund recognised his friend.

'Frantz!' Sigmund said and laughed as he embraced him.

Frantz grinned as he waved the mouthpiece of his pipe along the line. There were forty dockers: strong and hard men. Edmunt was sizing them up for spare breast-pieces and steel caps that cluttered the armoury. Each man was issued with a sword and most of them were given bucklers.

'We want a hot spot!' Frantz said and Sigmund smiled.

'They'll all be hot!' Sigmund promised.

SIGMUND WAS BUSY all afternoon. At the palisade gate Osric had deepened the ditch by over two feet. He spat on the floor as Sigmund approached. Sigmund didn't look at him.

'I need this finished by evening,' Sigmund said, 'then I need your men to make sure the barricades on Eel Street, Altdorf Street and Tanner Lane are secure.'

Osric nodded. 'We will do that, sir. Don't you worry.'

Sigmund was surprised at Osric's manners.

'Good,' he said. 'Keep it up.'

Sigmund walked out of earshot, inspecting the depth of the ditch.

Osric watched him go then turned to his men. 'Get working you lazy bunch of whore-mongers!'

Baltzer stared at his sergeant. 'What's all that about?'

'What?'

'Yes-sirring that bastard,' he nodded with his chin towards Sigmund.

Osric wasn't going to admit that he felt sorry for Sigmund. 'I thought I'd give him a day off,' he said. 'Now get digging!'

HELMSTRUMBURG HAD BOOMED under the care of the burgomeister, but precious little had been done to keep up the city defences, Sigmund thought as he climbed up the bank to the palisade. It was about eight foot high: fine against man-sized warriors, but many of the taller beastmen they had fought were nearly seven feet tall. It would not be difficult for them to clamber over. If the enemy came here in force then they would not be able to defend this stretch.

The gate was solid enough, but there was no gatehouse from which the men could rain down missiles on the enemy. Osric had two teams of carpenters hastily erecting a covered walkway over the top of the gate so that men could throw rocks down onto anything that tried to assault the gate, but it was rudimentary at best.

'There will be a fierce fight here,' Sigmund said. 'I want your men to be ready.'

'They'll be more than ready,' Osric said and refused to look at Baltzer.

SIGMUND WALKED ALL the way around the town wall. There were cracks running through the long straight sections. Some of the battlements had fallen off, but the walls should hold, Sigmund thought, as long as there were enough men to defend them.

Hanz's spearmen were stationed on the north gatehouse. The discipline of the professional soldiers was a fine example to the volunteers. They were calm and assured, but well-honed and disciplined.

Everywhere he went, Sigmund encouraged the men. When he got to the east gate the men had found a crack in the crossbar and they were busy hammering strips of iron around the circumference.

Sigmund encouraged them. 'That'll never break now!' he said, and his upbeat tone disguised the doubts he had. He tried to ignore the smouldering ruins of his family mill. The Guild of Blacksmith Hammerers had been assigned this stretch of wall. They looked to Sigmund as he passed them by and he nodded to each man.

Strong-arm Benjamin was standing at the end of the wall, staring up at the water tower, which marked the wall's end. The tower stood twenty feet above the walls and there were a number of arrow slits in the stonework, but there was a number of inch-wide cracks running up it.

'It's a sorry sight,' Strong-arm said, nodding towards the stonework.

Sigmund nodded.

'One cannon ball would bring this tower down.'

Sigmund nodded. 'Luckily beastmen do not have cannons,' he said.

SIGMUND RETURNED TO the barracks as the sun began to set, and realised how tired and hungry he felt: but there was no time for exhaustion – he had to check the state of preparation.

'We have armed all the men we could,' Edmunt said. 'There are maybe three hundred volunteers, by my count.'

Sigmund nodded. The armoury of weapons and shields and every scrap of amour. The stone-floored room had an empty echo to it as Sigmund walked up and down, looking at the empty racks. There were a lot of men wondering if this was their last night around town. Simple, honest men who never wanted to lift a sword in anger, now forced to defend their homes and family.

It was different for professional soldiers. This is what they were paid to do: kill or be killed, and not to worry about death, shadowing them day and night.

WHEN SIGMUND CAME out of the armoury Edmunt had his whetstone and was sharpening his axe. He rubbed the steel dust away and the axe head had a fresh curve of polished steel along the edge, like it was smiling.

Edmunt kissed his blade. 'I've given it a name,' he said.

Sigmund stopped to listen.

'Butcher,' Edmunt said.

OSRIC'S MEN HAD been billeted in the houses along the palisade, many of which had been emptied of furniture already. Hanz's men were billeted at the north gate. Only Gunter's men were still sleeping at the barracks.

The drill yard was quiet with so few men here. As the sun began to slip out of sight, Sigmund took in a deep breath. He needed to be alone for a few minutes.

He went into his room and swung the door shut. He put his feet up on his camp bed and put his arms behind his neck and tried to clear his mind of all the small details.

Who was the enemy leader, he wondered and what was he doing now?

Sigmund shut his eyes and tried to imagine where he would attack Helmstrumburg, were the situations reversed.

The palisade, he thought. Obviously it was the place most easily stormed.

But was that too obvious?

If he didn't attack the palisade then where would he attack?

It was hard to say. The water tower? Maybe he would send rafts in, and try to gain entry into the harbour.

There were so many weak places that the beastmen could attack, and he didn't have enough men to cover them all. Where will the beastmen attack, he asked himself again and again? He was sure they would attack the palisade. He had no liking for Osric, but he had a hard bunch of men. They would hold up any attack, for a while at least.

AFTER SIGMUND HAD finished a simple meal of bread, cheese and ale, he put his feet up and lay down on the bed, eyes shut, working through the list of all the things he had done that day, searching in case there was something he had missed.

There was a knock on his door but Sigmund did not move.

'Yes?' he called.

The door opened. 'There is a man to see you,' a voice said. It was Edmunt.

Sigmund opened his eyes, pushed himself up from the bed and walked to the door. Outside, he saw one of the trappers standing in the yard.

Sigmund recognised Vasir and gave a tired smile.

'Vasir!' Sigmund said, feeling that the man had been sent at this opportune moment to give him insights into the enemy. 'What news?'

'Many tracks. All my men found spoor.'

Sigmund nodded and Vasir licked his lips. 'From the signs there must be more than five hundred, but I'd say they were waiting for something. I'd say they were expecting more, if you was to press me sir.'

Sigmund nodded. Some power seemed to be organising the beastmen. Was it the stones?

Vasir seemed to hesitate. 'And one of my men went to your father's mill,' he said. 'He found three skinned bodies. Not one of them was your father.'

Sigmund nodded. He had grown up with the men who worked in the mill. They were real country folk: hardworking with little to say, unless pressed. Their deaths should never have happened. It was his father's fault, and he felt his anger flare up. But there was no point in being angry at a dead man.

Vasir's eyes flicked back and forth as he watched the captain. Vasir took a bundle from the inside of his jacket, and unwrapped it and held it out to the captain. 'And he found this!'

Inside there was a silver pistol with a curiously wide barrel. Sigmund took it and stared at it incredulously. There was only one man in Helmstrumburg with a pistol like this.

Sigmund rushed over to Gunter and let him know that he would be out for half an hour.

'Do you need help?'

Sigmund shook his head. 'No. It is a personal matter,' he said, his face dark.

Sigmund hurried across the drill yard and into the evening streets where a hush seemed to have fallen. He hurried through the dark streets, picking up speed as he went, and ended up running across the marketplace. He ignored the calls from Blik Short and his Old Unbreakables and took the stairs of the Crooked Dwarf two at a time.

Guthrie was out, but Josh was there.

'The two Reikland merchants!' Sigmund demanded. 'Where are they?'

Josh pointed to the front of the inn. Sigmund sprinted up the stairs and pounded down the corridor. He kicked the door open and drew his sword.

The room was empty, except for Theodor, who saw the naked foot of steel and jumped from the bed, his hands outstretched.

'You!' Sigmund said and stepped forward, knuckles white on his sword handle.

Theodor leaped up. 'I know why you are here,' he said, backing up to the wall as Sigmund advanced. 'I know why you are here and I can explain!'

But Sigmund kept coming forward. He only stopped when the point of the sword was an inch from the Reiklander's chest. 'Captain Jorg!' the man blurted. 'Your father is alive! I know where he is. If you kill me, you will never find out!'

Sigmund did not remove the sword, it pressed into Theodor's skin.

'I was there to help your father,' Theodor said. 'I helped him escape. There was a terrible fight. Look!' he pulled aside his shirt, showing Sigmund a ragged cut along the bottom of his ribs. 'I got this! Your father would not have given me such a wound.'

'You could have done that yourself,' Sigmund said.

'I promise you your father is alive! I saw him last night riding away from the mill. But we cannot talk here. My companion might come back at any moment and that would be disastrous for you, me and everyone in Helmstrumburg!'

'Where is he?'

'I don't know. He might return at any moment!' Theodor said.

Sigmund started out of the door, but Theodor pulled him back.

'Please – I need to explain!'

THE BARGE CARRIED him out of Helmstrumburg and along the dark banks – the lights of town retreating behind him.

The burgomeister waited until he was safely past town then paddled desperately to shore. The current was too strong so he threw himself into the water. It was deeper than he thought and he took a mouthful or two of water before he found the muddy bottom and struggled to shore.

His clothes dripped as he hauled himself ashore.

'It's me!' he shouted. 'The burgomeister!'

The moonlit trees were silent. A few leaves moved in a breeze but he saw no one. Where were they?

'I have come!' he shouted, but even though he felt he was being watched, he saw nothing.

THE TREES WERE like a silent wall. Occasionally one of the soldiers thought he saw something, but each time it appeared that it was nothing more than a bird, flapping in the undergrowth – or sometimes a fox, bolting across the open ground.

But even though they saw nothing, the men on the walls had the feeling that they were being watched. And watched they were: even though the beastmen were too stealthy to be seen. Closer than any of the men could imagine, the smaller beastmen lay still, watching the preparations on the town walls.

In the shelter of the trees, a white figure stamped his hooves and snorted with barely contained rage. Only half of his force had arrived. The attack which he was to have led was late.

A stooped figure shuffled towards him, bent low in suppliance, shaking its rattle in homage to the beastman warlord.

'My lord – Brazak's and Drakk's herds have arrived!'

Azgrak snarled with fury and turned from the town. Drakk was the brood-brother of the Red Killer. He had inherited the Red Killer's herd. There were fresh heads plaited into Drakk's human-hair belt. His legs were brown with caked blood. On his snout there were fresh gouts of blood. In his left hand he dragged the headless corpse of a child.

Brazak walked next to him, his suppurating skin now accelerating to a rolling boil of pus and slime. The stink was overpowering.

Azgrak's fingers clenched and unclenched on his axe shaft. He bared his fangs, let out a roar of fury, and the warlords stopped. It took a moment for the noise to die down. 'You are late!' he snarled.

The pace of Brazak's boiling skin slowed for a moment, and Drakk let go of the foot of his meal.

'There were many humans to kill,' Brazak snarled and Azgrak opened his snout and roared in fury.

'We were meant to attack today!' he raged. 'You are late!'

He tossed the head of Red Killer onto the floor in front of them. Drakk sprayed in supplication, but Brazak was too slow to show his deference to the warlord.

Azgrak was a white blur. Brazak's festering skin stopped all of a sudden, and his hooded head bent slowly forward as if he was bowing to the albino, but it tumbled forward, off his shoulders and onto the ground. A second later his legs gave way and the whole festering sack of flesh followed.

Azgrak turned to Drakk but the shaman crept forward, skull rattle shaking. 'The omens for tomorrow are good!' the shaman hissed. 'The guilty have been punished. Oh fearsome warbeast, do not kill all your finest warriors!'

Azgrak could barely restrain his anger, but instead of striking Drakk, he bent his horned head back to the moon and roared – and the leaves above his head shivered.

'Tomorrow, Helmstrumburg will burn!' the shaman hissed, but Azgrak brandished his axe at the town of the enemy.

'No,' he spat with fury. 'It will burn tonight!'

CHAPTER TEN

THEODOR'S FACE STRAINED as Sigmund put the point of his blade to the merchant's throat.

'Speak!' Sigmund commanded.

'We cannot stay here. My companion might return at any minute! Trust me, let us go somewhere where we cannot be disturbed!'

Sigmund heard footsteps on the stairs and saw Josh's terrified face peering up at him. Sigmund bundled the Reiklander out into the corridor and down the stairs to the bar.

Josh saw the drawn sword as they came towards him and ran down the stairs, but Sigmund called out to him and he stopped. 'Open the cellars!' Sigmund said and Josh hurried to obey. The captain's tone did not leave any room for discussion – and he had a drawn sword in his hand.

Sigmund shoved Theodor through the door that led to the cellar. The temperature dropped and there was a distinct scent of fermentation.

'Josh! Keep this door shut and guard it. Understand?'

Josh nodded and then Sigmund winked, and turned to go down.

The cellar was dark. Sigmund paused, about to call for a light, then a flint was struck, and Theodor lit a candle. In the flickering light, Sigmund could make out the face of Theodor and the barrels neatly stacked against the cellar wall.

'What is all this about?' Sigmund demanded. 'And why the need for secrecy?'

'I work for the Count of Talabecland,' Theodor said, and as he spoke Sigmund heard his fine Reikland accent disappear and be replaced by one from Talabheim.

Sigmund was not impressed. As he stepped forward, his sword edge glimmered in the candlelight. 'And what does that have to do with Helmstrumburg?'

'There are terrible forces at work,' Theodor hissed.

Sigmund had heard the same warnings in the mouths of mad men and doomsayers all his life. He could not believe that he had come all this way and with such secrecy just to be told this. 'Terrible forces,' Theodor continued, 'for whom skinning a man and his family alive is just the prelude.'

'You have seen these things, I can tell,' Theodor said.

Sigmund remembered the nausea he felt when he'd been inside the cabin of Osman Speinz. It hadn't so much been the sight of the butchered bodies that had disturbed him, but the crude symbols daubed in blood.

When he tried to bring them back to mind the symbols were a blur in his mind, as if his conscious mind refused to dredge them back.

'It is only with the greatest of efforts that I have remained sane,' Theodor told Sigmund, but his mouth was moving strangely. Sigmund suddenly felt as if reality were about to fail, that he was being pulled towards a world of insanity.

'Four years ago I became involved in a Chaos cult,' Theodor spoke the word in a low hush. 'And – Sigmar save my soul – I have seen things that would make a living man lose his sanity!' Theodor paused for a moment. 'There is some great event for which the powers of Chaos – *Chaos*!'

he said. 'Hell-spawned incarnate! Abominations beyond comprehension! Chaos – the primal slime that is always trying to slither out and dissolve us all into a sickening stew of madness!'

As Theodor ranted, Sigmund heard the door creak at the top of the stairs.

'Captain Jorg?' a voice called. It was Josh.

'What is it?'

'Sir, I am sorry to disturb you but Edmunt is here.'

'Tell him to wait in the bar. I will be up shortly.'

Josh's footsteps hurried back up the stairs and the door shut again. Sigmund looked back to Theodor.

'Trust no one! There is some great event to which they are working,' Theodor said. 'Tribes are gathering in the north. Beastmen rise here. On the borders of our allies in Kislev, raiding parties have struck again and again. On the Sea of Claws dragon-prowed boats cleave a path south. It is as if all minions of Chaos are being moved by a single will. We are ever vigilant, but we are always one step behind! It is only by chance that I was allowed to come to Helmstrumburg. And thank Sigmar I was. The situation is dire, Captain Jorg! Danger approaches!

'Long have the beastmen waited and watched the stars. Sigmar's star has come like a signal to them, that the time to retake their ancestral heartland is here. For did you not know that your town was built upon a site sacred to the beastmen?'

'I knew this,' Sigmund said. 'But what does this have to do with Sigmar's star?'

'Chaos is a power that is impossible to describe,' Theodor said. 'It glories in destruction and violence and yet – and yet,' he sighed, 'it has powers of organisation beyond the realm of sane understanding. Even as the northern tribes gather, so too do the mutants of the Drakwald, and so too do the beastmen around Helmstrumburg. If the beastmen seize Helmstrumburg they will be able to blockade not only the road that links Kemperbad and Altdorf, but also the River Stir!'

Sigmund shook his head at this nonsense. Whoever saw beastmen on boats? The men of the Stir River patrol would drown every one of them.

'They are not planning to blockade the river,' Theodor whispered. 'They are going to dam it!'

'Not even dwarfs could dam the Stir!' Sigmund snorted.

'They are not planning to dam it with trees or any means known to man. With the powers of the gods of Chaos, they were going to block the Stir with the corpses of Helmstrumburg!'

Sigmund could see that Theodor believed every word he said, but his claims defied imagination.

'And how would the town be destroyed by Chaos?'

'Sigmund Jorg, you do not know how far your town has sunk. There are cultists through every level of society here. Those that they could not buy through money or terror they have bought with gold. Even the burgomeister has sold his soul – unwittingly – to Chaos!'

'It was only as we were approaching Helmstrumburg that I realised the true extent of the danger. If I had known how deep the rot had sunk I would have asked for more troops. All we can do now is to put our faith in the Heldenhammer and our own right hands.'

'But what does all this have to do with my father?' Sigmund asked.

'The beastmen have a prophecy that their lands will be returned to them when the descendants of their warlord and Ortulf Jorg fight again.'

'Then I could fight him?'

'You could,' Theodor said. 'But you are a young man, untrained and unschooled in war. The beastmen do not fear you as much as they fear your father. They are happy for you to fight because they believe that they can kill you, and your death will bring their victory. In fact, they want you to fight because a Jorg has to die – and they believe it is you. Your death will bring about the return of their land.'

'What can I do?' Sigmund asked.

'You have already done much, Captain Jorg. I have sent out word to allies, but if you cannot hold back the first assaults then they will not come in time! You must hold back the beastmen and you must not die.'

ON THE WEST gate of Helmstrumburg Edmunt watched Morrslieb set over the Stir. He felt the weight of Butcher, hanging at his belt, and the familiar feel of the halberd in his hands. The moonlight glittering on the rippling water was a beautiful and chilling sight: and made him think of the battle to come.

'Do you ever worry that this will be your last night?' Elias asked. The red lantern flames made him think of the blood that would soon be spilt.

Edmunt looked at him, surprised. 'Not yet,' he smiled.

Elias nodded. He wondered whether that was last time he would ever see Morrslieb set.

AS THE NIGHT deepened around them, Gunter left the guardroom and went from man to man, on sentry on the gates or along the walls, offering brief words of encouragement.

When he came to Gaston the grizzled veteran winked. 'If you see anything then shout,' he said.

Gaston nodded and his sergeant passed along the wall.

Gaston took a deep breath and checked the sheath of his sword. It was sticking a little, but if he twisted the handle and pulled it came out clean. He practised drawing his sword a couple of times until he was satisfied, then ran a finger under the chin strap of his iron cap and rested on his halberd shaft.

It was the waiting that he hated most of all.

SQUIRE BECKER WAS supposed to be waiting for orders in the marketplace, as instructed, but as night fell he led his men through the evening streets towards the north gate.

Short, plump and effete, Squire Becker leading a squad of twenty men would have seemed comic at any time other than this. But as they passed townsfolk in the street the people made way for them and thanked them for their courage.

'Sigmar bless you,' one old woman said, and she stepped forward to mumble a prayer to Sigmar. Squire Becker heard the words and snarled as if stung. His face curled in fury and disgust. He drew his sword and cut the woman down, as if she were a common thief and his men did not pause as they trampled over her.

The people in the street stood dumbfounded – disbelieving their own eyes, but after the men had passed the trampled body of the old woman still lay there in a pool of blood.

One man shouted to the men of the free company, but they marched on down the street towards the north gate.

Squire Becker and his men were deaf to the hue and cry behind them. They turned a corner and saw the north gate where spearmen and handgunners were standing. The time was almost here and they had a job to do.

FROM THE WOODS that covered the lower slopes of Galten Hill moved a silent army: a thousand horned creatures, animal snouts sniffing the air and smelling victory.

Their belts were heavy with human heads or hands, or other gory tokens. With each victim they had daubed their fur with blood. It caked their fur together in a matted mess. Many of them had come fresh from slaughter – and the blood on their snouts and shoulders and weapon edges still dripped fresh scarlet blood.

One creature led them from the woods: an albino monster – patches of white fur showing through the dripping red gore. Behind him came the largest of the beastmen warriors, which dwarfed the smaller beasts like grown men dwarf children. They carried two-headed axes and massive clubs of twisted wood, knotted and hammered with metal spikes. Some of them wore plates of iron between their horns, or the shield of some long-dead knight strapped across their chest, but most of them did not wear armour of any kind: their ferocity and animal cunning were protection enough.

With the army came all kinds of creatures from the deepest forests, abominations that had not been seen in the Stir Valley for a thousand years.

There were bull-headed minotaurs with great axes in their hands. They snorted and pawed the ground, eager to rip open the throats of their enemies and suck their hot blood.

There were creatures that were half-man, half-horse. Their heads were horned like rams, and in their hands they carried simple wooden shields and sharpened poles, the ends hardened in the fires of their caves, where they had stood for long hours, listening to tales of the ancient times when beasts ruled this land.

There were creatures plucked straight from the nightmare of the most insane: many-limbed, twisted and shuffling parodies of life – Chaos spawn. And dashing through the tree trunks, blacker than midnight, ran packs of slavering four-legged creatures, which might once have been wolves or dogs, but had been corrupted by Chaos. Wickedly spiked spines tore through their twisted bodies, driving them mad with torment.

As the warhost gathered, two contingents split off from the main band and began to make their way around the city walls. Nearly two hundred beastmen went, keeping well out of sight of the men on the walls, but as close to the walls as they dared.

While Azgrak would lead an assault of power and savagery, these two bands would rely on stealth and cunning to break into Helmstrumburg. When all was set, Azgrak took a crude horn from his belt and blew a blast so great that it made the walls of Helmstrumburg tremble.

The warhost of Azgrak the White charged.

OSRIC WAS SITTING in the guardroom at the palisade gate, playing dice with Baltzer and Blik Short, the leader of the Old Unbreakables, when the first horn blast sounded.

'What in the name of all the gods was that?' Osric said, but he was half way to the door when the call was answered by a thunderstorm of other horns – each brazen voice adding to the cacophony that made the timbers of the gate-house shake. Osric grabbed his steel cap and halberd and took the stairs to the palisade three at a time. 'To arms!' he shouted as his men poured out of the guardhouse and grabbed their weapons. 'To arms!'

Baltzer grabbed the money from the table and slipped it into his pouch with the dice before he ran out with his weapon in hand.

The bells of the Chapel of Sigmar began to ring the alarm, wild and frantic bell-tolls summoning all the able bodied to battle.

Blik Short marched out and his company of retired soldiers stood smartly to attention: only their guts and grizzled hair betraying their age. 'Onto the walls, men!' Blik said. 'Fight well!'

The retired soldiers hurried up the walls and soon the palisade wall was lined with halberdiers and men of the free companies.

Osric stared out into the night, but could see nothing, despite the sound that was like the thunder of a hundred galloping horses. Then he saw – first one horned head, sprinting towards the ditch – and then a hundred.

'Sigmar's balls!' Osric cursed. It seemed that the land was thick with a thousand sprinting goat-men: their crude banners flapping and moonlight glinting like frost on the tips of their spears. It looked like a wave of hatred that would sweep Helmstrumburg away.

HOLMGAR LEANED ON the battlement of the north gate and stared out into the darkening sky. He and Vostig sat together, their handguns ready and charged – even though neither man expected battle tonight.

'Have you ever been to Nuln?' Holmgar asked after a long pause.

'I have,' Vostig said. 'It's a fine city.'

Vostig stood and went over to the swivel gun and started to polish the brass back to a shine.

'It was a shame to let such a piece go to waste,' he said.

Holmgar nodded. Occasionally he'd seen other weapons like repeating handguns or pistols which could fire eight shots before needing to be reloaded, but rather than being different breeds of firearm, they seemed to him to be different animals entirely.

As Vostig polished the swivel gun lovingly, Holmgar shook his head in wonder. As he stood upright, he saw Squire Becker come round the corner of the street that led to the gate. He didn't have much faith in their fighting ability, but the more men Sigmund sent to help them, the better.

'Who'd have thought that Squire Becker would stay and fight, when he could have bought himself a passage out of here?' Holmgar mused and Vostig nodded, then frowned. Squire Becker had a drawn sword in his hand.

And if Vostig was not mistaken, the sword was dripping blood.

Just as Vostig opened his mouth to shout a warning there was a horn blast like a clap of thunder and Holmgar dropped his sword in shock. At the same time Squire Becker broke into a run and behind him his men lowered their spears and charged.

RODERICK WAITED IN the bar until Sigmund came out, pushing one of the merchants with him.

His legs were mud-stained, but he smoothed down the front of his blue jacket and assumed his usual air of pomposity. His stomach was hollow, his palms sweated. The last person he wanted to talk to was the arrogant captain.

'I demand to speak to you,' Roderick declared.

'All right, but make it quick!' Sigmund said, and signalled to Theodor to step aside for the moment.

Roderick pursed his lips and wiped the sweat from his upper lip. 'This evening I went to see the burgomeister, only to see him leaving town on his barge!'

Sigmund shook his head. He had expected no more.

'And he was helped,' Roderick leaned in close to whisper, 'he was being helped by the friend of that man there!'

Sigmund clapped Roderick on the shoulders.

'I have disliked you, for so long, Roderick, but now it seems you are an honest man after all. I already knew the burgomeister was a traitor. The most important thing we can do now is defend the town, soldiers and town watch alike. Will you join us? Will you give your life to save Helstrumburg?'

After a second's pause, Roderick replied, 'Yes.'

'Find yourself a sword and that band of cut-throats you call the watch, and join us on the palisade!' Sigmund said.

As Sigmund clapped Roderick on the back, there was the distant sound of a horn call. The attack had begun! 'The palisade!' Sigmund shouted and he shoved Theodor in front of him. 'Edmunt – run to the west gate – I will be with Osric!'

The town square looked more like an army camp than a market place. There were camp fires lit all across the square, and around them huddles of men gathered for warmth. They heard the horn and knew what it meant – Helstrumburg's doom had come upon it.

Sigmund strode down the steps of the Crooked Dwarf.

'Guthrie?'

There was a holler from the camp fire to the left. 'Stay here till I call for you! Squire Becker! Where is Squire Becker?'

'He's gone to the north gate!' one man from the Crooked Dwarf Volunteers shouted.

Sigmund cursed. Damned pompous oaf! He had told him to wait for orders.

'Frantz!'

A voice answered and the familiar shape of his friend came through the darkness.

'Bring your men! We are going to the palisade!'

* * *

OSRIC HAD NO idea what he told his men – but as the horde of beastmen closed in, he exhorted them to bravery and courage and swore he would track down and castrate any man who failed to do his duty. Every second word was an expletive, but his men barely heard him – they were staring with horror at the tide of horned shapes running through the gloom.

At the top of the ditch on the right of the gateway Baltzer crowded in behind Osric and adjusted his money pouch to stop it swinging against his hip. Schwartz shut his eyes and squeezed out a prayer to Ulric to lend him strength and fury, while Friedel flashed back to the assault on Blade's Reach Tower, when the greenskins had charged like this – and he told Sigmar that he would gladly sacrifice another finger as long as he could come out of this alive.

On the parapet above the gateway, Vasir's trappers laid their quivers at their feet and tested the string on their bows.

The beastmen came on, without order, in bands behind their tribal leaders. Some of them carried ragged standards, thankfully hidden in the gloom.

On the other side of the gate Blik Short drew his sword and called out to his Old Unbreakables, 'Hold fast!'

The old men drew their swords and waited.

At fifty yards Vasir and his trappers started to fire arrows low and straight at the enemy. Many of their arrows struck home – but with each beastman that dropped two more surged to take its place.

Within seconds the attackers were at twenty yards. The leading beastmen reached the far lip of the ditch they had so laboriously deepened. The slime they had dug out was slippery and a few beastmen fell – either shot by Vasir and his men's bows, or tripped up with treacherous footing – but they were trampled underhoof as a solid mass of bodies followed after.

The leading beastmen charged down into the ditch and barely slowed as they charged up the steep bank, a few of them flinging spears at the men on the palisade. There was

no plan or strategy to their assault. They did not come with
ladders or grappling hooks or battering rams, it was little
more than a ferocious stampede. They were wild animals
that knew no better strategy than to simply overwhelm the
palisade by force of numbers.

As soon as they reached the foot of the palisade the beastmen leaped up, like wild dogs, caught the top of the
parapet, and hauled themselves up.

Osric stabbed down and caught one on the up leap. The
power of his thrust and the power of the creature's own
momentum drove his halberd blade straight through the
crude armour through the creature's stomach. It hung on
the blade, trying to thrust its spear into his face. Osric threw
his halberd down and with it tumbled the beast. Then
Osric drew his sword and stabbed the next beastman
through the windpipe.

Friedel felt the palisade shiver at the impact of the attackers. A thrown spear barely missed him, and he stepped back
from the lip of the parapet. Two hands caught the top of the
palisade in front of him. Friedel had no idea whether it was
one beastman or two, and stabbed each with his blade –
noticed with a mixture of horror and curiosity that he had
cut off a beastman's finger and it was lying, claw and all, by
his feet. Then a beastman jumped and caught the top of the
parapet and Friedel beheaded it with one ferocious cut.

AT THE NORTH gate Squire Becker and his men – Chaos
cultists all – fell upon the astonished Vorrsheimers. They
screamed horrific curses and clawed and slashed and gored
like rabid beasts. The spearmen barely had a chance to
reach for their weapons before three of them were lying
dead or dying.

Squire Becker and his men trampled the bodies in their
haste to reach the cross-bar. They struggled to lift it from
the heavy brass braces as more soldiers streamed from the
walls and the guardhouse – but it was too late. The heavy
doors opened outwards to the night on the enormous
black iron hinges.

'Get those doors shut!' Hanz shouted, and a ferocious struggle ensued. Both sides tried to maintain their hold on the gates as they tried to kill each other. On the walls above the gate Holmgar lifted his handgun, blew on his fuse and then aimed his handgun at Squire Becker. There was a cloud of smoke as he fired, and when it cleared he saw that he had not hit Squire Becker but the man next to him: the shot had scattered his brains over the inside of the gateway.

The spearmen outnumbered the cultists and cut them down – but even in their death struggles they hung onto the gates and would not let them close.

'Get these doors shut!' Hanz shouted again, but at that moment there was a thunder of hooves outside the walls and a herd of monstrously large beastmen came from the darkness, running towards the open gate.

Holmgar struggled to clear the smouldering embers from his gun. There was a ragged patter of handgun shots, but the war party must have numbered nearly a hundred: even if all the shots hit home they would make little impact. If this war party took the gate the whole forest would stream into Helmstrumburg.

Holmgar fired his shot and was already looking for a way of escape when a huge boom of thunder shook the walls. The whole gateway was wreathed in smoke. Holmgar had a terrible intuition that some traitors had mined the wall, until he heard Vostig laughing and remembered the swivel-gun.

In front of the gate there was a twitching pile of bodies and body parts. One beastman was struggling to crawl away, but the lower half of its body had been shot clean away, and only a few tangled remains of bone and sinew trailed after it before it expired with a low moan.

AFTER THE INITIAL shock Hanz's men tumbled out of the guardroom and charged. Squire Becker and his cultists were driven back from the gateway by sheer weight of numbers. But they fought ferociously, and even when they had fallen to the ground, they still bit and scratched at the legs of the Vorrsheimers.

Another two spearmen fell before all of Squire Becker's men were killed. Vostig was busy reloading his swivel-gun with a couple of handfuls of shot. Holmgar peered down at the warband of beastmen that had been standing there. There were rumours of war machines from the master craftsmen of Nuln that could deal death to a hundred men, but Holmgar never thought he would see such a thing. It was truly wondrous!

THE BEASTMEN HAD attacked all three gates at once, but it was on the west side of town, where the palisade enclosed the new town, that they attacked with their main strength.

By the time Sigmund reached the palisade the fight was well underway. Osric's men had weathered the storm of beasts, but it was obvious to Sigmund that they could not hope to hold the palisade against such numbers.

Already there was a stair of dead beastmen along the palisade that the creatures behind were using to clamber up to the walls. Osric's men cut and thrust until their arms felt like lead weights.

Blik Short had lost two of his Old Unbreakables, but the old warriors held their stretch of wall with stoic courage: not ceding an inch to the beastmen that threw themselves onto the palisade. As they watched, a massive beastman clambered over the palisade to the far right and used a huge battle axe to cut down two of Osric's men. Into the gap followed four of the smaller beastmen and soon the wedge began to widen as more and more beastmen scrambled for the opening, intent on seizing the palisade by sheer weight of numbers.

Frantz and his dockers were impatient to join the battle but Sigmund held them back until the beastmen assault along the rest of the wall faltered. All hurried to the opening and then he drew his sword and charged. Osric's men, who were about to break felt the impact of Sigmund's charge on the pressed mass of beastmen and struck back with renewed vigour.

Sigmund slashed left and right. A spear stabbed at him from out of his field of vision and he felt the blow on his cuirboili breastplate and was knocked sideways. The spear-thruster sensed an advantage and readied another stab, but this time Sigmund caught the shaft. At the same time as he pulled he slashed down with his sword and lopped off both of the beastman's forearms, then ran him through with his own spear.

Next to him, Frantz desperately parried an axe blow with his buckler, but the power of the blow jarred his hand and arm. He struck back in fury and gutted him with a slow thrust.

ABOVE THE GATEWAY, Vasir strung another arrow and looked for a suitable target. Through the mass of bodies he could see a number of bull-headed creatures – minotaurs – pushing their way through the press. They were over eight feet tall and they carried twin-headed axes in their massive fists.

Vasir's first arrow hit one in the chest, but even though the arrow embedded itself into its flesh the creature didn't seem to notice. He looked in his quiver, he only had three arrows left. The beasts were just below him now, bellowing like enraged bulls and swinging their axes into the timbers of the gate as if they meant to chop a hole through.

There was no way Vasir could miss. The next arrow hit the same creature in the shoulder and it dropped the axe for a moment. The next hit it in the lower back as it bent over, and the last caught the creature in the knee – but instead of keeling over the beast lowered its thick neck and charged the gate like a maddened bull. Vasir felt the whole gateway quiver under the impact. The bull charged again and this time his platform swayed violently. He clutched the palisade for support but the creature charged again and part of the walkway broke free.

'Back!' Vasir shouted but the other trappers had already started to jump to safety. Two men tipped over the front of the parapet into the path of the minotaurs. The foul creatures grabbed them by the limbs and literally tore them apart.

* * *

AT THE BASE of the water tower on the east wall Theodor waited in the shadows as he saw the figure that he knew would come creep across to the disused shed. Theodor silently adjusted the grip on his pistols and moved to lessen the distance between him and his prey.

He could see a smouldering fuse in his prey's hand, and heard the rattle of a key as he undid the lock. There was no reason to wait, but Theodor did so for his own satisfaction. The shed door swung open and his prey uncovered the lantern and – gasped in fury.

The barrels which were to have blown a hole in the wall for the beastmen to charge through had gone!

Eugen spun around as Theodor stepped from the shadows, twin pistols raised and primed, fuses smoking dangerously.

'You have failed, Eugen,' Theodor said in his Talabheim accent. There was special emphasis on the word 'failed'. Confronting his former master was more than satisfying, it helped expunge the memory of what he had pretended to be for so long.

Eugen hissed and drew his sword, but there was no chance to fight. He fired the right-hand pistol then paused to let the smoke clear and shot the left. The first was a death shot low in the groin, the other high on the left arm: shattering the bone as the heavy shot pulverised the arm and left it hanging useless.

Eugen staggered and fell – blood pumping from his pulverised arm and groin, his breath already beginning to rattle with the onset of death.

Theodor stared down at him for a moment, then spat in the face he hated above all, slowly reholstered his pistols and then turned back the way he had come, where the din of fighting was growing in volume.

THERE WAS NO attack on the east gate, so Gunter sent Elias to find out how the men on the west of town were faring.

The streets of Helmstrumburg were empty as Elias ran. He found Sigmund standing behind the palisade gate with a bloody bandage around his head and a sword still in his hand.

Sigmund's face was flushed, but there was no evidence of panic as he watched the fighting and issued orders. He saw Elias and recognised that he had come from the east gate and he turned and hailed him. 'What news?'

'Sir – there was no fighting on the east when I left it.'

Sigmund nodded. The situation was confused, but it seemed that the beastmen had thrown their whole weight against the west gate and palisade, and although they had driven the beastmen back over the wall, Osric's men were outnumbered and exhausted. The palisade would not hold.

As they stood the gate began to quiver with impacts, and the trappers scrambled for safety. Sigmund calmly watched the hinges that kept the gate attached begin to start from the gate posts.

'Elias!' he said. 'Get everyone behind the barricades! I want all the men that Hanz and Gunter can spare to join us there!'

Elias sprinted off again, almost relieved to be running messages rather than fighting. But he was sure that there would be much more fighting for him before the day was done.

THE PRESS OF beastmen on the palisade was such that it began to creak dangerously and the men of the free companies started to run from the walls. A blood-splattered figure loomed up from the melee of bodies and Sigmund recognised Osric.

'I need more men!' he roared but Sigmund had none. 'Fall your men back in order to the barricades!'

Sigmund grabbed Frantz and gave him the same orders. 'Back!' he shouted above the chaos and din of battle. 'Eel Street!'

Frantz nodded and took twenty-seven in all back down the street. The gateposts snapped and through cracks in the gateway Sigmund could see the monstrous bull-men, their bodies splattered with human entrails and gore. He felt the spirit of the men begin to waver and stood up to give the order.

'Fall back!' he shouted. 'Fall back to the old wall!'

Someone grabbed his forearm and Sigmund almost cut the man down – but it was Blik Short – with a dirty bandage around his thigh. There was such a din it was almost impossible to make the words out. 'We will cover your retreat!' he shouted.

'No – fall back!' Sigmund bellowed, and hurried onto the next group of men.

As THE MEN of Helmstrumburg fell back, beastmen scrambled over the broken palisade and charged in – striking left and right. Instead of an orderly retreat men dropped their weapons and started to flee. The beastmen struck them down as they ran, and the whole retreat threatened to turn into a rout until Osric rallied twenty of his men with Baltzer drumming the retreat. They formed a bottleneck across the end of Eel Street and presented a thicket of iron blades.

On Altdorf Street, Sigmund managed to rally enough men to block the top of the street. They battled the beastmen that came streaming through the shattered gateway. As he fought, Sigmund saw the minotaurs that had shattered the gate push through their way through the crowd of beastmen.

The men he had rallied began to scream in terror at the size of the creatures and Sigmund thought he would lose control of his troops until he saw a squad of men stride out through the chaos and stand across the path of the bull-men like a wall.

BLIK SHORT LIMPED into place across the top of Altdorf Street keeping in step with the ten men he had left. The bull-men saw them and raised their huge axes and charged.

'Hold fast!' Blik shouted but his men needed no orders. Between them these veterans had seen a hundred battles, and survived. If this was to be their final battle then it was a good way to die. The men of the Old Unbreakables gripped their swords and shields and readied themselves.

This was a good day to die.

UNDER COVER OF the Old Unbreakables, Sigmund managed to cover the retreat of the men to the barricades on Altdorf Street.

Osric's men slowly retreated down Eel Street, where the banner of the Helmstrumburg Halberdiers flew. The men of Gunter's squad cheered Osric's men as they fell back and then scampered through a hole that had been left in the barricade.

The beastmen thought they had been pursuing the halberdiers, but suddenly they were faced with a barricade over eight feet tall, bristling with halberds and handguns. Vostig gave the order and his handgunners fired – shredding the front rank of beastmen. Twenty spearmen then burst out from the houses behind them and fell upon the beastmen. The surrounded attackers barely had a chance to raise their weapons in defence before they were cut down.

ON TANNER LANE Gaston stood with twenty halberdiers covering the retreat of the men that fled from the palisade. A few halberdiers from Osric's company joined them, but the men of the free companies did not stop running until they were behind the barricade – but it was far from finished.

Gruff Spennsweich had refused to join any of the free companies, determined to stand and protect his daughters: but events had spiralled beyond his control and there were shouts in the street – as men fled from the palisade.

Gruff ran to the front door. He could see men running down the street and the horned heads of beastmen running down from the Altdorf Gate. He ran inside and fetched a wood axe. 'Out!' he shouted and his girls ran out into the street as Gruff stood in the road to cover their retreat.

Valina dragged the twins out and they ran down the road – civilians and free company all streaming back behind the barricades – while Gaston's men blocked the advance of the beastmen. Gruff had one thought – to protect his daughters, and even as Gaston's men pulled back, Gruff stood in the street, lashing out at any beastmen that came within reach.

'Get back!' Gaston shouted, and he tried to pull the farmer back, but Gruff shook him off. He had been driven from his fields and now he refused to be driven any more.

Valina could see her father in the street. She turned and shouted for him to run away but he stood in the street, keeping three beastmen back with sheer ferocity and blind courage. But as he fought, a huge creature came behind him and struck him on the base of his neck. There was a spurt of blood and the farmer fell, his body quickly lost to view under the trampling hooves of the beastmen.

CHAPTER ELEVEN

To THE HERDS of beastmen the narrow streets seemed like tunnels. People barricaded themselves into their houses, or hid upstairs and hurled stones, pots and even pieces of furniture down onto the startled beastmen from the upper storeys.

Bewildered for a moment by the tunnel of houses and the hail of missiles that rained down on them, the beastmen's attack started to falter, allowing the last defenders time to scramble to safety. But it didn't take the beastmen long to react to their new circumstances, and they started going from house to house, battering down doors and falling on the trapped populace with claw, horn and blade.

The screams of the dying chilled the defenders at the barricades, but they were forced to endure the savage spectacle for nearly half an hour, as living people were flung from the upper windows to the waiting packs of hounds below, who fell on them with horrific hunger, tearing them apart before the helpless defenders.

Vasir looked away as an old man and his wife were low-ered from the upper windows of their house. The old man was wearing a nightgown, his wife was half-naked. He was calling on Sigmar, but she was screaming incoherently. Just inches below them the snouts of the jumping hounds gnashed and slavered – but the beastmen suspended them just out of reach and the pack of hounds started to bite and snap at each other in their excitement.

'They're doing this for sport!' Vasir cursed, and cursed the fact that he had used up all his arrows.

'They're worse than animals,' Hanz said but none of them went out to help. They stood helpless. Some made the sign of Sigmar. When the old man and his wife were dropped into the pack, Hanz and Vasir looked away but they could not stop their ears. The screams were mercifully short, but the horrific sounds of slavering and rending lasted for nearly a minute.

ON EEL STREET only Edmunt stood atop the barricade and watched the whole grisly spectacle, Butcher in one hand and the banner of the Helmstrumburg Halberdiers in the other.

He devoured each detail, remembered each scream, the face of each Helmstrumburger that died at the hands of these creatures. His stony glare did not shy away from even the most horrific of details. Each horror would be returned, he vowed silently, each death paid for ten-fold.

Butcher swung back and forth as he warmed up his wrist. 'There is a lot of work to do today,' he told the heavy axe head, and the smile of sharpened steel flashed in the sun-light. ·

WHEN THE BEASTMEN had cleared the last defenders from the houses, they surged up Altdorf Street, the charge led by the slavering hounds that bounded up and onto the barricade, snapping and tearing at the defenders' throats.

Hanz held his shield in front of him and braced his spear-butt under his foot. The static spear blade caught a hound full in the chest, and the momentum of its leap impaled the beast, but even as the blade drove deep into its organs, its snapping jaws closed with a snap onto his forearm.

Hanz let out a horrified yelp of pain as the razor-sharp fangs sliced through skin, flesh and bone. He dropped his shield in horror, seeing his right arm ending in a bleeding stump. Another hound leapt over the barricade and caught him full in the throat. Hanz flew back into the crowded defenders, the spined hound still goring at his exposed neck. The men of the free companies fell back in horror but Sigmund leapt forward with sword drawn and stabbed the loathsome creature three times before it died.

Sigmund kicked it away from Hanz but the Vorrsheimer's throat had been ripped out, the only thing keeping his head onto his shoulders was a few blood-smeared vertebrae.

It was a testament to the discipline of the Vorrsheimers that they held the initial assault and the death of their sergeant, but at the crucial moment that Hanz was punched from the line, Edmunt stepped forward, Butcher lashing out to left and right: spraying blood and brains over defender and attacker alike.

The beastmen shied back from him: cowed by the ferocity of a warrior who was not afraid to die: another child of the forests, meeting wildness with wildness, ferocity with hatred. Behind the fury of his onslaught, the line of spearmen held their footing and drove the last few hounds back. As the beastmen struggled to clamber up to them, there was a hedge of shields and spear blades against them.

SIGMUND LED THE men on Altdorf Street, the halberdiers lashing out at the leaping hounds, until blood ran down their shafts and stuck to their hands.

No one spoke, their breaths came in ragged gasps as their arms began to hang from their shoulders. Sigmund stabbed and cut, but a shard of a shattered sword caught him on the brow and opened up a cut, and within moments the streaming blood began to blind him and he fell back.

'Water!' Sigmund shouted as he tried to wipe the blood from his eyes. He felt firm hands guiding him back, away from the barricade, and then a cool wet cloth wiped away the blood and renewed his sight.

'Osric!' he said in astonishment, but the sergeant would not look him in the eye, and turned and hurried back to the barricades. A short fat man ran to Sigmund and started to lead him back to the crude field station in the front room of a nearby inn. It was Fat Gulpen, the town crier – his fat face now topped with an ill-fitting steel cap.

Sigmund shook him off. 'It's just a scratch! Bind it up!'

There was a stinging pain as Fat Gulpen started to wrap a dirty cloth around his head.

'Hurry!' Sigmund snapped. 'I need to get back!'

WHILE THE BARRICADES on Altdorf Street and Eel Street held the initial onslaught, the charge of the hounds on Tanner Lane drove the men there from the barricade, and they began to stream back to the second line.

The daughters of Gruff Spennsweig helped to drag wounded men back, but one man that Valina was helping was caught by the foot by a spined hound, whose skin was splitting to reveal ribs. She screamed and let go of the man. The hounds fell on him and in an instant he was hidden by the snarling pack.

As she ran, Valina felt something hold her back. She screamed, turned and saw the same spined hound had clamped its jaws upon her skirts. She yanked and the dress tore and she was free. She started to sprint back towards the second barricade but felt jaws clamp themselves onto her left ankle. She tripped and fell and put her hands over her head, but the gesture was futile. For an instant she was aware of fetid breath and paws as the creatures leaped onto her – and then she screamed.

* * *

ON TANNER LANE, Gaston grabbed running men and forced them to stand and fight. As dying men screamed it looked as if the whole retreat might collapse into chaos, but he managed to rally twenty men to hold the street.

After the hounds came the beastmen, clambering over the abandoned barricade, and charging.

The spiral-horned creature that had cut down Gruff picked out Gaston and charged. Gaston saw the raised axe and felt an incredible calm. This is it, you are going to die, a voice in his head said, just make sure you take him with you.

Gaston looked like a hero of old, with his long moustaches, as he drew his sword and stood ready. The axe went up for the killing blow and Gaston leapt forward, driving his weapon into the face of the spiral-horned creature. All the force from his legs was transferred onto the point of the sword and the spiral-horned head jerked backwards and was almost torn from the body.

The blade caught the creature just under the chin and punctured the soft under-tissue of the creature's neck and palate, snapping its jawbone and spraying yellow teeth into the air. The blade carried on through the beast's upper palate and went straight into the brain, buckling only as it hit the massively reinforced skull. But Gaston held his ground and the creature's skull snapped free of its spine and the war-axe flew forward without aim or direction.

The men began to rally and soon Gaston's forlorn hope had strengthened to nearly forty men; they retreated to the second barricade in four ranks.

Friedel stood shoulder to shoulder with Gaston. He was one of the few men to still have his halberd in his hand. He kept the creatures well back, but as he stabbed his blade into the neck of a creature that was crawling towards Gaston he felt a searing pain in his leg, stumbled and fell.

Gaston tried to reach down and drag the wounded halberdier back under the protective hedge of blades but before he could, three beastmen dragged the wounded man out of his reach and fell on him.

Freidel's screams only silenced when they tore his chest open and tore out his heart. A moment later they had twisted his head from his shoulders and hurled it back at the retreating men.

WHEN THEY FELT the Tanner Lane 'barricade behind them, Gaston could feel the discipline of the men behind him begin to falter as they turned and scrambled for safety. There was no one to cover their backs and a number of men were pulled back down and cruelly slaughtered.

Only the courage of Gaston and the men with him allowed so many to get back onto the barricade and then farm-lads with pitchforks covered their retreat, penning the beastmen back like animals as Gaston – the last – clambered onto the barricade to safety.

ON EEL STREET, Butcher struck again and again, until the beastmen paused before coming near Edmunt, but the weight of numbers was almost overwhelming. Men were stumbling back from the front line and collapsing from exhaustion. Women gave out water and such little food as they could find, but there was no way so few defenders could hold back such a flood.

The tightly thronged herds began to part and the human defenders could see terrible creatures start to push their way into the top of Altdorf Street: things that had crawled straight from the world of nightmares – Chaos spawn.

Sigmund stood silently behind the lines, assessing the situation then he called to Strong-arm Benjamin. The burly black-haired man ran over.

Sigmund pointed. 'See that building there?'

There was a tall thin house, the second and third floors of which over-hung the street. Benjamin nodded.

'Find a way in and set the place on fire!'

The street between the barricade and the house in question was full of baying beastmen. 'How?' Benjamin asked.

'Through the houses!' Sigmund said, and Benjamin understood.

He took his twenty smithy men and clambered up to the top floor of the house next to them. It was a lodging house, with many doors and simple wooden steps leading up to the third floor, where the rooms had sloping ceilings.

Clothes were scattered on the floor. The occupants had fled. The blacksmiths began to pound at the plaster wall. Their heavy hammers made short work of the plaster and wattle walls, and soon there was a round hole that was large enough for them to duck through.

Benjamin's men went from attic to attic, leaving ragged holes in each wall, until they reached the house that Sigmund had indicated. The second and third storeys hung well out over the street. If they were discovered, the beastmen would find a tunnel all the way to the defenders' barricade. But for the fire to catch hold it would have to be on the ground floor.

Benjamin had two of his men gather lanterns from the deserted rooms as he stole a glance from the upstairs window. The street was black with bodies, the palisade seemed like a cliff holding back a stormy sea. The Chaos spawn were moving inexorably through the beastmen and Benjamin realised with horror that they eating their way through the goatmen.

Benjamin led two of his men down the stairs, listening for the tell-tale sound of hooves – but the house appeared to be deserted.

As they came down onto the first floor the banners of the beastmen were hanging in front of the windows. The air was thick with beastman musk. Their hearts pounded in their chests.

On the ground floor the lattice windows had been shattered. Beastmen were jostling each other, eager to get to the fighting on the palisade. But their attention was all focussed forward – none of them noticed the men in the houses just yards to the side.

Benjamin held the lantern in his hand. He gestured to the other men and they began to pour oil over the beams and timbers of the house.

Benjamin crept to the front room and unscrewed the flask he had, and shook it over the overturned furniture. But as he did so there was a pungent scent of roses.

Scented oil! He cursed and looked with alarm at the beast-man, and for a second he was sure that he had escaped. But the noses of the beastmen were far more sensitive than his. The sudden draft of scented oil made a number of them turn and they bleated with shock and delight at seeing a human inside the building. Within seconds there were three beast-men chasing Benjamin through the rooms then the front door swung open and a stream of beastmen charged in, their hooves skidding on the smooth tiles.

Benjamin reached the bottom of the stairs and realised that there was no way he could escape. Shaking the last of the scented oil over the stairs, he smashed the lantern on the banister and held it to his chest.

The oil caught flame and Benjamin screamed as he charged forward, a living torch. The beastmen skidded and slipped in their panic as the fiery apparition ran towards them – then the whole ground floor went up with a *whumpf!* of hot air – and they were incinerated in the inferno.

As THE BATTLE raged Josh raced back and forth along the old stone wall between Altdorf Street, Eel Street and Tanner Lane. There were ten young lads relaying messages from Sigmund to Gaston and Edmunt.

Captain Jorg was calm as he listened to each breathless report. He issued orders calmly but deliberately.

'Gaston has fallen back to the second barricade,' Josh said and Sigmund nodded and shouted to Guthrie, who stood at the back of the lines with his Crooked Dwarf Volunteers. They were a sorry-looking band of warriors, but they were all he had left. 'To Tanner Lane!'

Sigmund looked back to see what was happening in Alt-dorf Street and saw the house that Benjamin had gone to suddenly erupt in flames. A wave of panic spread through the beastmen and the pressure on the front line eased.

The flames began to lick up the front of the house, and soon the whole bottom floor was aflame. The fur of those closest to the flames began to crinkle and singe. Two of the Chaos spawn had been driven off, but one – with blue spined legs like a spider that helped drag its bloated body forward, seemed oblivious to the heat and kept onwards, its skin blackening and bubbling as its watery insides started to bubble and boil. The intense heat drove the rearmost attackers back, while those at the front were trapped. They pressed forward, desperate to escape the heat and soon the beastmen at the foot of the barricade were so tightly packed that they could not even swing their weapons or even raise their shields.

Elias stabbed again and again, but the beastman below him refused to fall.

'He's dead!' the man next to him shouted. 'They're too tightly packed for the dead ones to drop!'

As the inferno increased the heat was so intense that beastmen at the back of the press went berserk and began to attack their comrades in an effort to escape the heat. The fur on their backs blackened and began to smoke. Suddenly, the upper storey crashed down in a tumble of burning timbers. The whole front of the house toppled right across the road, burying the spawn, and killing many of the beastmen and cutting off about fifty beasts that were still fighting at the barricade.

Sigmund drew his sword and pushed through the startled defenders.

'Charge!' Sigmund yelled and suddenly the attackers were beset by a mob of furious men: halberdiers and free companies and handgunners all mixed. The terrified beastmen began to bleat in terror. Some tried to hide inside the buildings, a few tried to run through the burning ruins, one or two making it to the other side as flaming torches – their fur and skin peeling back from their bones as they roared their agony.

* * *

THE FLAMES QUICKLY spread and soon houses were alight on Tanner Lane and Eel Street. In the next half an hour three more houses toppled as the flames spread from houses to house and Altdorf Street and Eel Street were impassable.

Only Tanner Lane offered the beastmen a chance to close with the enemy. Men stumbled back from the fighting and staggered towards a makeshift field station that the apothecary, Gustav, was running in the front room of a merchant's house.

There was a queue of wounded men lying on the pavement outside. Beatrine helped to drag wounded men back from the barricades. Floss held the men down as Gustav inspected the wounds.

'Get some rest,' Gustav said to two young men whose wounds were beyond help – and they were piled in the corner of the room and given a little kirsch to soothe their passing.

The next man that was lifted onto the former dining table was a halberdier whose arm had been almost severed by an axe cut. Gustav nodded to Floss and the other helpers and they held the man down: a leather strap over his forehead pinning his head to the table.

Gustav reached for his knifes, already dripping blood and began to sharpen them. 'You'll be losing this arm,' he said to the soldier who nodded and bit his mouth shut.

Gustav cut quickly and cleanly about an inch above the cut, cleared the twitching muscles away from the bone that had shattered and was oozing bloody marrow.

'Saw!' Gustav said. Floss handed him the saw then shut her eyes as the apothecary lowered it to the man's arm and began to saw.

THE SECOND BARRICADE on Tanner Lane was not as high or as formidable as the others, but at least the lane was not much wider than a single cart. The fighting here was bitter and merciless. A pile of beastman bodies began to pile up outside the barricade, while Beatrine and her sisters helped drag the wounded men away.

Gaston didn't know how he could continue to lift his sword – when the burning houses began to shed charred timbers and the beastmen seemed to sense that they would be cut off and retreated.

Gaston watched them leave, until the street was empty except for a carpet of twitching beastmen. The men did not dare to pursue, the flames were so intense that there was no way through. They collapsed where they were and Guthrie sent some men to bring beer from his inn. They came back ten minutes later with a barrel strapped to the back of a mule and the men passed the steins around, drinking deeply.

As the men rested Floss took a knife from the table side and clambered over the barricade. She had been driven from her home. Her father and her elder sister had been killed. She bent over the first wounded beastman. It was small, not much larger than a boy, with soft brown fur with a dark stripe down its back. Except for its fanged mouth, its face had a strange, almost feline softness to it. It had been stabbed in the chest, and its breathing was coming slowly and raggedly.

Floss's skirts were knotted up. She could feel the heat of the burning house on her left cheek as she bent over the wounded animal and cut its throat.

The next beastman saw what had happened and struggled to get away. When Floss knelt at the side of its horned head, the creature bared its teeth to frighten her away, but she had seen more blood that afternoon than most soldiers. The vertical pupils of the beastman struggled to see what she was doing – then the knife kissed its throat and its hot blood spurted over Floss's hands.

On Altdorf Street, Sigmund ordered a third line of barricades to be built and men and women worked frantically to empty their houses of every scrap of furniture, piling it up across the street. They barricaded the doors of their houses and knocked passages through the upper floors so the street would become a death trap for the hordes of wild animals should they break through.

When he had given his orders, Sigmund clambered up on the old stone wall and hurried the thirty yards to Tanner Lane.

The lane was clogged with dead bodies. The barricade was lined with exhausted men. 'The lions of Tanner Lane!' Sigmund dubbed them and the men gave weak smiles.

Sigmund recognised Guthrie and grinned. 'You made a warrior after all!'

'I will never fight again,' Guthrie said with a smile. 'I only ask Sigmar to save me today!'

When Sigmund got to Gaston he laughed out loud and embraced the man.

'Last time I saw you, you were on the palisade!'

Gaston smiled weakly. He had lost almost all of the men here – and he hardly knew how he had survived himself.

'Sigmar blessed me!' he said.

WHEN SIGMUND GOT to Eel Street the air was much lighter. Everyone had a handful of stories to tell about how they had escaped and they were recounting them, laughing with the shock and relief that they were still alive.

'Captain Sigmund!' a voice shouted and Sigmund turned and saw Theodor. The merchant's pistols were blacked with powder and he had a tear in his jacket where a knife had narrow missed disembowelling him. He saw the cut on Sigmund's forehead and blanched. 'You should not be in the front rank! You're the only hope these people have!'

'There's two hundred men fighting here. Each one is hope for Helmstrumburg.'

Theodor took hold of Sigmund's arm. 'Believe me! Your men are deserving of the highest praise, but you cannot hold the beasts of the forests forever. They will find a way to come around the defences. And when they do – their hounds will eat well!'

Sigmund's lip curled in disgust at his talk, but then it struck him that the man was right. They had weathered only the first storm. These beastmen were not driven by any sane desires. They had a single purpose that had smouldered for a thousand years: to drive the humans from the town.

'These creatures are driven by a force older than Helmstrumburg. But we might destroy their unity if we destroy the herdstones!'

'How can we do that?' Sigmund demanded. 'I have no men to spare and it would take a hundred men a day to destroy those stones!'

'Did you get my note?'

'What note?' Sigmund frowned.

Osric he realised what they were talking about and grinned sheepishly. Four barrels of blackpowder would have made a nice packet, but if it saved the lives of his men then it was probably worth it.

'Is this about four barrels of blackpowder?' he said.

SIGMUND MANAGED TO find a number of carpenters from the men on the barricade and sent them down to the docks with Theodor. He had five of Frantz's dockers go to the Crooked Dwarf and bring back ten empty barrels.

Then Sigmund went to the north gate, where there were about fifty free company and twenty spearmen. Since the attempted treachery of Squire Becker, there had been half-hearted attempts to attack the north gate – but they had been easily beaten back. The beastmen had not been expecting to find the walls held strongly against them.

Sigmund found a similar story when he met Gunter. The veteran had a bandage around his chest, and there was a red patch on his right side, near his armpit.

'A lucky arrow,' he laughed, giving no sign of the pain he must be in.

Sigmund described the battle at the palisade and the barricades and Gunter nodded in approval. Bringing the beastmen into the streets was probably the best thing to do. It limited their numbers and gave them no way to use their speed to outflank the halberdiers.

'We are going to try and destroy the herdstones,' Sigmund said.

'You're doing what?' Gunter said. 'That's madness!'

'We cannot beat them.'

'We are beating them!'

'This is our only chance! I have seen the numbers that these beastmen control. We can fall back from barricade to barricade. We can burn each house to gain a respite, but it is as if the whole Drakwald Forest has emptied itself. And there are only so many houses in Helmstrumburg. When we have burnt them all then we will line up, shoulder to shoulder on the docks, and be killed?'

Gunter didn't say anything.

'If we do not return by nightfall, take over command of the defences.'

Gunter nodded. 'Good luck!' he said and the two men embraced and then Sigmund strode down towards the docks.

THERE WAS A crude raft on the dockside when Sigmund arrived, and twenty of Osric's men standing round four firkins of blackpowder. With them were the best fighters that the barricades could spare.

The Vorrsheimers had sent Stephan, the young spearman with the scar on his cheek.

Next to him stood Elias, who had stopped feeling like a new recruit at the palisade. Already he had lost count of the number of times he had killed. Black-haired Schwartz grinned as Sigmund approached and Sigmund nodded to Theodor. He had seen the man fighting and knew that he was a man to be counted on.

Osric had found a shield from somewhere and had a drawn sword in his hand. Baltzer had a cut on his cheek, but was otherwise unwounded. The short thin man leaned on his halberd for support, regarding Sigmund with ill-concealed contempt.

Theodor had his pistols loaded and ready.

Frantz stood next to him, with an unlit clay pipe in his mouth. Four or his dockers stood behind him, still armed with their swords and shields and steel caps.

The dockers had put up a magnificent fight on Altdorf Street, but Sigmund didn't want them here. He wanted trained soldiers only.

'Who is going to carry these barrels and let your lot do the fighting?' Frantz demanded.

Sigmund paused to consider. 'Fine. Now you all know why we are here?'

Baltzer and Stephan shook their heads.

'Putting it simply, we are going to cut the head from the serpent,' Sigmund smiled.

THE DOCKERS LIFTED the raft to the water's edge and lowered it in. It bobbed on the water and the soldiers began to slip into the water, holding onto the sides as they slid their weapons onto the top of the raft to stay dry.

When all the men were in the water, Sigmund lowered the firkins of blackpowder and they were strapped onto the top of the planks, well above the water. Last of all he handed Stephan a hooded lantern.

'Keep that well away from those barrels!' Osric warned 'Or we'll end up in Tilea!'

THE MEN PADDLED the raft out of the harbour then caught the current of the midstream water and began to drift downstream.

Sigmund clung on to the wet wood as he passed the houses of Helmstrumburg. There was black smoke billowing up from the burning houses. Half the new town seemed to be burning. When they were alongside the palisade he saw all the dead bodies that filled the ditches and that were piled up in drifts against the palisade. They had killed so many beastmen, yet there were still so many left.

EDMUNT TOOK OVER command of the barricades and as the houses burned there was no danger of attack. He went from barricade to barricade assessing the damage. The men saw him and felt heartened: people were already whispering that this was the man who had held Eel Street all alone. They imagined Butcher would be an enormous battle-axe, such as men used in ancient times, and when they saw the simple woodsman's hatchet they were amazed.

Edmunt paid no attention to the whispers. He talked to the leader of each free company and took stock of how many fighting men each still commanded, laughed at their stories of bravery or sheer luck, made them feel like heroes, just by having spoken to him.

As the lull continued a few doors opened and here and there an old woman or child stumbled out into the dead-littered streets. Somehow they had managed to hide from the beastmen and only the approaching flames had finally driven them from their hideouts. They clambered to safety, shaking with terror.

Edmunt sent a number of his men onto the north wall to spy on the beastmen, then took ten halberdiers and a number of the blacksmiths and went from house to house, hunting any beastmen that had been trapped in the buildings. They came back with nine horned heads that they tossed into a pile in front of the barricade.

As EDMUNT HUNTED trapped beastmen Gaston walked slowly along the lines of wounded men who were propped up against the walls of Tanner Lane.

'Well done, Johann!' he told a man he had known before enlisting, who had a bandage around his left ear. 'That's the poorest excuse of a wound I've ever seen!'

'I can't hear you!' Johann retorted.

Gaston grinned. The next man was one of Osric's. He had a stab wound in his leg. A dirty strip of cloth was seeping blood but the man had a tankard in his hand and was happy to be still alive. 'You couldn't face taking orders from that thieving lowlife any longer?'

'I just couldn't let your boys keep running away!'

The next man was slipping in and out of consciousness. A girl was trying to stop the blood from a cut to his head. She saw Gaston and smiled shyly, but Gaston passed on.

He was too shaken to notice how pretty she was, and it wasn't until he was three paces along the line that he caught himself and turned back to smile.

'He looks to be in good hands!'

'Thank you, sir.'

'What's your name?'

The girl put a hand to her hair, where she used to have ribbons. But she had used all her ribbons as tourniquets on the wounded men.

'Beatrine,' she said, and blushed.

Gaston nodded. He put a hand to his moustaches and smoothed them down, feeling a knot. It was only after he had pulled the hair free that he realised that the knot had been a splatter of blood that had scabbed the hairs together.

'We are lucky to have such pretty nurses,' he said and promised himself that if he came through this day that he would seek this girl out.

SIGMUND AND HIS men clung to the crude raft like survivors from a shipwreck and steered themselves far out into the river stream away from the banks and spying eyes.

The water lapped against them, and here and there the men could feel long weeds reaching up to tug at their legs.

'There's something in the water!' Baltzer hissed.

Osric reached up and took a knife from the raft, but no one looked reassured. If the forests had hidden all these beastmen for so long, then what might the waters of the Stir hide?

Sigmund kept his eyes on the land. There was no one he would rather not have on this mission than that cut-throat. His mind started thinking about the things that Theodor had told him. He didn't believe in river monsters. He was sure that he and his men would reach the land. Who else would fight the beastman leader?

He laughed silently at himself. Now he was starting to believe the prophecies too.

As they followed the current of the river the beastman army came into view. They were all lined up the bottom of the hills and there were more scattered through the woods and orchards, well back from the river banks. There were countless creatures grouped in their warbands, their gruesome banners flapping in the breeze.

The men on the raft went silent. They kept as low as possible, paddled further into the wide waters, wishing that they were not so exposed on the plain water surface. If any of the beastmen thought their raft was anything more than a piece of floating debris then the alarm might be sounded, and their attempt would be little more than suicidal – and Helmstrumburg would be doomed.

As THE FLAMES kept the beastmen back, Edmunt led his men into a huge coaching inn on Altdorf Street, called the Blessed Rest. The bar was empty, but the sound of hooves on floorboards showed that there were beastmen inside, disorientated by the corridors and doorways.

Edmunt and his men were familiar with this drinking house. Many of them were patrons. They silently crossed the room and took a back staircase to the servants' rooms in the back. From there they hunted, room by room. They found three beastmen in one room. One of the blacksmiths killed one, while the halberdiers stabbed the other two beastmen. One of them died but the other was only wounded. It shrank back, goat legs curled up to its stomach as it put its hands up to its horned head, and opened its mouth in something approaching a nervous smile of sharp teeth.

Butcher hit it full in the forehead and the strange expression froze on its face. Edmunt turned away as he pulled Butcher free and wiped it on the back of an overturned couch. He didn't notice the hand sticking out from underneath the piece of furniture.

There were two doors at the end of the oak-panelled room. Edmunt tip-toed to the left-hand door. There were strange sounds coming from inside the room. He nodded to the blacksmith and they came close to the door, then Edmunt kicked it open and rushed inside, axe ready to strike any that might be waiting inside.

The sounds were coming from a four-poster bed at the end of the room. Edmunt kept his axe ready and crept over the shredded bolsters and ripped clothing. There was something kicking and struggling on the bed. Edmunt bent low and edged towards the bed, ripped a curtain and brought his axe up to strike – but his axe stopped and he let out a strangled gasp.

Staring up at him was the skinless face of what he guessed had been a middle-aged woman: the eyeballs bulged and the lipless mouth opened and closed. He saw that her tongue had been torn out.

The hands and feet of the woman had been struck off and the wounds cauterised with hot irons. It seemed the beastmen had started torturing this hapless victim and then been disturbed or had broken off to find more prey.

Edmunt averted his eyes and pulled the sheets over the woman's body. But one of the woman's mutilated arms came up and touched him. He turned to face her and saw pleading in her unblinking eyes. Pleading and understanding and – in an instant – he saw forgiveness in her face, for what he had to do.

'What is it?' the blacksmith hissed from the open doorway.

Edmunt shut his eyes and brought Butcher down into the skinned forehead, keeping his eyes closed until he had pulled the axe free, and let the curtains drop.

'Nothing,' he said.

IT HARDLY SEEMED credible to Sigmund that they had sailed this way in the *White Rose* just two days before. In some stretches of the river it was hard to believe that a ferocious battle was raging not more than a few miles away. Tranquil and undisturbed, chickens still pecked through the broad apple orchards. Behind an unburned hut, the first shoots of spring wheat were showing – but then another beast camp came into view and the effect was jarring. Beastmen had no place here. Smoke billowed up from Helmstrumburg, and every now and again the roar of battle or the blowing of a horn or ringing of a chapel bell came to them over the water.

As the raft floated on, Sigmund wondered if they might drift downstream all the way to Altdorf. Finally, when it seemed the men could endure the cold and the wet no longer, they came alongside the mound and the four black standing stones, sharp and angular against the scattered forest.

From the river, Sigmund counted at least ten beastmen as well as a strange shambolic figure that was capering around the top of the mound.

Sigmund tried to see what the figure was doing, but then the raft drifted past the ridge of land and the mound was hidden. Out of sight, they all paddled and kicked hard to bring the raft to the shore.

The jetty was unoccupied. The land behind the ridge of land was much as they had left it two mornings earlier: bushes and the occasional trees silent and still. The slopes were empty. It seemed that all the beastmen's attention was focussed on the battle in the town. The only creatures were those that were around the mound.

Sigmund thanked Sigmar. It looked like they had a chance of success.

THE MEN KICKED and steered the crude raft towards the jetty. Osric caught the nearest upright and the raft swung round as he held them against the tug of the stream. For a moment it seemed that Osric would not be able to hold on and they would spin out of control back into the river, then Sigmund reached out and caught one of the uprights and they managed to drag the raft close enough to the edge for the men to pull it ashore.

They moved quickly and quietly, grabbing their weapons, while Frantz and his dockers grabbed the precious firkins and hefted them onto their shoulders.

Instead of going over the ridge, Sigmund led his men along the river bank, where the bushes and trees would offer them as much cover as possible. When they reached a patch of ferns Sigmund signalled them all to get down. He could see the beastmen guards, and recounted fifteen.

The hooded figure was still capering around the top of the mound. It was hooded and bent, and gave the impression of being incredibly old. But contrary to this, the thing leaped round the stones with a strange agility and purpose, as if it were performing some arcane ritual.

Sigmund's mouth went dry. He had no doubt that he had to stop the ritual, but he also had to get close enough to allow them to kill the sentries without an alarm being sounded.

WITHOUT WINDS TO fan them, the fires in the town had died down by late afternoon. Without the cover of the burning buildings, Edmunt and his men returned to the Eel Street barricade, eight more beastman heads hanging from their belts.

When they had slipped through the hole that the defenders had made in the barricade, each man dropped the heads onto the floor. The horns knocked against each other, gory necks dripped fresh blood, glassy eyes stared blindly up at the crowd of horrified onlookers. Some of the women started to cry, but the men stared at the things – not so much with hatred, but the certain knowledge that every beastman had to die, or the men and their families would.

Edmunt looked exhausted, but he was unable to rest. When he wanted to shut his eyes the face of the woman in the Blessed Rest came back to him, skinned and still living, and he touched the haft of Butcher at his belt.

The blade was dulled now, and he sat down, accepted a tankard of ale and a hunk of bread, and ate as he took out his whetstone and sharpened the blade into a smile.

As the fires died down it was only a matter of time until the beastmen attacked again. Edmunt had posted sentries high up in the buildings by the barricades and a boy shouted down, 'They're coming!'

There were shrieks of terror from some of the women, while the men took up their weapons with a weary resilience.

SIGMUND CRAWLED THROUGH the ferns until he was within ten feet of the nearest sentry. The beastman leant on its spear as it turned its snout back and forth sniffing the breeze. There was a stink of musk. Sigmund loosed his sword in its sheath. He was so close he could see the flies that were crawling around the creature's eyes. It stamped its hoof. The flies flew up into the air and it swatted at them with its hand. The mix of human and animal was horrifying, as if the wild beast had been mixed with the worst of human emotions: hatred, violence, and lust.

Sigmund had his sword out. He drew his feet up under him, ready to leap up.

The flies continued to buzz around the creature and it swatted them again. Sigmund leaped from the ferns, his sword a whirlwind of death as it struck the head from the beastman guard, and kept running as he struck the next down.

Behind him the whole river bank rose up in anger. The beastmen bleated in shock as twenty men leapt up, their swords dealing death to the left and right. Osric gutted one beastman and lopped the arm off another, forearm and hand still gripping the knotted club as they all flew into the air. Then Osric paused to drive his sword through the wounded beast's heart.

Baltzer kept behind Osric and caught one creature on the back of the neck, his sword snagging as it caught in its spine.

Theodor's first shot hit a beastman under the chin and snapped the horned head back violently. The second hit another beast in the shoulder and it swirled as it fell, to have its throat cut as it lay helpless. The remaining beastmen ran to the base of the mound to protect their shaman. There was a ferocious struggle as the men tried to cut their way through – but even in death the beasts clutched the blades of the men of Hemstrumburg.

Sigmund could feel the air begin to crackle with energy as the shaman's voice rose in pitch, but even as his hair began to stand on end Stephan broke through the wall of fighting and roared as he charged the hooded spirit-charmer. It was only the roar that alerted the shaman to the danger. It turned and saw an Empire soldier charging towards it, spear held ready to thrust through its heart.

The shaman brought up the skull rattle and there was a clap of thunder. An invisible force struck Stephan in the chest, ripping open his ribcage and flinging him back onto the floor: pulsing heart exposed to the sky.

As Osric and his men struggled to cut down the last of the beastmen, Sigmund saw the shaman step up to the broken body of the spearman and reach down.

'No!' Sigmund shouted, but Stephan's body spasmed and the shaman stood with his forearm dripping blood, and a pulsing heart clenched in his fist.

SIGMUND CUT THE last beastman down, ran up the slope and grabbed the fallen Vorrsheimer's spear, and hurled it at the cackling shaman. The steel head seemed to hang in the air before it struck the shaman full in the chest. Its body spasmed as a foot of steel impaled it. Bloody froth poured from the creature's lips, its goat-legs buckled and it fell to the ground. Its rattle cracked with the impact, and human teeth fell out.

As the foul creature died, one of the beastmen in the clearing put a horn to its lips and raised the alarm.

'Blackpowder!' Sigmund shouted, and Frantz and his dockers sprinted up. At any moment there could be hundreds of beastmen charging through the trees. They used their knives to crowbar the firkin lids off, then placed one at the base of each of the four standing stones and then began to uncoil the fuse.

Already the first beastmen were streaming back to the standing stones. Sigmund screamed at Osric to block their approach.

Osric and his last ten men grabbed spears and shields from the fallen beastmen and spread out to cover the men working furiously at the mound. The first beastmen to arrive seemed to have been scattered in the forest. They did not come all together, but singly and without order.

Osric and his men formed a ragged screen, parrying and blocking the desperate blows of the beastmen who saw the dead body of their shaman and attacked with new ferocity.

SIGMUND RAN OVER the mound, trailed a fuse, then he suddenly tripped and fell into a hole that the beastmen had been digging. He gasped with shock when he saw that at the bottom of the hole, next to his right foot, was the enormous skeleton of a long-dead human warrior. A horned helm had slid across the skull's face, scraps of cloth and armour had fallen through the collapsed bones. In its right hand the skeleton held an ancient broadsword, rimed and green with age, and in its left the old brass boss of a wooden shield, the thick linden timbers rotted away.

Sigmund felt a chill run down his back. The treasurer's book had said how Ortulf Jorg was buried with all the men who had fallen that day. This giant must be the man who killed the beastman leader a thousand years ago – and now Sigmund was here, destined to fight their leader himself.

And this, perhaps, was his ancestor.

Sigmund stared at the bones, as if looking for some sign or feature that he might recognise – but there was nothing. He heard a desperate shout and looked up to see Osric and his men fighting a desperate battle to hold back the berserk beastmen. He ran down the slope and fumbled to ram the fuse into the hole in the firkin. As he worked, he could feel the power of the stones as they began to hum, and his head hurt so much he could barely concentrate.

'The lantern!' Sigmund shouted and Frantz's face went ashen as he realised that they had left it in the ferns.

Frantz began to sprint off, and Sigmund saw one of Osric's men being cut down, the beastman leaping over the dead man and charging Sigmund.

Sigmund's sword hummed as he drew it. He took three strides forward, catching the creature at the base of one of its horns, slicing deep into its skull, but the creature ran full into him, and its momentum knocked him clean from his feet. Sigmund heard a gunshot and then another. He kicked the dead beast off, and was up, sword ready, when he saw Theodor, fumbling with the wheel-lock of his pistols as he reloaded.

Sigmund scrambled to his feet, but instead of charging, the beastmen hung back. Sigmund thought that perhaps the death of their shaman had broken the creatures' resolve, and the battle was over – but then he heard a roar that sounded like a bear. Through the silent tree trunks strode an albino giant, curled ram's horns spiralling down to its throat, shoulders that bulged with a primal ferocity.

The creature swung a two-headed axe from hand to hand. Over its chest was the crudely fashioned breastplate of some vanquished knight, battered out of shape and looking almost toy-like strapped onto the large chest of the beastlord.

Schwartz ran at the creature, but a swing of its fist sent the man flying, his neck broken and his head swinging uselessly on the shattered spine, staying at a twisted angle as he lay dead.

'Back!' Sigmund shouted to Osric and his men. 'Get back! There's no point you fighting it,' he told them. 'It wants me!'

Osric's men turned away and the sergeant dragged a wounded man with him, lest he should fall into the hands of the beastmen. They stumbled as they ran, through the standing stones, past Sigmund towards the bushes.

The albino beastman paused at the edge of the standing stones. Its fur was white from head to hoof and the only colouring was its pink eyes, which blinked painfully in the light. The beast opened its mouth and roared with pleasure at the prospect of killing the one that was foretold.

Sigmund said his prayers to the gods as the creature took a step towards him. Sigmund could feel the weight of the creature as its hoof stamped down, then pointed its axe and seemed to speak in some crude language.

Sigmund gripped the sword hilt two-handed to stop his fingers from shaking. His only thought was how he might wound this beastman before it struck him down. As the creature took another step forward there was the deafening shot of a pistol to the left – but Theodor's aim was poor and the first shot either missed or had no effect.

'He's mine!' Sigmund shouted, but Theodor drew his sword and strode up to the creature and fired again. This shot hit the creature in the thigh causing a red stain to spread over the white fur. It raged with fury and turned to face off against the second attacker, pink eyes blinking with anger. It ran at Theodor and swung its axe, but he leapt out to the side and stabbed the creature high on the shoulder at the base of its neck.

The beastman leader charged Theodor again and twice more he caught it with precise stabs in the shoulders, as if goading the beast to an insane rage, but on the third run the cunning creature feinted a charge to the left. Letting go of the axe shaft he caught the tail of Theodor's jacket and even as he tried to pull away, the beastlord dragged him into his deadly grasp.

Theodor looked like a child in the clawed grip of the monster as it flung him to the ground then grabbed his feet and picked him up.

Theodor's face was contorted with terror. Sigmund dropped his sword, grabbed a fallen halberd and stabbed it into the knotted muscles of the beastman's back, but the blow seemed to have no effect on the enraged creature.

It swung Theodor round in a deadly arc and then brought his body down against one of the standing stones. There was a sickening crack as the man's spine snapped and his head exploded with the impact, splattering brains and blood over the stones.

Sigmund stabbed at the creature again. It was occupied with the dead body, goring it against the stone, ripping Theodor's inert body apart, and covering its horns and brow with gore. It was so consumed with animal hatred that even when Theodor's body was little more than a broken mess of flesh it still butted and gored and bit.

'Hey!' Sigmund shouted and only another thrust of the halberd brought the creature's attention away. It blinked the blood from its eyes and seemed to realise that the man it had caught was dead.

As Theodor's mangled corpse fell to the ground, the massive beastman turned to Sigmund and charged.

Sigmund jabbed at it in much the same way as Theodor had done. The halberd gave him a much longer reach: he goaded the beast and then danced back a couple of steps.

The beastman ran at him a couple of times, and each time it did Sigmund was ready for a feint or a sudden swerve. The creature paused to catch its breath and then suddenly ran at Sigmund, head down to butt him. Sigmund was caught unawares and the sharp point of the horn caught him on the left thigh. He let out a strangled gasp of pain as the blunt horn opened a ragged cut up his hip and he only just escaped the reach of its claw.

Sigmund dragged his foot as he struggled up the mound, using the halberd as a prop to keep him upright, and the beastlord halted and snorted with satisfaction. It scented fear and weakness. Now the hunter had become the hunted.

Sigmund got to the top of the mound and it struck him how fitting it was that he would die here on the spot that his forebear was buried. As he felt warm blood running down his leg he felt a stab of disappointment that he had failed to kill the beast.

Edmunt and Gunter would save the people of Helmstrumburg. They were no longer his care.

For a moment he had an image of the town: burning as its people were slaughtered in the streets, the wild beasts tearing them apart. He put his hand to his belt to draw his sword, but the scabbard was empty. He had dropped his weapon in the fight at the base of the mound. And the halberd was now his crutch. Without it he could barely stand. He was defenceless.

Sigmund laughed bitterly. Trapped, wounded and defenceless. This was not how he had imagined his death. He could see the beastman's nostrils flare as it strode up the hill towards him.

Sigmund's hand slipped on the halberd shaft and he half fell into the open grave of Ortulf Jorg. Catching his balance, one of his hands fell on the hilt of a weapon. He looked down in amazement and saw the sword of Ortulf, slayer of the beastlord.

The leather bindings on the grip had long mouldered away, but the weapon itself was sound. Sigmund lifted the weapon from its thousand year-old rest and it balanced perfectly in his hand.

The beastlord saw its foe arm himself and roared as it raced up the final yards.

Sigmund rested on one knee. He only had time for one blow. He waited until the last moment then drove the sword forward. He felt the blade bite, then clawed hands tore into the flesh of his side and shoulders. The weight of the beastman hit him and he was picked from his feet and rolled down the mound, his enemy's body crushing the wind from his lungs. He slammed against one of the standing stones and everything went black.

CHAPTER TWELVE

THE WEAPON'S HAFT was sticky with blood. Butcher rose and fell again and again, dealing out death to any that came within reach. A dappled beastman ran through a pitchfork-wielding farm lad next to Edmunt, and the young boy gasped and clutched the spear and fell back with it still impaled in him. The beastman had just started to grab a broken sword when the blunt end of Butcher caught it beneath the chin and snapped its mouth shut, crushing its teeth together. Blood spurted from its nose, eyes and ears, and the creature's head flew back as it fell into the ranks of those beyond.

Anyone else's arm would have refused to rise again, but Edmunt had spent all his life chopping wood, and if the truth be told, he thought grimly, the beastmen heads broke more easily than many pieces of wood. As he fought, he felt the men around him beginning to tire of death and killing – even after so many hours, and he called out in a hoarse voice. 'Have courage!'

But even as he spoke, the beastmen began to back off. Edmunt stared in disbelief, and laughed out loud, called out insults on the goat-men's courage.

Why would they back off at this moment, when the defenders were almost spent?

There was a moment's pause in the fighting. The men had barely had time to draw breath when a man sprinted up a side street and screamed: 'They've broken through on Altdorf Street!'

There were cries of horror and dismay. Edmunt leaped from the barricade and led fifty men down a side street where dead and wounded were piled in the shade. But in Altdorf Street the ragged defenders stood on the wall staring down the street with the same astonishment.

Edmunt hurried to Tanner Lane, but the beastmen had fled from there as well.

'Have we won?' Gaston asked but Edmunt shook his head. He had no idea.

Guthrie misheard the two men's conversation and clapped his hands. 'We've won!' he shouted, but no one wanted to believe that it was true. All of a sudden Gaston found tears on his cheeks. He turned away and wiped his cheeks and nose. He had no idea how he had survived when there were so many men around him who had been killed.

Sigmund felt a pain in the small of his back. He managed to move his hand under the weight of the beastlord and feel about behind him. He winced as he moved and then his hand brushed a curved wooden object.

His stunned brain took a moment to work it out: a barrel.

Sigmund frowned. For a moment he had thought he was lying in his bed at the barracks, and he couldn't understand what the weight on him was, or why his leg hurt, or why there was a barrel in his bed – then he remembered. He was about to be killed.

Sigmund held his breath. At any moment he expected the beastlord to pick him up and to tear him apart as it had done Theodor, but the huge stinking body on top of him lay still.

Sigmund reached for his sword, but his right hand was stuck. He tried to push himself up but the dead weight of the body pressing down on him was too hard to shift. He managed to get a little purchase and tipped the beastlord away, wriggled to the side, then dragged himself free.

The dead beastlord was an awesome sight. Its head lolled to one side, snout open and pink eyes glassy in death.

Sigmund found it hard to believe that he had survived the fight until he saw three inches of sword blade sticking out of the back of the beastman and understood. The impact of the creature had driven the sword through its body with a force that Sigmund could never have matched. The blade had impaled the creature's heart, killing it instantly.

Sigmund managed to push himself to his feet and mumbled a prayer of thanks to Sigmar. He swayed for a moment, thought he might pass out, and had to put his hand out to steady himself.

He could see that the fuse and the barrel were still in place. All he had to do was light the fuse and the whole mound would go up in smoke. For a moment he felt a wave of elation. They had won!

Then he remembered that he had nothing to light the fuse with and he felt a moment's panic, followed by a sense of crushing defeat.

A band of beastmen had come over the top of the mound. The cruel twist of luck made him fierce and ferocious. Sigmund was determined to sell his life as dearly as possible. He picked up a fallen halberd, but staggered against one of the stones and it felt warm to the touch, throbbing with some arcane pleasure, making his head spin. The touch revolted him. He fell back and felt hands supporting him.

'Now then!' Frantz said. 'I've got you.'

'Frantz!' Sigmund hissed. 'We don't have a light!'

'I have it here,' Frantz said and lifted the lantern they had carried all the way from Helmstrumburg.

Sigmund was weak from blood loss. He laughed weakly. 'Then light the cursed fuses!' he hissed, 'and help me get out of here!'

They started to move, then Sigmund grabbed Frantz. 'The sword!' he said and insisted they go back to where the albino beastman leader lay dead.

With Frantz's help Sigmund pushed the dead beastman over so he could reclaim the sword.

'Light the fuses!' Sigmund hissed as he dragged the sword from the beastman's body, and Frantz bent to the nearest fuse. In the distance, his blurry sight could make out band after band of beastmen rushing towards the standing stones.

'Take this and go!' Sigmund told Frantz, and held out the sword, but the docker hurried back, grabbed Sigmund and helped support his weight as they dashed down towards the bank of the river.

'Leave me and go!' Sigmund yelled at his friend, but Frantz kept dragging him along. He looked over his shoulder and saw more and more beastmen swarming over the mound. Sigmund's arm was weak. He brandished the sword but it was unsteady in his hand. There was no way that they could escape.

Osric and his men were crouching in the bushes. The beastmen began to swarm after Frantz and Sigmund and Osric cursed. 'You're going to hate me for this,' he told Baltzer and leaped from cover and shouted to distract the pursuing beastmen. Baltzer swore at Osric, but he leapt from cover and all the men charged.

At that moment the first barrel exploded. In a split-second three more explosions followed, throwing earth and debris and beastmen bodies up into the air.

Osric had no idea where his sword went, but suddenly he was off his feet and tumbling through the air. He landed heavily in a prickly bush. The thorns ripped into his skin and clothes and he felt a hot blast scorch his head and face.

Sigmund grunted as he was flung face forward into the grass. Frantz barely had time to put his hands over his head before clods began to rain down, and then a fine rain of dirt, as a great cloud of smoke and dirt fell back to earth.

'Sigmar's balls!' Osric swore.

Stones, beastmen, even the mound had disappeared. The force of the explosions had stripped the trees of branches. Their naked trunks stood, the nearest ones on fire with a fierce crackle as the rising resin turning them into enormous torches. At that moment there was an unearthly, haunting and ear-splitting scream.

The unearthly howl of pain lasted for nearly five seconds, then it was gone. Sigmund sat up and stared at the devastation. The lack of blood was making his head dizzy and the pain in his leg was almost overwhelming. Worst of all, the echoes of the scream made his insides shiver.

He felt someone sit up next to him.

'We did it!' Frantz laughed and clapped him on the back. Sigmund felt pains shooting all through his body, but despite the pain he started to laugh.

THE SILENCE ALONG the streets of new town was disconcerting. How could an army disappear so quickly?

Edmunt sent runners up Tanner Lane and Eel Street to see what the beastmen were up to. They were barely fifty feet from the barricades when the ground shook and they heard a distant rumble, like thunder, and saw a cloud of dirt and smoke erupt from the site of the burial mounds further down the river.

'They've done it!' one of the spearmen shouted, and Edmunt climbed up onto the barricade to see the huge cloud of debris that climbed hundreds of feet into the air, then began to dissipate and drift out over the Stir.

Edmunt picked up Vasir and crushed the trapper in a fierce bear hug.

ON TANNER LANE Beatrine heard a boom and had no idea what it meant. Someone shouted that it was the signal that reinforcements had arrived; another that the captain's men had succeeded in finding cannons.

Whatever the noise meant, a wave of relief swept through the defenders. She clapped her hands and felt tears rolling down her cheeks. Gaston turned around, looking for the pretty girl with blood stains on her dress – and picked her up from the ground and swirled her round, kissing her cheeks.

ON ALTDORF STREET Gunter saw the cloud of dirt that rose into the air and nodded in satisfaction: it appeared that Sigmund had accomplished his mission.

Then there was a sudden gust of wind and with it came a howl – as if there were maddened spirits blowing through the town. The sound was so unearthly and terrible that it made the weak-minded shake with terror but Gunter's presence kept the rest to their posts.

In a moment it was gone – and the people began to wonder what it meant.

'I think we've seen the end of these beastmen!' Gunter shouted. 'Clear this barricade away!'

The people, soldiers and civilians alike, began to pull the jumble of furniture and carts apart but the individual pieces of furniture and cart had been so compressed by the beastman attack that it bowed in at the centre, and they saw to their amazement that the barricade had been moved three yards from its original point.

The pressure of the beastmen had also locked the individual pieces of furniture into a solid mass that was almost impossible to pull apart.

Gunter clapped his men on the back and sent Josh and Hengle to the marketplace to bring a barrel of beer for the thirsty defenders when he heard a low rumble, almost too deep for human hearing, that grew steadily louder.

Gunter thought he was imagining it at first, but the sound was distinctive and he climbed up onto barricade to take a look.

'Shit!'

There was a horde of horned warriors charging down the road. Maybe they hadn't blown the stones after all? 'To arms!' he bellowed, and punched one man who was busy offering thanks to Sigmar. 'They're coming!'

* * *

THE DESTRUCTION OF the stones had sent the beastmen into a berserk fury. Whatever order the warbands had once possessed was gone. They were like a stampede of terrified animals, their eyes rolled wildly in their heads – but they didn't flee – they were in a frenzy of hatred and fury that went beyond all reason or understanding or even concern for their own safety. It had but one purpose: destroy Helmstrumburg.

EDMUNT HELPED THE scouts he had sent out to clamber to safety. 'Stand fast, men!' Edmunt called out. 'Stand fast!'

His men stepped up to the fighting steps, but having believed that they were saved many of them could not bear the thought of returning to battle one more time. Their numbers had been severely weakened during the repeated assaults and the beasts were charging with more ferocity than ever now.

Only the halberdiers and spearmen stepped up without hesitation. This was their job. They gripped spear, shield and halberd shaft and waited grimly.

The horde of beastmen flowed over the barricades in a crashing wave, overwhelming the defenders by sheer reckless force of numbers.

At the barricade on Eel Street there was a spray of blood as Edmunt lashed about him with Butcher, but the beastmen seemed impervious to pain and ran into the whirling axe-head as if they wanted to be killed.

Again, Edmunt's blind ferocity steadied the men about him, but they were exhausted and the beasts began to overwhelm them.

The barricade on Altdorf Street was breached first. Gunter strode into the gap meaning to plug it himself, but he was gored and cut down. The tide of beasts drove straight through the reinforcements and most of them were cut off and slaughtered as the beasts charged the second barricade.

Vostig and his men were holed up on the second floor of the buildings between the first and second barricades. They had been firing at the massed beastmen until their guns were too hot to shoot, but suddenly the sea of horned heads was through the barricade and washing around the feet of the buildings they were in.

Holmgar was in a narrow house above the barricade with two of Vasir's trappers. He put his handgun down and stared in horror: stunned at the speed with which the beast-men had broken through – but the men on the barricades had been fighting beyond the point of exhaustion. He heard windows smash downstairs. Hooves sounded as the beasts began to rampage through the ground floor and then he heard the sound of many hooves on the stairs. The gun barrel was too hot to hold. He drew his sword, but he was never much use with it. The trappers looked at him, as if expecting him to know how they could get out of this.

Holmgar gave a wan smile. He knew his time had come.

'It will be a pleasure to die with two such fine men,' Holmgar said rather politely, but the trappers grinned and the three men shook hands.

The sound of hooves came closer. They paused at the door. Holmgar stared at the handle as it turned to left, then right. The door opened, then he charged for the last time.

THE MEN ON Tanner Lane began to shout in horror as they saw a Chaos spawn come slithering down the street. It was higher than a man on horseback, but its body was an enormous sack of pulsating flesh. It slithered forward like a slug, squeezing its bulk between the buildings, feeling its way with round, slug-like probosces. Sucker-rimmed orifices along the length of its body opened and closed without reason.

Gaston tried to hold his men but there was no way that they were going to stand and fight a creature that had crawled from the Realm of Chaos itself. The wounded men who lined the streets shouted out in terror but no one stopped to save them.

The defenders ran to the second barricade, but Gaston turned north into Altdorf Street, hoping to alert Gunter. Seeing beastmen spilling down the street towards him, he turned south towards the river where he saw the pretty girl he had noticed earlier leading three younger girls down the street.

Gaston caught them up. The older girl was terrified; the younger ones were hysterical with fear.

'Follow me!' Gaston ordered and kicked open the door of one of the tanneries that lined the river. The stink of ammonia was overpowering, but he forced the girls to the back of the building, where the sluice gates ran straight out into the river.

As they hurried round the stinking vats Gaston turned and saw the great slithering creature pass the front of the tannery. It blotted out the light for a moment and he had a terrible feeling that it would turn in after them. They could make out a white proboscis taste the air, but the scent of urine was so strong it masked their scent.

'Jump!' Gaston shouted, but the girls were too terrified.

'The river will take you downriver. Stay afloat and you will be fine!'

'We can't swim!' Beatrine said and her sisters nodded in agreement.

'Shit!' Gaston said.

Floss saw men running past her and ran to the window of the makeshift field station – and then saw the spawn flow over the barricade as if it were a branch in the stream.

It moved so quickly there was no time to get out of the house. Apothecary Gustav's apron was completely blood-soaked. A pile of legs and feet and arms lay at the floor. Flies buzzed over the blood and dead men.

'It won't be able to get in!' Gustav said but Floss was in a complete panic. She tried to duck through the door, but a proboscis darted towards her and she screamed and ducked back into the room.

Men were crying out in horror at the creature.

'Be quiet!' she screamed at them, but there was nothing they could do. There was a horrific sound of slobbering as the spawn slithered over the wounded men outside. They held their breaths, willing the creature not to notice them, then a tentacle reached in through the doorway.

It tasted the air and it smelled good. The spawn began to feel for an opening.

Gustav's blue-crystal spectacles fell from his nose, and the knife fell from his numb fingers as the creature began to morph and squeeze itself through into the room.

Floss backed up against the wall. The tide of suppurating flesh expanded to fill the front wall. It pulsed with pleasure as it devoured all the meat – living and dead – in the room. Gustav never left the surgeon's table. The Chaos spawn enveloped him, spectacles and all. The colour of the beast reddened as the digested blood started to flow through its membranous tissue. Its orifices opened and closed with increasing rapidity.

Floss screamed and squeezed her eyes shut as if this was a terrible nightmare she could wake herself from, but she felt something warm and jelly-like slither up her body, and her screams were muffled as the creature enveloped her in a warm and deadly embrace.

DESPERATE TOWNSPEOPLE BANDED together and managed to ward off the lone beastmen by sheer weight of numbers. Here and there, there were soldiers who managed to retain some order. There were running battles through the streets with the beastmen. But where the beastmen outnumbered the humans then they fell on them with quick and savage brutality: cutting off heads as gruesome trophies.

As the barricades began to fall, Hengle ran across town. He sprinted up to the north gate where fifty men nervously waited for news. Twenty of them were spearmen and the rest were free companies. 'The barricades have fallen!' he shouted and the spearmen marched towards the nearest intersection with the new town, shields locked, spears levelled.

Hengle then ran to the east gate. 'The barricades have fallen!' he gasped. 'The beastmen are in the old town! Come now before all is lost!'

* * *

WHEN THE SURVIVING men of Sigmund's party went down to the river they found that the raft had broken free and drifted away out of sight. There was no choice but to brave the woods and walk back to town.

Frantz helped Sigmund keep up as the two remaining dockers and Osric's eight men marched along the Altdorf Road towards the east gate of Helmstrumburg.

'I need a beer!' Sigmund said, wincing from his cracked ribs.

Everyone except Baltzer laughed. He looked at Osric and shook his head in wonder. Then Baltzer suddenly remembered the money he had stolen the night before. He put his hand to his belt and felt the pouch still there, despite all that had happened.

It was a long walk, but the closer they got the more concerned they became. As they approached the town they walked past a gruesome banner of a human skin, left as a warning, or maybe a statement of conquest. The hands and feet were still attached, the head been flayed and scalped, tied to the crossbar by its hair.

They kept their distance, but as they filed past, the face of the skin came into view. The mouth was little more than a distorted hole, the eye sockets were empty – but the face was unmistakably that of the burgomeister.

None of them spoke. What promises had he been seduced with? What lies had eaten his soul to fall in with Chaos?

When they came within sight of Helstrumburg, instead of familiar faces running out to greet them, they saw plumes of smoke billowing up all across the town.

Exhausted and demoralised, they stopped at the tree-line to assess the situation, and take a brief rest. The sounds of shouting men and screaming woman; the clang of steel on steel drifted out to them – they could see that the outer defences had been overrun. For a long moment none of them spoke.

'They've broken through,' Osric said at last and the men stood and stared in disbelief.

* * *

ONE BY ONE the bands of human defenders were overwhelmed by the sheer number of beastmen. The attack stalled as the creatures satiated themselves on a festival of brutality.

As the beastmen penetrated deeper into town, terrified families ran towards the docks, thinking to throw themselves onto the mercy of the Stir, but beastmen ran them down. The lucky ones were slaughtered straight away. The screams of old men, women and children filled the streets as all manner of bestial torture was meted upon them. When they saw what was happening, some people threw themselves to their death from the upper windows of their houses rather than be taken alive.

Gaston hid in the tannery until the beastmen had passed on into town.

'Stay here!' he ordered, but the girls clung to him. 'You will be safe – I promise! If the beastmen come, then jump into the river! Understand?'

The girls nodded.

Gaston hurried to the half-open doorway. The street was full of dead. There were no wounded men left in the street, the beastmen had made sure of that. A man who had lost his leg had had his throat cut. His body lay slumped against the opposite wall. There were a couple of men who had been cut down as they ran. One of them had dropped a halberd. Gaston snatched it up. He turned into Mad Alice Lane, a narrow alleyway, no wider than a hand-cart, that led towards the docks. He crept forward – in case any beastmen were ahead – but the alley was quiet and empty.

Gaston hurried on. If he could get to the docks he might be able to find some sort of boat, and at least save some lives.

ON THE ALTDORF Road, the survivors of Sigmund's band stood and stared at the ruined town. At last Sigmund's strength began to ebb. Frantz lowered him onto the grass at the side of the road, and he winced as adjusted his position.

'Osric – if you find any survivors you might be able to bring them out on the Kemperbad Road.'

'You want us to march survivors through the forest all the way to Kemperbad?' Osric demanded. 'They'll never make it.'

Sigmund struggled to see more clearly. 'We can't just sit here and wait!' he declared and tried to force himself to his feet – but he had bruised ribs, a cut along his thigh and his shoulder was bruised from where the beastman lord had seized him.

'That's exactly what I propose we do!' Osric said. His men remained silent but Sigmund could tell from their expressions that they all agreed with him.

As they stood watching the palisade gate they heard the drum of hooves on the ground and Osric's face blanched. Beastmen reinforcements!

The vibrations increased and they could hear the hoof beats, hurrying down the Altdorf Road, growing closer and closer.

'Looks like we're going to die after all,' Osric said. His men stood up and Sigmund smiled. He didn't like Osric at all, but he respected him.

'Port arms!' Sigmund gasped and his men took whatever weapons they had to hand and stared through the scattered trees, waiting for the stampeding herds of beastmen.

They could see flashes of steel between the trees. Frantz helped Sigmund to his feet and put his sword into Sigmund's hand.

'It will be good to die with you!' Sigmund hissed through clenched teeth and as he spoke a trickle of blood ran from his left nostril.

They stood – nine ragged halberdiers, and three dockers – waiting to sell their lives as dearly as possible.

IN THE STREETS of Helmstrumburg, Edmunt was alone. He paused for a moment, then turned the corner on Franke's Lane – right into the path of thirty beastmen. The creatures recognised the giant human who had killed so many of their number and let out hoots and calls of excitement as they sprinted after him.

The beastmen shook their spears and blew their horns as they galloped after Death Bringer, as they called the giant. He was only yards ahead of them when he suddenly took a left turning. The beasts followed and found that they had run their prey to ground.

Edmunt stood in the courtyard of a brewery: the gates and windows all shut and boarded up. There was nowhere else to run.

The creatures stamped their hooves with glee as their quarry turned to face them. They spread out to surround him. They would take their time with this one. His head would adorn their banner poles. His skin would make a fine rug for their caves high on Frantzplinth.

When Gaston got to the docks there were hundreds of people seizing barrels or pieces of planking and jumping into the river.

Mixed in with them were a number of fighting men. Gaston seized the men around him and dragged them back from the water's edge.

'Fight!' he shouted. 'Fight!'

He pulled seven men back, but by his actions he managed to shame or shock nearly twenty men. If someone would lead they would follow. There were a number of boys who wanted to come, and if they could find weapons then Gaston welcomed them.

Trapped in the cul-de-sac of the brewery yard, Edmunt took Butcher from his belt and smiled. Death comes to all of us, and the best way to face it was with a weapon in hand. Taal, give me the strength of a bear, Edmunt prayed and waited.

The beastmen came forward, weapons ready. One of them barked something in a crude language, and they spread out wider. Edmunt had his back to the wall. He waited for them to come closer.

Then the beastmen heard footsteps – and turned. Across the entrance of the courtyard stood a motley crowd of warriors. They outnumbered the beastmen nearly two to one. Spears, pitchforks, swords and halberds: their faces were grim as they began to advance on the beastmen, which began to snort and stamp apprehensively. The buildings reared up around them. A few of the beastmen tried to scramble up the walls, but slid down the smooth, unnatural surface. The brewery walls were too tall. There was no way out.

'Welcome to Helmstrumburg,' Edmunt smiled and his men charged.

WHILE EDMUNT'S MEN baited the beastmen into traps, Gaston's men fought a running battle, disappearing down the snickleways and then reappearing behind the creatures.

As the reinforcements from the north and east gates arrived, the street to street fighting actually served to diminish the advantage of numbers that the beastmen possessed. In the narrow streets, with their tall, overhanging houses, the wild beasts became disorientated. After their experience in the new town, they were apprehensive to enter the buildings – and the people took advantage of that to hurl missiles down upon them.

'THE RAGGED COMPANY!' Sigmund hissed as the moving shapes drew closer. He was light-headed from lack of blood and wished he had his full strength to fight this – his last battle.

But the first figure that came into view was a knight on horseback, not a beastman. The knight was clad in dark steel armour, his horse's barding was polished to a shine, the edges gleaming with gilt inlay. The pennant on his lance fluttered red and white, emblazoned with a silver griffon. Templars of Sigmar: the Knights Griffon.

Sigmund's head span. He gripped his sword to help his mind focus. He was glad that they would be able to hold up the beastmen long enough to let the knight escape. But then two more knights appeared. And two more.

'Warn them!' Sigmund hissed. 'Warn them that the beast-men are coming!'

His face was white and Frantz put out his arm to support the captain, and Sigmund's fingers clenched on the docker's arms.

'Warn them!' he hissed and Frantz laughed.

'What did whitey do to you?' he said and patted Sigmund gently on the back. 'These aren't beastmen!'

Sigmund didn't understand for a moment. His head span as he tried to understand that there were no more beast-men. The hooves they had heard were horses'.

At last it sank in and Sigmund started to laugh and the noise was like a hacking cough. He spat up blood and wiped his mouth. Looking up he saw a column of Knights Griffon, their squires and porters coming behind on speck-led horses laden down with packs.

After them came a group of twenty men with black and gold painted breastplates and jauntily cocked hats with dyed pheasant feathers trailing behind them. Their legs were protected by greaves. The leader had a handgun strapped to his saddle; his men carried holsters on their saddles. Each man had a cavalry sabre slung over their back.

Their horses were five or more hands shorter than the knights' warhorses. They tossed their manes as they can-tered behind the trail of knights.

Sigmund struggled to stand up as the foremost knight approached.

He saluted the man slowly. 'Captain Jorg, Helmstrum-burg Halberdiers! We are glad to see you!'

The knight pulled the reins and looked down from his great helm at the blood-stained captain.

'Have they still not given you lot a proper uniform to die in?' the man said with the hint of a smile.

The man spoke with an aristocratic accent that made Frantz stand to attention. Sigmund strained to see the face and then grinned. It was Marshal von Dvornsak, of the Valkenburg Kommondaria, the knight who had ridden to save them from the greenskins at Blade's Reach. The pistoliers' captain rode up, a handsome man who looked down with curiosity at the halberdier. 'This is Captain Jorg,' he continued, explaining to the captain. The marshal gave Sigmund a wink. 'If it wasn't for him getting his men into trouble then my men would have nothing to do!'

The old marshal's lips had the hint of a smile, but Osric disliked both him and the pistoliers' captain. They were all arrogant blue-blooded bastards.

Sigmund struggled to keep himself upright. 'How did you know to come?' he gasped.

'We had word from Talabheim,' the marshal said.

Sigmund understood. Theodor said that he had sent word out for reinforcements. He wished that Theodor had lived to see this moment. Of all men, it seemed that he had done most to save Helmstrumburg.

'Now, where are the vermin, what are their numbers and their disposition?'

Sigmund tried to explain, but was still weak and dizzy. Osric took over, telling the knights' commander what had happened, and as much information as he could about the layout of the town, and the number and type of the beastman forces. Marshal von Dvornsak nodded and waved his men on.

The pistoliers moved alongside them. A few of them gave the halberdiers curt nods, but most of them passed by without even an acknowledgment.

'And those bastards will probably claim they liberated Helmstrumburg,' muttered Osric, as the mounted column trotted past.

AN ORDER WAS given and the squires spurred their horses forward to take the lances from the knights. Marshal von Dvornsak split his men into three squads of ten – sending one each down Tanner Lane, Altdorf Street and Eel Street, swords drawn. Behind the knights' massive warhorses came the pistoliers, their light geldings chomping and tossing their heads at the stink of blood and the musk of the beastmen.

The horses moved slowly through the shattered remains of the barricades, picking their way carefully through the heaps of dead men and beastmen. On Tanner Lane they came across the Chaos spawn, still inside the field station, contentedly digesting the remains of over thirty men.

The Chaos creature's pulsating flesh flared blue and sickly green as the first pistol shots punctured its overblown carcass. The horses started to panic as it began to squeeze back out of the door, following its own sticky trail of slime, but the pistoliers casually reloaded and then fired again; it was impossible to miss at such short range. It was a deadly fusillade, riddling the Chaos-spawn with lead shot.

Within twenty seconds the fearsome beast stopped moving. Its flesh began to deflate and change colour, until it was translucent, then sections tore open, the half-digested forms of the people it had devoured spilling out onto the street.

The captain of the pistoliers commented as he pointed at one of the forms – 'What a shame...' he said and the men looked and saw the remains of a young girl with dark black hair.

With a shake of his head, the captain spurred his horse on and the pistoliers turned their horses down the street after the knights.

As soon as the beastmen realised that the roads out of town had been blocked they began to scramble for a way out of the tight and alien confines of the townscape – back into the wild woods.

The only ones that did escape were those that managed to break through to the docks and leaped into the river. The rest were cut off by the knights and pistoliers, and then slaughtered.

One band managed to hide from the knights and flee out of town along Eel Street, but the knights' squires gave pursuit with spears and ran them to ground, one by one, as if they were hunting wild animals.

* * *

SIGMUND LIMPED INTO town and found his way to the marketplace, where the survivors were gathering. Edmunt picked Sigmund up in a bear-hug that was as gentle as he could make it, considering Sigmund's wounds. Elias nodded politely and even managed a smile. Vasir was there: a dirty bandage around his thigh. Guthrie was sitting on a barrel; he looked ten years older. Hengle saw his brother and sprinted to embrace him in a fierce hug.

'Where is mother?' Sigmund asked.

Hengle pointed to the Crooked Dwarf.

'She stayed there the whole time?'

'Yes! The beastmen never made it to the marketplace. Edmunt and the others were magnificent!'

Sigmund gave Edmunt a look, but the woodsman shook his head.

'But how are you?'

'I am alive,' Sigmund laughed, and then saw a pretty blonde girl – her skirts torn and singed – make her way through the startled crowd and stand next to Gaston. Sigmund smiled. He was glad that Gaston was still alive. He didn't know why but the handsome warrior's presence reassured him.

'Where is Gunter?' Sigmund asked, but the men looked down. The list of the fallen was too long to dwell on. Sigmund shook his head. He never thought that Gunter would be killed. The old sergeant seemed to have survived so much. He had been old and wise when they were just raw recruits.

'What time is the Crooked Dwarf open?' Sigmund said, forcing a smile through his exhaustion and shock.

The men laughed, but the laughter was weak.

EPILOGUE

FOUR DAYS AFTER the battle of Helmstrumburg, the knights from the Valkenburg Kommondaria rode out of town with the Kemperbad Pistoliers and the long train of squires.

The town stank of blackpowder and smoke still hung over the rooftops. Most of the new town had been burnt down; the blackened stumps of rafters and beams were stark against the skyline as people picked their way through the rubble, looking for food or for the bodies of their brothers or mothers or children.

The beastman bodies had been piled up in the moat and burnt: the land reconsecrated by the priests of Sigmar.

Sigmund's chest and shoulders were bruised black and blue – the hand prints of the beastlord neatly printed into his skin. The cut on his thigh was healing well. There were new patches on his uniform.

He saluted as Marshal von Dvornsak rode past and followed his men out along the Altdorf Road.

If it hadn't been for the knights, the town would have been lost. Sigmund knew that, but he disliked being indebted to another soldier twice – even if it was the handsome old marshal.

Sigmund stood on the steps of the Crooked Dwarf then ducked back inside the tavern, sat down at the table with Edmunt, and put his feet up on the table.

He had lost thirty-three halberdiers including Gunter, eight handgunners, thirty-four spearmen, including Hanz and Stephan. He had chosen a bright young man called Verner to be their sergeant now. He was liked by his men, and seemed to have a good head for leadership. He had certainly earned their respect in the battle and had rallied a band of thirty men in the street fighting. As far as Sigmund was concerned, there was no better test for a man.

There was a clatter of hooves in the marketplace and Sigmund pulled his hat down over his face.

'One of the pistoliers has probably forgotten a feather,' Edmunt said.

Sigmund took a sip of his beer. Josh brought a new barrel up the stairs. Guthrie was polishing the tankards. Unfortunately he had lost most of his regulars, but if you ignored the bandages and the missing faces, you could almost forget that there had even been a battle.

They heard a horse stop outside the Crooked Dwarf. There were footsteps outside as someone came up the stairs to the inn. The door opened and a uniformed man came inside.

Sigmund pulled his hat down over his face. He couldn't bear to talk to one of the pompous Kemperbaders.

'Captain Jorg?' someone said in a Talabheim accent.

Sigmund pushed his hat back and looked up at the new arrival. He was smartly dressed, with pistols at his waist and a sword at his belt – but he was not one of the men from Kemperbad.

Sigmund nodded.

'I have a message for you!'

Sigmund took the scroll and tore it open. It was from Landsmarshal Pesl.

'Your relief has been sent to Helmstrumburg. You are commanded to move with all possible haste to Fort Wilhelm on the Upper Talabec.'

At the bottom was a subscript: 'Andres Jorg sends his warm greetings.'

So his father was alive, after all. Sigmund put the message down and let out a long sigh.

'New orders?'

'Yes,' Sigmund replied.

'Do we have time for another drink?'

'Just one,' Sigmund said.

HE HAD FLOATED all the way from Helmstrumburg, but an eddy brought the man ashore on the mud flats outside Altdorf.

The man barely had the strength to crawl a little way up the bank, before passing out again and lying there – his once-fine clothes stained and drenched beyond recognition.

In the afternoon Old Mother Scultzen made her way to the mud flats to see what she might find. There were often a few beached fish that the herons had left, or perhaps a piece of wood that she could dry out and burn. But today she saw the body of a man lying with his feet in the gently lapping water. She hitched up her skirts and moved closed.

'Now then?' she said. 'What have we here?'

The man let out a whimper.

'What's that?' Old Mother Scultzen said. 'You'll have to speak up! I'm a bit deaf in that ear!'

'Help me!' the man repeated, louder this time and Old Mother Scultzen shuffled closer. 'I've been robbed!'

She backed off in fear, but Eugen held up his hand. 'I have rich… relatives who will reward you well!'

Old Mother Scultzen shuffled forward and saw the quality of the clothes he was wearing. Maybe he did have family who would pay for his safety? She shuffled another step forward, and peered down at the dishevelled figure.

The man feebly tugged a ring off his fingers and held it out towards her. She snatched the ring and bit it to make sure it was real before she decided to help him. She would get men from the village to help carry the man back to her hut. She knew just the thing that would cure him: fish head broth! And then she would see about the relatives.

'Wait there!' she shouted at the prostrate man. Eugen shut his eyes and nodded, lacking the energy to move his legs out of the water. There was nowhere else he could go.

ABOUT THE AUTHOR

Justin Hunter grew up in North Yorkshire in the UK, and has lived and travelled widely across Asia, North America, Europe and East Africa. He currently divides his time between living in the UK, Ireland and New York, where he plays with the Warmonger Club. *Forged in Battle* is Justin's first Warhammer novel

MORE SAVAGE FANTASY FROM THE BLACK LIBRARY

The Call of Chaos
1-84416-144-7

War on all fronts in this epic fantasy graphic novel!

www.blacklibrary.com

MORE SAVAGE FANTASY FROM THE BLACK LIBRARY

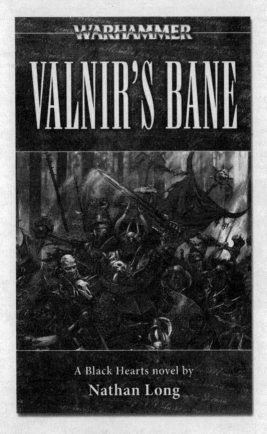

Valnir's Bane
1-84416-166-8

www.blacklibrary.com

READ TILL YOU BLEED
DO YOU HAVE THEM ALL?

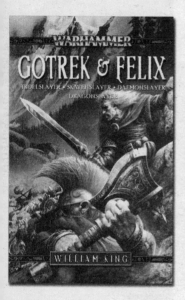